PSST.

HEY, BUDDY...
GOT A MINUTE TO SPARE?

HAVE I GOT A STORY FOR YOU...

Leshi sighed. "I'm getting the sense that you didn't volunteer for this mission."

Webrid struggled not to lose what little cool he had left. "Why would you say that? A frontal lobotomy on a street corner and an abduction by a violent gang on a strange planet was exactly what I had planned for this week."

WHAT OTHERS ARE SAYING:

The book's joy lies in the humorous prose ("Her wink could have clipped the wings off a beetle") as Webrid blusters his way across the galaxy.

— *Publishers Weekly*

GREEN LIGHT DELIVERY

ANNE E. JOHNSON

Candlemark & Gleam

For Ken,
who cherishes my imagination
and encourages it to dance.

1

anpril Webrid, carter for the Bargival district, handed a clod of jamboro cake to the blue-skinned businessman. He took a dendiac note in payment. "You stayin' here?" Webrid asked, "or can I bring my cart into your space?"

Obviously pretending that he hadn't heard, the fellow closed his window and sucked the cake down whole through a slimy blue mouth.

Webrid hated these commuter types. Somehow, they never learned the basic courtesies of urban interaction. And they were always in Webrid's way. So he tried again, louder this time. "Can I use your space, mate?" He enunciated clearly. "How long you stayin'?"

"Bivisher! *Braaap!*" came the reply, the first word being an expletive, the second a burp.

"Fine. I'll go somewhere else." Webrid knew when he'd been licked. But he couldn't just keep rolling along. He needed to get off the street for a while, after several hours of selling cakes to commuters, pushing his cart through the hot afternoon smog.

As he thought about how tired he was, Webrid realized that someone was standing next to him.

"Yeah? I got cakes today, friend," was his automatic response. Then he turned his head and focused his eyes. This guy did not want a jamboro cake; he could tell that much for sure.

For one thing, this "guy" didn't appear to be biologically based. Webrid could see the wires at its joints. A great metal head lowered itself on a slender tube of a neck. A brace of digital cameras absorbed the features of Webrid's face, which made him squirm.

"Like what you see, sailor?" he joked, but only to hide his fear. This wasn't a Vox police robot. Not one like he'd ever seen, and he'd seen them all, what with parking tickets and contraband searches every few days. The Vox, always watching and listening, seemed to be after him constantly for one thing or another.

The robot's head came closer to his face. Webrid pulled back. Maybe it *was* a cop bot after all. "I ain't parked wrong. I'm on the move, in search of a legal space, officer."

The robot responded with a mechanical buzz and a series of clicks. A door retracted into its central chamber, revealing a speaker. Somebody—somebody biological— spoke. "Ganpril Webrid, Second-State Licensed Carter," it announced.

That voice! Icy snakes of déjà vu scuttled up Webrid's spine. Clear as the bot hovering before him, he pictured the squalid back alley where he used to play with his cousins when he was a kid. Webrid huffed and shook his head, chasing away the random vision.

"Ganpril Webrid," the voice repeated. "You have been called."

"Eh?" Webrid had just spoken this syllable when a delicate feeler came flying out of the robot's head and wiped across his forehead. It stung. "Hey, now, what's the idea?"

But the thing was gone. Upward. Out of sight.

Webrid felt a headache coming on, and a strange green light pattern was starting to flicker in one eye. The light coalesced into a shape. It was not a very familiar shape, but after a moment of painful concentration, Webrid thought he recognized it. A tree? There weren't any trees in Bargival, or on the entire planet of Bexilla. Webrid had only seen trees in pictures at school years ago. But now there was one floating in front of him, made of a green cloud. Then its particles dispersed, and there was nothing to see but the comforting grunge of the Bargival streets.

Webrid decided he needed a drink. Some company would be nice, too.

He noticed a fine, lean Entra woman clinging to a shop window. There was a possibility there, he felt, if only he could find a place to lock his cart. Webrid pulled over near the shop where the woman had her four midriff suction arms stuck tight against the pane.

"Hey, sweetheart," he called. It was always worth a shot. He clicked his right and left tongues in a sultry syncopated pattern that had taken years to perfect. "So, uh, you see somethin' you like in there? Maybe I know the guy that owns the place. I know pretty much everyone in these parts." No answer, so he kept up the schtick. "I don't believe I know *you*, though, sweetheart. Wanna turn around and show me? I just know your front side's as fine as your backside." He was some smooth talker, no doubt about it.

This gorgeous creature popped just enough suction to allow her to turn her head. She took one glance at him and snarked, "Buzz off, carter."

Now Webrid knew what he was dealing with. "I don't need none of your classist garbage," he snapped, and it was true. "I can get a date hotter than you without the attitude."

That was maybe *not* so true, but saying it made him feel better.

What was it with the social atmosphere in Bargival today? Sure, Webrid was used to being looked down on a bit. Because most carters had at least some Yeril blood, they were often hulking and hairy, with unsightly claws. Webrid was pure Yeril. Still, the good folks of Bargival appreciated their carters, even if they didn't want their daughters to marry one.

A carter was a useful member of the community, transporting things or people from one place to another. Sometimes Webrid provided a simple delivery service, but other times he'd be commissioned to sell the wares he was carrying, like today. Webrid's mother had been a carter, and her father before her. In fact, his grandfather had given him the velancium-alloy cart he still pushed through the streets of Bargival, thirty Standard Raralt Years later.

"People will laugh at you when you tell 'em you're a carter, boy-o," Grandpa used to say. "But once they need your cart, they won't be laughing anymore."

They were fine words to live by. Webrid usually grinned through any derision he came across, and most days even made a few dendiacs in profit. Being a carter wasn't such a bad life, normally, but today it was all getting him down.

His head throbbed, and another spray of green light shot across his vision. But Webrid wasn't the sort to run to the doctor. Instead, he focused on finding that drink.

He considered heading to Joolo's Skinny Dip Club. He often carted items to this particular establishment, and the management relied on his discretion. He didn't ask what was in the packages, but he could well imagine what a high-end pleasure palace would need regular deliveries of in unmarked polyurethane cartons. As an unspoken exchange for keeping his mouth shut, Webrid felt entitled to use the club gratis. Through the back door, of course. It wouldn't do either party any good to draw too much attention to an impecunious carter frequenting a fancy joint like that.

But tonight even the lure of bare Prushaskian flesh couldn't interest Webrid. His headache was getting worse, focused strangely in the center of his brow. And now everything he looked at had a slightly green cast. Or was that his imagination? Screw the drink—what he really needed was to lie down.

No surprise, he hadn't even been able to sell all these damned jamboro cakes he'd taken on commission. Bargival was just too hot and crowded this time of year for baked goods, and Webrid should never have agreed to hawk them. Since he couldn't afford to buy groceries now, they might as well become his dinner. Webrid took a dry cake from his cart and shoved it into his mouth. Heavy as a stone. No wonder they called it a clod. He gummed it without enjoyment, as if in penance for his poor business sense.

He headed home. Turning into his alleyway, he was comforted by the voice of Dengel, his neighbor's little son, greeting him from a window high up in the tenement building. "Hi, mister carter," the voice wafted down, like a silk ribbon. Webrid found the heart to lift up his arm and call back, "Hiya!" But that was all the energy he had. Slowly, he lowered his cart into its usual spot in the stairwell. Every muscle ached and his vision was interrupted by pale green wisps of light. At least that tree hallucination hadn't returned. Locking down his pathetic livelihood for the night, he lurched into the lobby.

Webrid put his palm on the handprint lock to open the door to his elevator. Of course, it wasn't working. He'd only called management about it four times. Sometimes if he polished the scanner with his sleeve and smacked it swiftly in the upper right corner, he could get it to flicker back to life.

Before he tried it this time, he said a little prayer: "C'mon, let me catch one break."

And it worked. The lift door opened, speaking in the Vox's soothing female voice, "Override," which it repeated in the Raralt Planetary Circle's six most common languages. "Override. Please command."

"Floor eighty-three," he said in a flat voice.

"Floor eighty-three," repeated the computer, sounding perkier than Webrid felt. Up they went.

Next morning, Webrid couldn't even remember going to bed. He had the hangover of a man who'd drunk six flagons of Valestin hundred-proof, but he was pretty sure he hadn't had a drop. The headache! The center of his forehead burned deep into his brain, and his right tongue was sluggish. A pulse of alarm shot through him. Maybe he'd had a stroke? Was his medical card still valid? Was he going to puke right then and there?

The answer to the last question was yes. His stomach felt better afterward, but his head felt worse. Hauling his sorry carcass upward like he was fighting the gravity of Rada-2, poor suffering Webrid felt his way to the bathroom. There must be some drugs in there. Pretty much anything would do at this point.

Before he could reach into the medicine cabinet, Webrid caught his reflection in the mirror. He assumed he was delirious, so he leaned in closer. But the sharp green light between his eyebrows wouldn't disappear no matter how much he squinted.

"Wha'ZAT?" he quite reasonably demanded. He swatted the air in front of his face. "WhaTIZZ-at?" He weaved his head from side to side, as if a laser was shining at him and he could move away from it. But the dot was stuck there in the center of his forehead, clearly giving off its own light.

Grabbing a cotton swab, he poked at it, as he might at a dead rodent. "Aaah!" That hurt. The light source was implanted in his head somehow, and the flesh around it was raw.

"Malady?" asked the Vox. Apparently his healthcare dues were paid up after all, because the medicine cabinet was trying to help him. "Malady?"

"How the hell should I know?"

"Malady?" It wasn't going to stop.

"Great freaking headache."

"Headache," it confirmed.

"Damn straight."

Two aspirin clinked into the dispensary slot. When Webrid laughed at the understatement, he thought his skull would split from the pain. "You're killin' me here."

With a shaking hand, he grabbed the pills. But doubt came with them. "I didn't pay," he said, thinking of his healthcare tax. He distinctly remembered not paying.

The medicine cabinet obligingly said. "Payment of fifty thousand dendiacs processed as of yesterday. Thank you for participating in the Bargival Common Weal, Ganpril Webrid. We look forward to healing you."

Fifty *thousand* dendiacs? Webrid hadn't had that kind of money...well, ever. That was payment for the highest level of healthcare, four levels above what he could occasionally afford. He hadn't thought he could get more confused, but this was doing it. Then the ceiling said, "Ratchor Miggs visiting." Webrid's headache got worse.

"I'm not home," he said, realizing it was pointless. His landlord would know he was in by the use of his key card last night. That wretch Ratchor also had his own key, so not answering the door would do no good.

"Ratchor Miggs visit..."

"Okay, okay. I'm coming," he moaned, crawling along the hallway toward the door. He tried to think of another excuse for his late rent, but he couldn't even remember how many months' worth he owed. Heck, he was lucky to make it down the hallway without passing out. There was a cloth hat on the hall table, so he put it on and pulled it down low over his glowing forehead.

With a mind emptied by pain, Webrid opened the door and braced for an eviction notice. Instead, he got a fruit basket.

"You take this." Basket in hand, Ratchor Miggs stretched his wooly face into an unfamiliar shape. It took Webrid a minute to realize that his landlord was smiling.

"Um, for me?" he asked, puzzled.

"Ya, ya, ya. I say thank you."

"You say *what*?" It wasn't just Ratchor's Prellgan accent and double row of teeth that was making him hard to understand.

"I say thank you," Ratchor repeated with a patience, even an obsequiousness, that was altogether new.

Webrid decided to play along. "Well, you're welcome there, sport."

"You take basket."

"Okay." He took it.

"I say to you thank you. You pay year advance."

"Uh-huh," said Webrid, mystified.

Rather than forcing his way into the apartment, as Ratchor normally did when trying to extract his rent money, the fibrous landlord bowed and backed away. The door slid shut, mercifully blocking Webrid's view of Ratchor's pate bobbing up and down.

Webrid chose an over-ripe geffir fruit from the basket and wrapped his left tongue around it pensively. No angle of contemplation could cast a sheen of sanity on the day's events thus far. It was time to ask the Vox service for some answers. Sure, the Vox's constant peeping put the populace on edge. But it could also be a useful source of info.

"Bank balance?" Webrid asked the ceiling.

A fuzzy voice answered, "Bank balance, twelve million dendiacs."

Webrid wanted to say, "Repeat," but his face was frozen. Twelve million dendiacs was more than he, his parents, and his grandparents had made in their combined lifetimes.

Being Webrid, he didn't assume he'd won the lottery. Instead, his spirit plummeted, imagining the crash he would surely feel after this colossal mistake was discovered and they took all the money away. "And I bet they'll charge me interest, too, or fees," he groused, hobbling back to the bathroom.

That pinpoint of green light shining from his forehead surprised him all over again when he took off his hat and saw it in the mirror. It was a little less sore now. Instinctively, he dug a clawed finger at it. It looked like a pimple, something that he should be able to squeeze out. But all his impromptu surgery did was break some blood vessels and launch him into a whole new universe of pain. It took the limit of his muscle control not to hit his head on the steel sink as he collapsed.

"Message."

Webrid re-entered the conscious world. The Vox said it again.

"Message."

"Who?" he asked hoarsely.

"Joffl Mar of Briziu Bakery."

At first, the carter panicked. This was the guy who'd hired him to carry and sell the jamboro cakes. He'd be wanting his money, but all Webrid had for him was a few dendiacs and half a cart of stale clods.

A green beetle skittered across the bathroom floor, making Webrid jump. Expecting it to hide when he got nearer, Webrid was shocked that it stayed still for him to get a closer look. It was, in fact, a spot of green light. Now he remembered how he'd ended up down there. Sure enough, cupping a hand over his forehead made the light disappear from the floor.

"Info!" he commanded. "Transfer fifty dendiacs to the account of Joffl Mar." That was more than generous, he congratulated himself.

"Transfer complete," said the Vox.

"Oh, and a message," Webrid added. "Tell Joffl Mar that he can go tie them blasted cakes around his neck and jump into the Rebeten Lava Flow."

"Message sent."

For the first time in ages, Webrid the carter was filled with a sense of well-being. He also realized that he needed to get the hell out of town.

nd Cheed is nice this time of year." The Vox had been blathering on as Webrid packed furiously.

"Travel details," he requested.

"Planet Cheed, three hours' journey from Bargival Central Spaceport via Rogdin Shuttle Lines. Shall I book passage?"

Webrid wondered if having a laser implant in his forehead would upset spaceport security. "Cheed details," he said.

"Cheed requires no portable air supply. Southern hemisphere is a popular tourist destination."

"And northern hemisphere?"

The Vox was silent for a moment, as if retrieving obscure information. "Northern hemisphere: Wilderness. Uncharted. No civilization."

"I'll being staying in the south, then. Book passage for tonight." To his own surprise, he added, "One-way ticket."

He also booked a few nights in a hotel—a really swank hotel—just so he had a place from which to mull his next move. The more Webrid packed and planned, the more it became clear that he was kissing Bargival goodbye forever. But this miraculous windfall of money might also be the end of his freedom. If he accessed it, he was traceable. The Vox could always find him. Somehow he needed to get his hands of a lot of those dendiacs and disappear from the system.

"Maybe I could withdraw..."

The Vox said, "Withdraw from which account?"

Damn, he had to stop talking to himself. The Vox could hear him scheming. Webrid laid a clawed hand over his mouth and twisted his tongues together just in case. Obviously, a large withdrawal of cash would be noticed. That would cause an investigation, followed quickly by a manhunt when the authorities realized the money wasn't really his.

"I wonder what poor bastard was expecting this dough," he said aloud, then clapped his hand across his mouth again, so hard it stung. Cursed habit, this muttering. It would take him down yet.

Although it felt good to have a destination, and exciting to be breaking from his life's daily drudgery, Webrid was conflicted about his decision not to return. His family had been in Bargival for three generations. Webrid had only been out of the city once in his life, to visit some old relatives as a child. He'd never been off the planet Bexilla. It could be accurately said that he didn't know what he was doing.

Looking around at all the belongings that didn't fit into his suitcase, Webrid was amazed by how much he owned. He was reminded again of the vision from his childhood alleyway that had overtaken him the day before. It had been years since he'd thought about the old days, and the housing block shared by all his Yeril cousins, aunts, uncles, and grandparents. And, of course, his domineering mother. Not so well these days, old Mom, although Webrid never went to see her. A mix of nostalgia and nerves brought on a soliloquy. He spoke out loud, of course.

"My folks are from Bargival." He picked up a bowl his mother had given him. Although it was chipped and stained, he'd kept it all these years. "Still, my ancestors must've come here from somewhere else. So maybe," he said to a shirt he couldn't quite bear to leave behind, "just maybe, I'm a natural-born traveler and I don't even know it."

Webrid ran his hand over a scuffed-up table. "But all this stuff, it's my history." The table, he suddenly realized, was made of wood. Therefore, it had to have belonged to his grandfather.

Reminded of the cloudy green tree that had haunted him the day before, he thought of a crazy aunt he hadn't seen since he still had his baby claws.

"What was her name?" he asked the table, pointing at it like it was one of his Yeril cousins. "You made her so mad. She hated when anything was made of wood. Had a thing for trees, like they were alive, had feelings. That was some crazy dame. Naggrid, right? Yeah, Auntie Naggrid." He shook his head. "Whatever happened to weird Auntie Naggrid? *She* must've gone traveling, while I've been stuck here."

Webrid smacked the table angrily and hurled his full weight down on one of his suitcases. But that sucker was not about to close. "Maybe this is why my life stinks. 'Cause I'm not doing what I was born to do. Who says I hafta be a carter? Huh? I gotta explore my options." On the last word, he rammed his rear down onto the suitcase again.

Rather than bouncing back up, Webrid just sat there. His speech took on a brooding tone. "But my people are carters. It's in my blood somehow. I don't know nothin' else." He stood, inspired. His voice grew louder. "How could I be so stupid? I'm a carter." He shouted it. "I'm a *carter!*"

Realizing at last that he could be heard, he mouthed the next statement silently through a goofy grin. "And being a carter is my permanent ticket out of here."

He called out, "Yo, Vox! Cancel that booking tonight." Webrid's heart raced at his own brilliance. "And give me info on getting a carter's license on Cheed."

The Vox took its time while Webrid paced manically around the room. Between self-congratulatory smirks, he considered the inevitable bureaucratic hoops he'd be put through. He was prepared for a massive licensing fee, interplanetary taxes, ten hours' worth of forms to fill out, a business ethics exam, a road rules exam. It was all worth it. He'd smoke some leposso stems to stay sharp and just barrel through all the nonsense in a couple of days.

"Bring it on!" he roared at the ceiling. He was prepared for anything they might throw at him. Anything but what he heard next.

"Ganpril Webrid. First-State Universal Carter's License valid. Fees paid in full for three Raralt Standard Years."

Webrid, struck dumb, plunked down onto the suitcase. It clicked closed under him, but that didn't matter now. He'd never even known anybody with a first-state universal license. It meant he could work anywhere. Any city. Any district. Any planet. Those licenses cost half a million dendiacs per year.

Far from being elated, Webrid felt punched through with defeat, as if he'd been violated. He certainly didn't feel free. Someone was trying to control his destiny, and he resented it.

"What's going on?" he asked.

"Please rephrase query."

Webrid sighed and thought. What exactly did he want to know? "Who bought that carter's license for me?"

After a few seconds, the Vox answered, "Rempener Dras."

"Who?" He'd never heard that name before. The Vox repeated it.

And now a question he should have asked hours ago: "Is there another carter named Ganpril Webrid in Bargival?"

"No."

"On Bexilla?"

"No."

"Anywhere in the whole Raralt Planetary Circle?"

A pause, then: "No."

The carter tried a new approach. "Info on Rempener Dras."

No answer. He asked again. Silence.

"Vox, will you give me info on Remper.er Dras?"

"No."

Webrid wasn't really surprised. Sighing again, he stroked his grandfather's beat-up wooden table. "I could score some serious money for this. Nobody can get wood stuff anymore." But he knew that ugly table was as much a part of him as his own legs. "What do I need with money, anyway?" he said to it kindly. "Seems I'm a millionaire now."

Since he'd bothered to pack and his life was in a tumult anyway, Webrid decided to go on that trip to Cheed anyway, and got the Vox to re-book it. He thought he might take advantage of the fancy license, so he dumped his suitcases and a few boxes into his trusty cart. He left the jamboro cakes on the ground for the neighbors and pests to fight over.

After a few failed experiments with bandages, he pulled a leather cap down over his forehead to hide the fierce green light. What would happen when he was searched at the spaceport, he couldn't imagine. One problem at a time. At least the headaches had lessened.

Webrid decided to ride to the spaceport on a WideSide Trans-Shipping vehicle, a hovering platform normally used by commercial enterprises. The little boy, Dengel, hung around with bare feet and open mouth while Webrid loaded his belongings.

"Where you go?" Dengel asked.

"Going on a trip," was all Webrid would say.

"Good life," said the boy, waving. "Good life." It was a common colloquial phrase of farewell, but its literal meaning smacked Webrid hard when it came from those innocent lips. Webrid hoped the kid could tell the future.

"Please," he prayed silently to gods he'd never believed in, "let me have a good life."

On the WideSide craft, the carter found himself traveling with a young fellow taking an expensive double-engine loping car across the mountains for a race. The spaceport was apparently on the way. Spoiled brat would barely acknowledge Webrid's presence.

"I bet I'm richer than you," Webrid longed to say, but there was no point. While he was still dressed in his grease- and smog-stained workman's overalls, no one would believe he was a millionaire. He barely believed it himself, although he'd had no problem paying for this lift from WideSide. It cost what he used to earn in a month.

At the spaceport, security was a breeze. They did make Webrid remove his cap and had a robot scan his implant. But after gathering around its readout monitor and nodding solemnly, they let him right through. He heard them say the name "Rempener Dras," or rather intone it as if it were a holy word.

"This Rempen-Whose-It character has a mighty long arm with a mighty strong pull," Webrid muttered to himself. He looked at the electronic claim check for his cart. "What if they search it?" he whispered to a urinal in the men's room. But that was the beauteous nature of his situation: Webrid himself had not committed a single misdeed. For him, this was remarkable. On a normal carting day in downtown Bargival, he'd have earned at least a parking summons by now. Here he was, behaving like a model citizen, but spending like a Leprictian queen planning her daughter's wedding. You just never knew.

"Psst."

Webrid could have sworn he heard something.

"Psst!"

Definitely there was someone behind the disinfector where Webrid was cleaning his hands. He'd heard stories about spaceport restrooms, so he was loathe to turn around.

"Pssssssst!" It sounded more urgent now.

"Not interested, friend," Webrid said quietly, hoping to get out of the restroom without making eye—or any other kind of—contact with this person.

"You'll need a bnarli," said a tenor voice with a lugubrious Akardian accent.

Webrid, self-conscious about his lack of traveler's savoir-faire, was embarrassed that he didn't know what a bnarli was. It could be anything from a special boarding pass to a type of condom.

"You can buy one from me," said the voice, whose owner Webrid finally turned to see.

The hopeful salesman was undoubtedly Akardian. Webrid saw this race around Bargival all the time and recognized the chaplet of droopy ear-like projections growing around the man's head. His lips were droopy, too. Akardians tended to be gifted salespeople. Normally, upon spotting one, Webrid would push his cart to the far side of the street just to avoid a hard sell. Now he was cornered in a public restroom with an Akardian holding a...what?...a "bnarli" up to his nose.

"What *is* that?" Webrid pulled away. The thing had straps, which set his imagination racing.

Blue teeth like stalactites gleamed behind the drooping ears and lips. "Try it on. Yeah. Try it on. You're gonna need it."

"Are you kiddin', fella?" Webrid erupted. "What could I need that for?"

The Akardian tapped his forehead between two tear-shaped lobes, then stretched his finger out toward Webrid's implanted laser. He repeated these motions a few times until Webrid caught on.

"Oh." Webrid spoke almost soundlessly, indicating his lighted brow. "You know what this is?"

The Akardian nodded vigorously, making all his ears wobble.

"Well?" Webrid demanded. "What is it?"

"The light?" the salesman smarmed. "You require info, sir?" He pulled a black card from his pocket and spoke into it. "Open account."

To Webrid he said, "It's a thousand Ds for the info. Hundred more for the bnarli. You put the bnarli over here," he raked his fingers across Webrid's forehead, "and keep light safe, and you, too."

Webrid sighed, more at the principle of the thing than the actual money. He wasn't often bested by an Akardian shill. But he had no choice this time. He spoke into the card, "Ganpril Webrid. Transfer eleven hundred dendiacs." Once the card flashed an acknowledgement, the Akardian flashed a mouthful of teeth.

"So?" Webrid was not in the mood to be messed with. "I've paid you. Now spill."

The Akardian beckoned with a droopy finger, so Webrid followed him out of the restroom and over to a sparsely populated corner of the spaceport. Twirling his finger in a circle above his head, the wily hawker showed that they were safe from security cameras. He spoke in a lolling hum.

"Laser." He pointed to Webrid's forehead. "Laser is info."

"What kind of info?"

"Any kind. Why don't you know?" asked the salesman. The one eye visible beneath his ears was squinting suspiciously.

"Watch your mouth!" Webrid lashed out in a loud voice,

but when a couple of heads turned his way, he continued *sotto voce* with a forced smile. "I'm asking the questions here. This thing was put in me without my say-so."

"They tell you nothing?"

"Look, pal. I don't even know who 'they' are." Webrid thought back to the police robot—or whatever it was—that had called him by name and brushed a limb against his brow. And he thought of the green cloudy tree. "I've got no idea what's happening to me."

"Okay. I see. Let me show you this." The Akardian helped Webrid strap the bnarli around his head. It was similar to an eyepatch, but its surface was flat and made of pliable plastic. It lay comfortably over the implant.

"Nobody sees the light now," the Akardian said, probably not intending to sound philosophical. "You can stay safe, take it where it belongs."

"What do you mean, where it belongs?"

"You're carrying the light."

"Where?"

"It'll guide you."

"How can it guide me? Does it talk?"

"Don't *worry*, man. It'll guide you. This I know."

Webrid thought he could feel his chain being yanked. But then something sank in. "Hey, did you say I was carrying this for someone?"

A hundred ears bobbled in affirmation.

Grinning widely, Webrid put out his hand (claws upward, as good manners required) and shook the Akardian's floppy paw. "Pleasure doing business with you," he said, and walked off, oddly satisfied. Although he was still missing most of the details, it made a world of difference to know that he'd been hired as a carter for this laser light. That explained the massive influx of money, at least.

And now it was time to make his way to the spaceport

bar, to get properly tanked up before boarding his first interplanetary flight. He stopped first at a dendiac dispenser to get a pile of cash. For the moment, Webrid didn't care what the Vox thought about that. His client would protect him.

"This sure must be doozy of a gig they hired me for," Webrid explained patiently to a brimming bowl of Valestin hundred-proof. "High risk. Worth millions to somebody. But it's okay." He took a gulp. "I'm a carter. It's in my blood."

s it happened, Webrid was unconscious for his first interplanetary flight. He'd boarded the craft somehow, and had been helped to his seat just as the booze shut down his synapses. When he awoke, he tried to focus on the gentle, fur-covered face of a Zenivar flight attendant.

"Are we leavin'?" Webrid asked.

"We've arrived, sir," was the soothing reply.

So, that was it. What was all the fuss about? He emerged onto the southern hemisphere of the planet Cheed with the same blinding headache a hangover would have given him back home. "Why do people bother to travel?" he asked the bustling spaceport crowd.

"Baggage claim to your right, sir," volunteered an obsequious drone. That didn't directly answer Webrid's question, but it was good to know.

Still in a haze, Webrid claimed his ancestral cart. He followed the signs to the line for customs, and that's where panic pushed a fist into his belly. The laser! Whatever client he was carrying this thing for might have power over security on Bexilla, but surely not on Cheed.

Yet the customs authorities waved him through, even after a robot scanned his face. Unable to stop himself, Webrid ran his finger along his temple, feeling the strap of the bnarli. Did they think it was a medical device?

Having risked tipping a Zenivar to guard his cart, he stopped in the men's room to check out just how ugly his mug was looking. What he saw amazed him. The bnarli had taken on the hue of his skin, and an optical illusion made it seem to share his forehead's hairy texture. The patch was practically invisible.

"No wonder it cost a hundred Ds," he said aloud, then gasped as he looked around for lurking Akardians ready to sell him more weird accessories. Thankfully, there wasn't an Akardian in sight, and everyone else was ignoring him. When Webrid left the restroom, he found the little Zenivar still standing there with his cart, a flushed smile on her plush face. Webrid indulged for a moment in the fantasy that everything was going to be all right.

It was a short-lived reverie. A tall, sinuous magenta creature sidled up to him, smelling of fry grease and coal dust. The being stopped beside the cart, but said nothing.

"Whaddya need, mac?" snipped Webrid.

"Can't you even recognize a lady when you see one?"

Embarrassed, Webrid mumbled an apology.

The woman grinned, causing the tendons in her face to stretch. Looking up at her, Webrid wondered why her species had never evolved an outer layer of skin. Still, she was rather fetching, in an anatomy class sort of way.

"I noticed your cart," she was saying. "You're the guy with the thing, right?" She tapped her forehead.

Suddenly on the defensive, the carter growled, "I don't know what you're talking about, hon."

She cocked her head to one side and her fuchsia sinews

pulled tighter. It made her eyes sparkle startlingly. "My name's Leshi, Ganpril Webrid. I'll be seeing you later." And off she sprang, sucked into the whirl of the traveling throng.

"G'bye, Leshi," Webrid said, suddenly wishing he'd handled the whole thing differently. "Stop it!" he ordered himself. Of all the bizarre things that had happened in the last few days, getting an itch for this toothpick of a woman was the strangest. She wasn't Webrid's usual type at all. He preferred slinky, spitfire broads for hire, where you got what you paid for. This one was self-assured and inscrutable. Two days ago, he'd never have given her a glance.

"Then again," he said, steering his cart toward an exit, "the only thing that's the same from two days ago is that I'm still a carter." The thought filled him with peace. "We needed a change," he said, patting the metal side of his lifelong companion.

Stepping outside, Webrid let his lungs relish the sting of unfamiliar air. Other than that, however, there was no way to tell he was on another planet. The four globes of the Raralt Circle were so close together, and travel among them so common, that all were inhabited by the same melting pot of races and cultures. So much for change. Once again Webrid wondered why anyone ever bothered to leave home.

A long, boxy black van slid into the crosswalk in front of him, its expensive motor whispering a hum.

"Hey, I'm tryin' to cross, here," Webrid barked, suddenly feeling like he was back on the overcrowded streets of Bargival.

"Ganpril Webrid," said a voice. Above him? Behind him? Webrid glanced around.

"I am speaking through your inner ear, sir. Please enter the vehicle." A drone emerged from a sliding door and pulled Webrid's cart in before he could react. He should flee for his life, a part of his brain was saying. But his deeper nature insisted that, wherever the cart went, he should follow.

He scrambled after his cart, and emerged into a floating living room. At least he wasn't greeted with a steel bar to the skull. There wasn't even a threatening quorum of Planetary Circle Enforcement lawmen. "This don't seem like P.C.E.'s style," he said, admiring the velvet chair he sank into.

Maybe that Leshi lady had arranged it, he thrilled to imagine. "Naw, not her style, either. She's more the..." He realized that he didn't know what type she was.

But Webrid was not distracted by longing for long. He ran his hand over the chair's armrest. "This is the way to get kidnapped, I tell ya." He turned to his cart, securely tied down with soft straps. "Hey, I hope they torture us, too," Webrid said, and let out a guffaw. "I bet it'll be the nicest thing I've felt since..." His mind played a montage of recent bedroom interactions. "Well, in a while, anyway."

He was still chuckling to himself when he caught a view through the windshield. This vehicle wasn't skulking through back alleys to warehouses where he might get the stuffing beaten out of him and be left for dead. Instead, Webrid was being driven along the proud central boulevard of beautiful downtown Ksacheel, capital of Southern Cheed.

Sheepishly, appalled by his own imagination, Webrid said, "Info: Where are we going?"

The ever-present Vox answered (coolly, it seemed, or was that an illusion?), "Ganpril Webrid, you are riding in the Spaceport Shuttle to the Royal Ksacheeli Hotel."

Of course! The carter felt like a complete moron. He'd forgotten about the hotel shuttle. Lack of travel experience sure could be mortifying. Obviously, the hotel knew when he was arriving, and the electron-ID he carried in his belt identified him to the Vox.

The vehicle pulled up to a veritable palace, a massive edifice that looked as indestructible as it did elegant. Webrid should have been excited—or at least smug—to know he'd be staying in a joint this far removed from that hole of a tenement back in Bargival. But he felt hollow and homesick. It all seemed so foreign, a world where he didn't belong. Not the planet Cheed itself or this fine city, where a carter could surely carve himself a fine little business if he was willing to work hard. No, it was just that all this pomp and luxury rubbed Webrid the wrong way.

"Kinda wish we *had* gotten kidnapped," he muttered as a bevy of biological and robot servants got him settled into a suite of obscene splendor. The biologicals held out their bank cards and Webrid authorized a large tip for each. They all bowed, including the robots, and backed out of the room.

Then the carter sat alone, save for his trusty cart, and watched Ksacheel's lights come on as the sun fell. His chest ached under the weight of loneliness.

"Shouldn'ta come," he said in a low, sad voice. "What was I thinking? Just went crazy, I guess, what with all the money and the..." He felt the bnarli over his forehead but kept his mouth shut.

Suddenly loneliness turned to vague fear. He was lost in a strange land and desperately needed to be around something, anything, familiar. And he cheered right up as he realized how easy it would be. All he had to do was walk and walk until he came to a seedy part of town. Then he could have surroundings where he was comfortable and be around his own kind. Webrid might not have traveled much himself, but he'd met enough travelers to know that the working class was the same everywhere, a universal brotherhood.

So, without asking for info, the carter pushed his cart out of his swank hotel room. The only thing he left behind was his electron-ID card. He wanted some privacy for a few hours, until he felt ready to sample the rich life.

When the elevator opened, a group of large, tough-looking creatures swooshed past him and lumbered down the hallway. Webrid saw them crash through a door halfway down, right near his own room. "Either there's a helluva party starting up at my neighbor's, or somebody over-used his line of credit," he quipped to himself, basking in the glow of schadenfreude.

The elevator operator's rubbery eyebrows went up as the carter pushed his cart in. For the first time in his life, Webrid was ashamed of his profession. "Here's proof that I'm where I don't belong," he said once he'd escaped into the lobby and out onto the street. Although his stomach was rumbling, he rolled on past the chichi bistros where waitstaff in gold-threaded robes brought platters of steaming janz steaks and puddings to fill society's upper crust.

"I'll find me some street meat," said Webrid, longing for the sordid, salty sandwiches of home. He pushed through the unfamiliar grid, unwilling to slow down until the rents dropped. When the glitz had fallen off the storefronts and the siding was peeling off the houses, Webrid had reached his comfort zone.

"Zelaca?" he heard someone whisper. "Tomfooz? Expaltrin?"

A drug dealer! Webrid smiled, completely relaxed. "No thanks, friend," he said into the shadows, "but can you tell me where to find a sandwich and a bowl of Valestin hundred-proof?"

A single eyeball on a stem snaked its way around an alley entrance, examining Webrid and his cart. It blinked in satisfaction, and soon a rotund gelatin body on six stubby legs caught up with the eye. Its owner squished when he spoke.

"You cart for Eshalo?" it oozed.

Glad to be asked about his work, Webrid turned unusually voluble in front of this stranger. "Nope, I normally cart in Bargival. Just came over today. I'm on sort of a working vacation."

The drug dealer's eyeballs—Webrid counted five—swayed constantly like reeds in the wind, checking in every direction for police or customers. "Eshalo can use another carter most nights," dripped the dealer.

Webrid was warmed by gratitude. "Thanks, friend. Don't suppose you could point me to Eshalo's likely perch?"

With a light crackling sound, all the eyes looked in one direction, up the street. "Two blocks that way is Stim's Diner. Mister Eshalo or one of his runners is in there a few times a day. They all wear a purple triangle."

"Tribe sign," said Webrid, wanting to show that he knew how it was on the street.

"That's right." The dealer bared wide, glistening gums in what Webrid took to be a smile. "So maybe you can get your dinner and a job all in one trip."

"Well, I sure do appreciate it," Webrid said.

"Do you?" All eyes but one turned toward him. "Exactly how much?"

Shocked by his own naiveté, Webrid fumbled in his bag and pulled out a three-dendiac note, being careful not to reveal the fat bundle he'd peeled it from.

"All health and prosperity, friend." As he said the standard business farewell, Webrid saw the money disappear from his fingers just before the dealer vanished back into the alley. Webrid fought the urge to call a final "Thanks!" into the darkness, and instead put his back into forcing his cart up the hill toward the diner.

Stim's Diner was easy to spot, festooned by enough glowing signs and decorations to light a spaceport launchway. The light burned at a frightening intensity in such a squalid neighborhood. Webrid struggled to lock the wheels of his cart while squinting against the glare. He took a deep breath and opened the door to the garish restaurant.

hat can I get you, hon? I'm Stim, proprietress of this here establishment. You got a favorite species?" Her tentacles were as silvery as her tongue was saucy.

"So, it's *that* kind of diner," Webrid said. He hadn't meant for it to be out loud, but the deed was done.

"Aw, such a sweet, innocent little boy," Stim cooed, pumping her bosoms—or whatever those protuberances were—toward the carter.

But Webrid had a lot of experience in this sort of joint, thanks to his arrangement at Joolo's Skinny Dip Club back home. So he quickly recovered his cool and rearranged his bristled face into a leer. "I can see you've got a five-star menu, sweetheart. But I gotta fill my belly first, to stoke the ol' engines, you know?"

Stim swung her behind around and beckoned by wiggling it at Webrid. "We've got just the fuel for a growing boy like you." Her wink could have clipped the wings off a beetle.

The dining room was small, crowded, and stale-smelling,

just the way Webrid liked it. "Bring me a ground janz on a bun," he said to a bored kid with worm-like hairs on his forearms. "And a bowl of Val-Hundred." The kid barely nodded before slumping away.

His booze in front of him, Webrid glanced around the room for anyone sporting a purple triangle. He had to be careful. Looking too long in any direction earned him glares that he knew could quickly morph into lethal harm. Wouldn't do to upset the natives.

So his eye rolled ceaselessly over this motley collection of underworld characters and folks on the make. "Buncha losers, outcasts from society," Webrid burbled into his bowl. "I love every man and woman here."

The wormy-armed kid plopped a steaming sandwich in front of him. The first bite tasted like heaven. The second would have been just as good, but a strong hand on Webrid's shoulder prevented him from leaning further into his dinner.

"Don't look behind," a deep voice said in Western Bexillan, a dialect Webrid knew but rarely used. "Get up and walk to the corner, under the picture of that Entra girl."

Webrid saw the painting of a be-suckered Entra referred to by his new companion. He also felt a sharp blade resting near his jugular.

"I don't know much about art," he said, trying not to move his throat too much, "But I do enjoy the company of a nice Entra lady when I get the chance."

"Move it. Now."

So Webrid stood up and pushed his way past the other diners toward the painting. The knife was now against his back, where he kept a number of vital organs.

"Go left," his captor said, once he'd reached the wall.

Webrid protested, although he knew it was foolish. "We're in a corner, man. I can't go left." As he said this, he took one little step left, just to be obliging. The floor gave way under him.

As Webrid swooshed through the darkness, he contemplated his almost-finished life. He hadn't married or had kids (that he knew of). Just as well. That wasn't his scene. He'd treated people pretty decently, overall. He did, however, regret not getting to spend much of the money he'd just come into. He was also sorry to leave his current carting assignment unfulfilled. That wasn't like him at all.

His last thought before hitting the bottom was how little he enjoyed amusement park rides. *Whump!* He landed with great force in something spongy. He then puked his guts out, just as he had the last time he'd gone on an amusement park ride. Afterward, Webrid lifted his head and swallowed a mouthful of acid.

"Hey," he croaked. "Lookit all the purple triangles. I was just trying to find you g..."

"Ganpril Webrid," said somebody he couldn't see. Those people he *could* see stepped closer toward him. They were a rough-hewn bunch.

"How you folks doin'?" he asked politely.

"Ganpril Webrid!" the voice shouted. "First-State Universal Carter." Apparently news traveled fast in the Raralt Planetary Circle. "Remove your bnarli."

Webrid had honestly forgotten the word. He grabbed his trouser clasp and tried to look fierce. "I ain't removin' a thing, ya pervert."

Three members of the Eshalo tribe, two men and a woman, jumped him and tore the bnarli from his head.

"Hey!" he cried from his knees. "I paid a hundred D for that. Give it back."

"You have no need for it now, Ganpril Webrid," said the voice. The tribe members closed in tighter. "The time has come, carter, for you to deliver that which you have carried."

This should have been a relief. Webrid should have

congratulated himself on a tricky but lucrative job well done and started planning the wild nights of booze and girls he'd buy in celebration.

But something was seriously wrong. Something besides the rusty, toothy surgical instrument that a woman was now brandishing at him. No, the deeper problem was one he couldn't have articulated. It was a sense, a carter's sense, that this was a scam. A heist. These people, he was sure, were not the rightful recipients of his cargo.

"Get away from me," growled Webrid, searching frantically for an escape, although he was surrounded. He struggled mightily, but the three heavies had him pinned, and that mad surgeon was dangling her snuff-film medical implement his face.

When he was a kid, Webrid remembered, one of the first times his mom had let him take the cart out alone, he'd been mugged. Some hoods, younger versions of this present trash, had taken all his money and smashed all his remaining straliem-juice bottles one by one. Then they'd toppled his cart, breaking an axle.

It was the most humiliating experience of his life, and Webrid had sworn that he would never allow it to happen again. Through a combination of tough presentation and hard-won street smarts, he'd succeeded. Until now.

This memory ignited a rage in Webrid's chest that roared down into his bowels like rocket fuel, forcing his body upward despite the hands on his head and shoulders.

"Nobody. Touches. My. Stuff." He spoke with the awesome power of a Bera-Erriger priestess commanding the dead to rise.

Webrid took an instant's satisfaction in the stunned face of the woman with the surgical tool. But as he watched her, his own smugness turned to awe. A green light, apparently coming from his implanted laser, reflected against her head.

It intensified and bored into her skull, dissolving it, baring blobs of blue-gray, glowing brain matter.

The light shut itself off and there was silence. Then a great chorus of howling and screaming erupted as all the gangsters tried to be the first out of the room.

Webrid, left alone, had three important thoughts:

"Now I know where the exit is," and,

"Oh, look. There's the bnarli on the floor. Maybe I better cover this laser before I melt anyone else's head," and,

"I'm gonna take my cart back to my cushy hotel and never, ever leave."

They were clear, practical thoughts. Orderly and cogent. Then terror took over. With his blood pumping so fast that his vision swam in a sea of white, Webrid somehow put on the bnarli, got out of the basement, ran up the stairs to street level, found and unlocked his cart, and started to push it. Like a dowser seeking water in the Redfire Desert on Bexilla, Webrid heaved through the black streets until he homed in on the lights of the city's main boulevard.

After what could have been minutes and what could have been eons, Webrid entered the glittering hotel lobby. He let himself be shepherded to the elevator, hardly able to focus his eyes. (Was that someone following him? No, he just needed to lie down.)

"I've got it from here," he slurred as he stepped out onto his floor. He assured the disappointed bellhops, "I'll make it up to ya tomorrow." He just couldn't stand the thought of being fussed over at the moment. "PJs, booze, bed," he recited over and over as he pushed his cart down the hallway.

His room was 1234. It took all his remaining intellectual powers to read the numbers on each door. 1228...1230...1232... The next door should have been his. Unfortunately, that door was lying on the carpet, having been ripped off its hinges.

Way past his ability to problem-solve, Webrid simply rolled

his cart over the prostrate door and sank into an armchair. He was paralyzed with exhaustion and confusion, but although his limbs were leaden, he couldn't shut off his brain.

"They came for me," he said simply. It was a stunning realization. But an upside occurred to him quickly. "I wasn't here."

He didn't stay relieved for long. "Maybe they knew I wasn't here. What did they want?" He scanned the room. Those suitcases he hadn't taken with him in the cart had clearly been opened and rummaged through, but no one could say the room had been ransacked. He hadn't brought anything valuable, anyway.

"My electron-ID," he murmured. He should have shouted this, but he was too shell-shocked to feel the heat of alarm. It took all his strength to haul his rear out of the chair and search for the card that linked him to his money, his medical care, and his past and future life and livelihood. That card *was* Ganpril Webrid.

And there it lay, on the bathroom tiles next to the belt where he stored it. His priceless card had been moved and inspected, but not stolen.

"Maybe it's sabotaged," he said, but he knew his imagination had gone overboard. Webrid had damaged his ID card before, and within seconds, the Vox had acknowledged the problem and ordered him a new one, which had arrived before nightfall.

Somehow, finding the card and his other belongings still present and intact was more frightening than if there had been an obvious burglary. Burglary Webrid could comprehend. Something much more sinister was happening here. He felt defenseless, like a little child lost in a big, crowded place. All he could think to do was to lift the hotel room's plastic door and lean it as upright as possible against the doorframe. It was useless as a physical barrier, of course, but it gave him the illusion of safety.

On shaking legs, Webrid slid between his cart and the easy chair. But rather than sit down in the chair, he draped his flabby midriff over his cart, resting his head on his arms. He puzzled as hard and as intricately as he ever had in his life.

He fought the impulse to test his ID card by asking the Vox for info. Sure as Webrid knew the whorehouses of Bargival wouldn't serve him on a tab anymore, he knew the Vox was behind this invasion. And there was something else he knew: The perps had expected to find him there along with his ID. Webrid's person, not his belongings, was the target of the break-in. In recent years, he'd heard rumors of things like this, whispers about a Vox-informed police state that swept citizens away; they were never heard from again. Maybe they weren't just rumors.

Webrid also choked down his wish to call the front desk, not so much to report this crime and damage as to order some food and drink. He didn't want anyone important to know that he was back. It might not take long for another hitman to arrive.

Sucking in deep breaths for energy, Webrid came up with a plan. He would run away without his ID. Yes, it would be dangerous and challenging. He would need to locate and infiltrate that extremist fringe of society that lived without official permission. He would have to give up all his security, and he was not a young man.

But, wait. They had found him at Stim's Diner in the low-rent district even though he hadn't been wearing the ID. How had they traced him? Could the Vox see him anyway? How could he ever be safe again?

"I don't wanna die," whimpered Webrid into the lid of his cart.

There was a knock at the door.

he knocking got louder and louder. Then there was a pause, followed by the crash of the door hitting the foyer floor again.

"I'm in here," called Webrid, resigned. His chin was glued to the cart lid by a film of saliva he'd drooled out. He could hear somebody step along the plastic door, but he didn't straighten up to greet his assassin. Courtesy seemed pointless now.

Webrid's face was toward the carpet, so he saw two long, narrow feet in malleable metallic sneakers. He'd seen these sneakers and these feet somewhere recently.

"Are you going to stand up at some point?" said the assassin.

"Guess so. Um-kay." He grunted with the effort, and his spine clicked in a few places. Even standing, Webrid had to look up to see his visitor's face. It defied imagining that this day could hold any more surprises.

"Are *you* gonna kill me?" he asked.

"Why would I do that?" said Leshi, the woman from the airport with the long magenta limbs. She truly was one spicy cut of meat.

Webrid shrugged. "I dunno. Just seems like some people want to... Never mind." Suddenly, as he looked into this familiar face, all his fear of sinister surveillance seemed ridiculously paranoid. Webrid remembered his manners. "You want a drink?"

Leshi glanced around the room. "You already have a bottle?"

"Naw, I'll order room ser..."

"No, room service is not a good idea."

"Yeah, you're right. Sorry." Webrid felt his stomach rumble. "I need a sandwich." Leshi just shrugged. Embarrassed, Webrid blurted out a question, just to fill the room with sound. "So, did you follow me from the spaceport, or what?"

Leshi pulled a writing screen from her pocket and typed something, then showed Webrid: "You're easy to find with that cart. We have to leave now." She put a finger to her own lips to warn him to be quiet.

"What about my..." He pointed to the belt holding his ID card. She shook her head firmly, then started to pack his things.

Defenseless and exhausted, Webrid watched as this pink serpentine giantess loaded his last two suitcases on top of his cart and wheeled it out the door.

"But I'm so hungry," he said, following her.

"We'll get you that sandwich," she whispered, quickening her pace.

"Elevator's the other way."

She ignored him and walked to a back hallway. With her willowy arms, she pushed open the two panels of a huge window that came nearly to the floor, miming to Webrid that he should help her lift his cart over the sill.

"We're on the twelfth floor," he said, feeling like he might cry. Leshi's face was so stern that it reminded him of his primary school principal. Looking at her made jumping out the window with his cart suddenly seem like a capital idea. He decided to just do it, without looking. But as he heaved his end and stepped over the edge, his feet hit a metal surface.

"Hang on," Leshi warned.

Finally, Webrid looked down. He and his cart were on a wide platform, and Leshi climbed on with him. About a story below them was a featureless gray box the size of a small building. The platform moved swiftly downward toward the box, which opened a hatch and swallowed them up. They landed with a *thunk*, capsizing Webrid and wobbling the cart, but not affecting Leshi in the least.

"Easy, now," somebody said, righting Webrid. Someone else pushed him and pointed. "Just have a seat over there. Leshi, help me with the cart."

In his present stunned state, Webrid couldn't have done anything but sit down even if a Valestin bottling plant were gushing booze just down the street. He sat and watched the activity around him, wondering a million things. Among them was why he had not fallen twelve stories out the window, and why he was now in a harshly lit beige office with desks and equipment as far as he could see.

People of many species scurried and slid from place to place. Some worked at desks, pecking their fingers at images on monitors, talking into mics and phones, sorting through papers.

"You wanted this?" A furry little Zenivar was standing next to his chair, holding out a sandwich.

Webrid tried to say, "Thank you," but was unable to get any sound out. Leshi was nowhere to be seen, but there was plenty of activity to entertain him. He chewed the cold janz roll without blinking his eyes. These days it seemed like the whole damn world could change in an eyeblink.

"Put it seven marls forward," a small-headed man in a

blue robe was saying to an even smaller guy. "Rommey might see us if we go any slower."

"It's tricky here in town," replied the little one. His cap of twisted rope reminded Webrid of a sex toy he'd had a problem with once.

"Tricky?" snapped the blue-robe. "You were first in your class. I think you can handle tricky." He walked away as the rope-headed one sat at a computer and pawed at its screen.

A few yards away, in the other direction, an Entra woman was in conversation with some scaly man. Webrid strained to hear above the slosh of janz meat in his mouth.

"...don't want him there," the Entra was saying. She and her friend both looked at Webrid, as if he were an oddly shaped cocktail table they were trying to fit into a living room.

"No place else for him," the man said, flicking a dust speck from the woman's upper right shoulder. Webrid knew a sly move when he saw one, and he sure couldn't blame the scaly guy for trying.

"They'll never let him stay." The Entra beauty let the words float through her silver lips. She shook her suckers to get the guy's hand off her. That was hot. Webrid felt like he was watching an adult visi-story, snacks and all.

"You show him who's boss, baby," Webrid said.

Both of them seemed amazed that Webrid could talk. But rather than engaging him in conversation like civilized people, they turned away and walked to the other end of the office.

This was starting to be comical. Webrid stood and spoke loudly. "Any chance of gettin' another sandwich? How's about some booze?" All the workers stopped talking and typing for a moment and looked at him, then went back to whatever they'd been doing.

Only that sweet little Zenivar paid him any attention.

There she was with another sandwich. "We have no alcohol on board, sir," she said. "Here's a bottle of straliem juice, though."

Webrid was truly touched. He didn't have much contact with Zenivars because they were all in service industries, serving people with money. Until a couple of days ago (how many had it been, anyway?), Webrid had been too near the bottom of the social food chain to be served by anyone.

"Thanks, dear," he said. "You're a real nice girl." She blushed through her fuzz. They did that a lot, he was noticing. "Could you tell me something?"

"I shall be glad to try, sir."

"When you say you have no alcohol on board, what do you mean by 'on board'?"

The Zenivar adjusted her apron. "This is the *S.R.S. Draspar*, sir."

That sentence was more opaque than a window into a Yeril's soul. "Ah-ha. Right. And remind me, what is 'S.R.S.'?"

"That's Swarattan Roving Ship, sir."

"Of course, of course," Webrid chuckled, as if at his own stupidity rather than the general stupidity of this situation. "And these," he said, pointing to the office workers, "are the Swarattans?"

"Well," she giggled heartily, "not all of them."

"Ha. Ha. No. Obviously."

With great effort, the Zenivar pulled herself together. "Will there be anything else, sir?"

"Yes," said Webrid, no longer feeling quite so affectionate. "Where the hell is my cart?"

"It's down a floor," said Leshi, who had appeared from somewhere. "You need something out of it?"

Not wanting to admit his attraction to this walking kabob, or how relieved he was to see her, Webrid focused on the Entra lady across the room while he said to Leshi, "All I want is my life back." His slid his gaze back toward Leshi, taking her in from sneakers to skull. "Don't suppose you can give me that, sweetheart."

Leshi sighed. "I'm getting the sense that you didn't volunteer for this mission."

Webrid struggled not to lose what little cool he had left. "Why would you say that? A frontal lobotomy on a street corner and an abduction by a violent gang on a strange planet was exactly what I had planned for this week. Now, I'll ask once more, where the hell is my cart?"

It was hard to keep up the "or-else" angle when Leshi widened her brown eyes in sympathy like that and undulated her long neck. Damn, she could be gorgeous. He could have fallen to his knees and proposed to—or at least propositioned— her right then and there. Instead, he huffed and glowered.

"Follow me," she said. "It's time you met Debley."

They walked amid the desks to an exit door and took an elevator down.

"This is a spaceship?" Webrid asked quietly, looking at the floor. He didn't want to seem too interested in his surroundings or in her.

"It can't leave the atmosphere," Leshi answered, just as quietly, "but it is self-contained, so it can go to any part of Cheed."

"There's parts of Cheed that some vehicles can't go through?" Webrid said, forgetting his pretence of ennui.

"The north," she answered simply. "Here we are." They stepped into a hallway and Leshi pointed right. "Your cart's around that corner."

Webrid ran. When he saw his oldest friend, with its familiar dings and scratches, he bit his lip to keep from crying out. But he didn't bother trying to stop a few tears from falling. He thought he might drown in a wave of homesickness.

"Come on," said Leshi gently. "I'll introduce you to my brother."

He couldn't speak or look into her eyes. Webrid silently pushed his cart down the hallway, wondering how he ever could have been so stupid as to fly to freaking *Cheed*.

"Just leave that there," she said.

But he pushed right on past. He would not be separated from his cart again. What kind of a carter abandoned his cart before a job was done?

Leshi led him through the hallway around several turns until they came to what Webrid reckoned must be the center of the floor. There was a sizeable control room of some sort, staffed by serious-looking people of various species, turning knobs and poking at screens. A brownish-red fellow, totally skinless and obviously Leshi's brother, strode forward. Like his sister, he towered over Webrid.

"I'm Feklari Debley, general of the S.R.F. Glad to know you, Mr. Ganpril."

"Just Webrid," he said, shaking the long fingers offered to him. "What's the S.R.F.? I'm a plain-spoken guy, and I've had it with the code names."

Debley laughed, but when Leshi shook her head, he frowned suddenly. "How can you not know the S.R.F.?"

"He was forced into this. Doesn't seem to know what's going on," Leshi said.

Hearing that was a relief to Webrid. Maybe they would finally explain things to him. Even a few crumbs of info would be welcome.

Debley was pointing at Webrid's forehead. "How's the bnarli working out?"

"Wait. You can see it? You know what it is?"

It was Leshi's turn to laugh. "Debley invented the bnarli."

"Right. Of course. Stupid me. Now, what's the S.R.F., you S.O.B.'s?"

"Swarattan Resistance Force," the two meat people answered together.

"Uh-huh. And I'm working for this resistance force, am I? What, exactly, am I resisting?"

Settled at a table in Debley's office, Webrid listened as Leshi and her brother "explained everything." In reality, they explained very little, and Webrid got a sense that even these two were out of the loop on certain aspects of his situation. The longer he sat there, the more convinced he was that all this truth they were spouting was a fancy cloth draped over a bigger lie.

"That laser in your head," Debley said, pointing, "contains data."

"What kind of data?"

There was just a beat of hesitation. "We're not at liberty to say."

"Yeah, sure. And why can't whoever wants the data just..." Webrid mouthed the next words, indicating the ceiling by rolling his eyes upward. "...just ask the Vox?"

Leshi laughed. "No Vox in here."

That sentence, and her nonchalance about saying it, stunned Webrid so much that he missed the next thing out of Debley's mouth. "Eh? Say again?"

"I said it's large amounts of general data, too much for the Vox to provide in a single individual query."

"So who wants it, a company?"

Debley said, "Not really," while his sister said, "Kind of."

Dragging himself to his feet, Webrid snorted. "I was wondering if you could please be a little more vague? If we go on like this, I run the risk of actually learning something."

Leshi seemed to float around the table in only three or

four strides. She laid her fingertips on Webrid's shoulder. Although the touch was weightless, it caused his knees to buckle, and he sat.

Her voice was soothing. "There's a part of the government here on Cheed that needs what's on the laser."

Finally, something that sounded real, or at least plausible. "Okay, fine," Webrid said. "So, if it's the government, why don't they just get it directly from..." He looked up, Voxward. "You-know-who."

Debley, still across the table and frowning at his sister, said, "That part of the government isn't necessarily supposed to have access to this particular data."

"Oh!" cried Webrid brightly. "It's a crime? Embezzlement or some such? Why didn't you say so?" He relaxed considerably.

Again, he heard "Kind of" and "Not really" at the same time.

Leshi started to explain, but was obviously treading carefully. "The plan is to do, um, something with this data that will affect everyone."

"Ah-ha. And how do you happen to know *that*?" asked Webrid, wiggling his eyebrows and trying to make his voice drip with innuendo.

It was Debley who answered. "Because we've had believable intel. I know people. I used to work for the government."

"Well, aren't you something and a half?" Webrid said. Hard to believe such a squeaky-assed nerd could have such a smokin' sis. "And that's where you invented bnarlis?"

Debley nodded.

"And did you also, my glistening friend, invent the transportation of data lasers inside an unwilling skull?" He clenched his jaw into a sickly-sweet smile.

"You were supposed to know about it. Give your permission." Debley was suddenly shy and squirmy.

"And now," Webrid continued, rising to his feet again,

"now you are the 'resistance.' Now, you treasonous bastard, you've kidnapped the messenger with the goods. Why don't you just dig this thing out of my head and kill me?" He banged the table with his fist. "Huh? Why not get it over with?"

Leshi and Debley looked at each other, then at their feet. Finally, Leshi spoke. "We can't read the laser. Yet."

nd so it came to pass that Ganpril Webrid, lowly carter of Bargival, found himself included on a clandestine tour of Cheed's uncharted northern hemisphere.

"There is no recognized law enforcement," Leshi was saying, "and probably no roads."

Her brother contributed, "And no hospitals. Only scattered micro-grids of power, privately owned."

"Lots of wildlife up there," Leshi interjected, "Emphasis on 'wild.' Some truly lethal plants and animals, apparently."

"Okay, hold it." Webrid couldn't bear any more alluring details about the vacation paradise where they were heading. "I get the picture. So, now you need to explain why I'm bound for this hellhole that I maybe won't escape from with all my limbs."

Leshi and Debley looked at each other but said nothing. They did that a lot.

Pushing his cart toward the exit from Debley's office, Webrid said, "You know what? Just forget it. Drop me in a commercial district so I can find work. Better yet, take me back to the hotel so I can get my ID and work legally."

"Did they buy you a universal license?" Debley asked.

That stopped Webrid cold. He turned, intrigued. "Yeah, they did."

Leshi and her brother spoke intently to each other, but Webrid eavesdropped closely.

"It has to be her." Leshi said.

Debley nodded his head. "Yeah. Rempener Dras."

"Hey, I know that name!" Webrid shouted across the room. "Who is that?"

Ignoring Webrid, Leshi said, "She's trying to get around Rommey."

Webrid tried again to be included. "Who's this Rommey? Someone mentioned him earlier."

"Who mentioned him?" they both demanded, sounding alarmed.

Webrid shrugged. "Some Entra lady, when I first got on this...this ship thing." He gestured generally at his surroundings.

The siblings shared that look again. Leshi finally spoke to Webrid, drawing near him, which wrecked his resolve to be cold and defensive.

"Rommey is Cheed Council Secretary, but he's also well connected in the underworld. All the tribes here pay tribute to him, but he's starting to make connections on Bexilla and other planets in the Raralt Circle. He's really bad news, so we really don't want him to notice us and stop this vessel."

"But this vessel's huge," Webrid said, mulling the appeal of further gang contact. "How's he not going to notice it?"

"We're coded as a floating office building."

Webrid had to laugh. "How did you choose this thing as your cover? That's kind of..." He almost said *crazy*. "Unusual."

"It was available when we needed it, so we figured we'd try it out." Leshi shrugged her spindly red shoulders. "It's actually pretty effective because it's so ordinary. As long as we move fast enough to keep up with our posted commuter schedule, we're fine. The Vox can't see inside, but it knows where we are. Picking you up at the hotel was a big risk. We couldn't list the Royal Ksacheeli on our itinerary, or the Vox might have been suspicious, since it knew you were there. So we could only stop for a minute, then make an official log about 'traffic problems' that slowed us down."

"Well, thanks, I guess," Webrid said, not feeling at all grateful. "How are you so sure Rommey cares what you're doing?"

Debley spoke with a bite in his words. "Did you enjoy your little visit with Eshalo's tribesmen at Stim's? They were surely working for Rommey."

Remembering the previous night made Webrid woozy. He thudded into a chair, with one hand on his heart and the other on his cart.

"I see you get it now," Debley sneered.

"Stop it, Deb," said his sister. "Poor guy must be exhausted."

Leshi laid her weightless hand on Webrid's coarse-haired talon. "Why don't you take a nap? I swear no one will take your stuff. We'll wake you in time to shower and eat before we begin the trek."

Webrid had been enjoying a single thought involving naps, Leshi, showers, and food. The word *trek* didn't belong. "Do we really have to trek?"

"Yes. We have to get you to the government outpost in the north," said Debley. His tone was resignedly civilized.

"The government? I thought they were the bad guys."

"The normal government is a lousy bunch, and the splinter group that holes up in the North is seriously bad," Leshi said. "But we need their equipment to read the laser."

Webrid pushed out a long, noisy sigh. "You know what?

I'm gonna take that nap now. Maybe this will all make more sense later."

The *S.R.S. Draspar* was really humming when Webrid woke up. He felt the engines vibrate, open and powerful. There were no windows in the little cot-closet where they'd crammed him. It was made even less comfortable because he'd insisted on having his cart in there with him.

"We must be really movin'," he said to his metallic bedfellow. "Let's go see what's up." It took a few tries to get past the cart and then open the door inward. Geometry was not among Webrid's strengths.

The hallway was empty, and Webrid had no idea how to find either the control room or Debley's office.

"Place this big, they oughta have signs," he groused, choosing a direction at random. There wasn't a soul to be seen.

After going straight for a while, Webrid steered around a corner. At the end of that hallway were wide electrical doors, green and polished, obviously an entrance to someplace important.

"Here we come, suckahs," he said. To be honest, he was miffed that they hadn't thought him worth guarding. "Would a sentry in the hallway have been too much to ask?" he mused as he rolled along. "Even if he was asleep on the job, at least I'd know I rated some attention. But no. I guess carters with the latest techno-gadget jammed in their heads are practically fallin' out of the sky."

While he said the last bit, the ship lurched and creaked. Webrid hunched his shoulders in contrition, directing a whispered "sorry!" upward toward the transportation gods. The engine started humming smoothly again, but the carter increased his speed toward the green doors.

The closer Webrid got, the more sure he was that opening the doors would require faking a handprint or decoding a number lock. How wrong he was. The moment the toe claws of one foot came forward and touched the doors, they slid open. Webrid figured he might as well push the cart in, since the doors were obviously welcoming him.

He was just noticing how unusually small, empty, and brightly lit the room on the other side was when the green doors and a second inner set slid back together and clicked closed behind him. Even then Webrid, while puzzled, didn't have the good sense to be alarmed. That response occurred to him belatedly, as the floor gave way under him.

Of course, his first thought was, "Oh, not again."

That was followed quickly by, "And with the cart this time."

And then, "But, hey, I'm not in freefall!"

Indeed, cart and carter were on an elevator platform, moving downward rapidly, but not out of control. After a few seconds, they stopped with a bump and a clunk. Webrid, by now unconcerned, assumed he would emerge on a lower floor of the *S.R.S. Draspar* and find someone to direct him back to the bridge and his "hosts," to use a euphemism.

The two sets of doors opened with a pneumatic hiss, and Webrid felt his ears pop. The center of his head had a dagger of pain spiraling through it. Webrid sat on the floor, clinging to his cart as if the eddies of a flooding river might carry it away.

The last thing Webrid heard before he passed out was a fuzzy echo of the voice of the Vox, saying "Ganpril Webrid."

"...with such awful taste," someone was saying, apparently under water. The next sentence was clearer. "Why'd they choose such a loser, anyway?"

Webrid could always tell when people were talking about him, even when he was only half conscious. *Especially* when he was only half conscious. And his ears were burning now. He tried to turn his head to volley back an insult, but found that his skull was restrained. All he could see was the whitest ceiling ever made. It was such a pure lack of color, the word "white" didn't even cover it.

"No germs, anyway," he mumbled with the one tongue that he could move.

Footsteps and the swoosh and crinkle of plastic fabric drew near him. "Look who's awake," somebody said. A head in a clear plastic casing appeared over Webrid, who was shocked to be looking at a coarse-haired, tall, dark Yeril man, Webrid's own species.

"Yerils can't be doctors," was all Webrid could think to say. Every Yeril he'd ever met had been a laborer of some sort.

"Listen to you!" said the Yeril, who did seem to be a doctor. The man turned to a beige female something by his side, also in a plastic suit. "I didn't think that kind of species self-disenfranchisement still existed, except among the oldest generation."

"Where's Leshi?" Webrid asked. He'd have shot a handful of claws through this doctor's plastic casing and into his teeth, but his arms wouldn't move.

"Leshi? I don't know who that is. You need to lie still." The doctor was talking slowly and loudly, as if to a learning-disabled child.

"Where's my cart?"

"You won't be needing that."

Webrid disagreed. He focused all his strength on sitting up, but, because his head was in a steel restraint, all the effort did was wrench his back.

"I need my cart." Mortified, he realized he was about to

cry. When had he become such a weak blubberer? Right—ever since he'd had that laser put in his...

"You took out the laser, didn't you?" Suddenly, he loved this doctor. He was sure his cart was safe. "And I'm still alive." A tear of gratitude tickled his ear.

The doctor and his assistant shared a meaningful glance. Now the beige woman stepped forward. She had a kind face, if slimy, and deep-set ebony eyes that made her look primed for the sharing of bad news.

"Do I have brain damage?" Webrid asked, preparing himself. "Am I gonna be a vegetable?"

Her smile was a little too warm. "No, you're fine."

"But? Please drop the other shoe. I hate waiting."

The doctor took over. "The laser is still in your head."

"Why?"

As if to postpone this angle of conversation, doctor and nurse removed the steel restraint from around Webrid's skull.

"Tell me!" Webrid croaked.

"We couldn't get it out without..."

"Without killing me?"

The doctor looked uncomfortable. "Well, sure, that was also an issue." Another significant glance at his assistant. "You see, the laser, will, um..."

"It only functions when it's attached to your brain," said the woman. She had begun unscrewing the arm restraints.

Webrid thought and thought. Then he got it.

"So, you were willing to kill me to remove the laser." Both of them turned away. "But you didn't, because killing me would have ruined the laser. Yeah? Is that about right?"

They walked out of the room.

"Oh, no you don't." Webrid struggled to stand up. "Where's Leshi? Hey! I'm talkin' to you!"

Grasping medical tables, shelves, or the wall with each

step, Webrid made it to the door. It was locked. He was defeated.

"Please come back and try again," he said with his mouth against the door. "Just kill me. Maybe if you take my whole brain, you can keep your stupid laser working. I just can't take any more of this. And please, please, *please*, bring me my cart." His knees buckled and down he slid to the cold stone floor.

The cold stone floor. Made of giant square tiles. As wide as a person's body. Not grouted together. With room for Webrid's claws to slide under and jimmy one loose. Sometimes there were advantages to being a working-class Yeril, used to looking after his own needs when he had nothing.

It didn't take long to lift a tile. He chose one right at the base of the door so someone looking in the window panel couldn't see what he was up to. As he'd guessed, there was an energy-duct shaft below. Webrid was just dropping a leg down when he realized he was naked. A white plastic full-body suit hung nearby, so he squeezed that on, popping a side seam in the process.

Energized by his desperation to find his cart, Webrid lowered himself into the shaft. He even thought to pull the tile back over him, as he'd heard ex-cons describe doing on heists. Granted, they'd been unsuccessful heists, but it was the only source he had.

Lines of light shot up between ceiling tiles from the rooms below, and there was plenty of insulated wiring to hang onto in the space under the flooring. The ceiling swayed and moaned under Webrid as he crawled forward. He knew he'd get caught, but it didn't matter. All he really hoped to accomplish was to escape from that surgical room and get help from somebody reasonable.

Having turned a corner in the shaft, he could hear voices

below him, so he froze and listened.

"The irrigation tax is a no-brainer," said a husky voice.

A whiny man's voice said, "But the 43rd electorate will fry our behinds next moon if we don't..."

"Seriously? 'Fry our behinds'?" the husky voice cut in. "And you expect to be taken seriously by the party? No wonder Dijeral's up in the polls. You'd better wow 'em tonight at the Ring Market. "

"Yeah, yeah. Don't worry. Come on, I'll spot you lunch. We'll try that Stew Stand."

Webrid was suddenly disoriented. The irrigation tax had been all over the news, a hot-button issue in the 43rd electorate on his own planet, Bexilla. There was a debate planned between the incumbent and a young upstart named Dijeral, to be held at Bargival's Ring Market Amphitheater. And a new restaurant called The Stew Stand had just opened down the street from the capital building in Bargival.

Apparently, Webrid was home again.

ebrid stayed as still as possible in the crawlspace until he heard the two politicians leave the room. Once he was sure they were gone, he removed a ceiling panel and jumped down onto a desk. It wasn't a pretty landing, but he didn't break any bones. Unfortunately, there was no way to get the ceiling panel back into place. Never mind. He would be found soon, he was sure. After all, he was about to wander the corridors of Bexilla's capital building dressed in a skin-tight white plastic suit.

"My head," he said, remembering the little matter of his lethal laser, which he didn't know how to control. Draped on the back of a chair was a red scarf. Webrid wrapped it around his head, hoping it would stay put. He'd never have believed he could miss his bnarli.

If he was lucky, he could make it out of the building. His luck, however, seemed to run out before it began. He had taken one step out the door and closed it when he heard, "Can I help you, sir?"

Webrid snapped into high fabulation mode. He'd had plenty of practice with police robots. "Maintenance!" he shouted, his nerves over-compensating.

"For the transcomm fibers?" asked somebody who was obviously not security. He seemed such a pleasant young man. Probably some mucky-muck's intern. "You're looking for the stairs to the first floor, then?" Webrid gave this guy six months before he got eaten alive by his colleagues. In politics, there's no mercy for the naïve.

"Thanks, fella!" Webrid cried, trying to keep the same hyper voice he'd started with. He opened the nearby door that the kid pointed out, but was stopped by an idea.

"Say, listen. I just got on shift. The last guy, he had a cart with some tools and supplies. Oscillia-Recto-Suctions and, and..." Webrid regretted getting too detailed, but now that he'd started, he was stuck. "And some rabbidiated D.S.Q. wires." That sounded good. "Where do you suppose ol' Ardrin might have stashed that cart?"

The novice scratched his chin, which was the widest point on his body. "Down the stairs, just to your left, is a big supply closet. I know because a few times I went in by mistake, thinking it was the vending machine room. But that's one door farther down."

Webrid grinned, and his pleasure was sincere.

"Oh, and they have real nice sandwiches in the vending room, if you're hungry."

"Thanks, man. You're the best."

The supply closet was easy to find, but there was no familial cart waiting for him in there.

"Why should it be here, you idiot?" Webrid berated himself. "Nothing in your life is ever going to go right again."

He sat down in heavy misery on an overturned bucket. His face in his hands, his skull pulsing with pain, he listened to his own breathing. A series of new sounds, whirring and clinking machinery, made him jump. It took him a minute to remember that the closet he was in was next to the vending room. Webrid noticed that there was a door leading directly from his closet into that room. He then noticed that he was starving.

Having waited until there'd been no sound for several beats, Webrid opened the door and viewed a snacker's paradise. It was one of those Mega-Vends he'd heard about, practically a supermarket of small meals, pick-me-ups, beverages, and treats.

Instinctively, Webrid reached for money in his pocket. But he was wearing a plastic surgical suit. That didn't matter anyway, since the Mega-Vend took only Vox cards. Webrid could clearly picture his Vox ID card on the floor of his room at the Royal Ksacheeli Hotel on the planet Cheed. No snacks for a hungry carter.

He didn't have time to really get into feeling sorry for himself, though. Voices were coming nearer. Webrid dived back into the supply closet and sat by the door to listen, trying not to breathe too loudly.

"Where is he?"

"Lab."

"So they couldn't get it out?"

"It's hardwired to his brain."

"Damn, that's rough. So they have to use him?"

"Yeah. A carter. Can you imagine? A dirty old carter the central pawn in a civil w..."

"Sshhh! Rilsy, don't say that!"

"Well, that's what it is. We're supposed to be one government—at least that's what I was taught at school. Now, all because of some lame forests, the whole Circle's coming apart. We haven't needed forests my whole life. Why do we need 'em now? Just burn the damned things. Not worth this hassle and expense."

"Some people think they're important."

"Some people think like my grandpa! We should run our government like that? Maybe you want to go back to life before the Vox, too. No info, everyone just scraping by in the dark."

There were beeps, clicks, clunks, and thuds from the vending machines as the conversation continued.

"They'll work it out."

"What are you, born yesterday?" Webrid heard the distinctive sound of a hand smacking a vending machine. "Darn it, they're out of Snefrons. Are those shintal crisps any good?"

"Yeah, they're okay. How come you're so sure the situation is that bad?"

"Dude, that Rommey group in Cheed was never supposed to have any, you know, real power. They're not supposed to, like, do stuff on their own. Definitely not stuff they don't tell the capitals about. They're up there, up in the forests, making plans without telling anyone."

"So, how'd the capitals find out?"

"Spies, man. How else?"

Webrid's mind raced through a lineup of everyone he'd ever met. They all looked like they could be bought.

"You think there's gonna be...you know?"

The answer came as a stage whisper. "I bet they're gonna deal with it using a hired hitman. Or a High-Training Team. They don't wanna use the army, that'd get people all freaked out."

"Yeah. I guess so."

"So, the thing in his brain is what, now?"

"Nobody's saying. But it must be really important. Top-secret message."

"I bet it's the data on..."

Webrid would have given his right tongue to hear the end of that sentence, but a shrieking alarm went off just then.

The oddly calm female Vox-voice was broadcasting over the din. "Urgent. Person of interest roaming building. Male. Yeril. May be dangerous. Lock-down in twenty, nineteen, eighteen, seventeen..."

Webrid scanned his surroundings. The vending room was out, since there were people in there.

"Sixteen, fifteen, fourteen..."

The main door of the closet went out into a big hallway. Even if he risked it, how would he exit the building from there in thirteen seconds?

"Thirteen, twelve, ten, nine..."

The floor was covered smoothly with a painted varnish. The ceiling was a possibility, but even standing on the bucket, he couldn't reach it. Was there a ladder?

"Eight, seven, six, five..."

On a little doorway just to his left, Webrid saw a wonderful word: TRASH.

"Four, three, two..."

Headfirst, he plunged out that tiny door.

Not surprisingly, he landed in a pile of trash. After righting himself, he felt a thrill in the realization that he was not in a trash room, but in an outdoor trash area. He had escaped! Still, he knew he had to get far away, and fast, or he'd be right back on that table getting his brains carved up.

Webrid climbed and crawled over every type of refuse, finally touching his foot to the ground. He was extracting his other foot from a bag of goopy sandwich wrappers when he noticed something a few arm lengths away. It was a wheel. A very familiar wheel.

Wading back in, Webrid reached his cart. Half of it was buried, but in no time he had rescued it and let it roll out onto the pavement. As he was crawling out of the refuse, he noticed two of his suitcases poking out of a gloppy knot of lunch containers. One of the suitcases still had clothes in it, which, to be honest, offended him.

"How come nobody stole this?" he asked, holding up his favorite green-dotted tunic.

He dragged the lot out of the trash pile. With a Snefrons wrapper, he wiped off the more offensive blobs of wet food. Using his index claw as a razor, he split his plastic bodysuit in several places until he could peel it off like a Prushaskian dancer at Joolo's shed her clothes. He put on one of his own outfits and enjoyed being able to breathe normally.

While loading the cases into the cart, Webrid decided to tempt fate just a bit more than he already had. He opened the smaller case and poked a claw into the lining. His wad of dendiacs was still there.

Again relief and umbrage swirled together. His captors had assumed he had nothing valuable because he was Yeril and a laborer. Classist creeps! "They know I'm no master criminal. They know I'm just a puppet with no control over this situation." Part of him wished that they had pulled apart his suitcase fiber by fiber. It would have done a lot for his self-image.

Webrid was messing with the cart's loose wheels, muttering to himself about what a raw deal most folks got, when a terrifying noise jolted him back to the here and now. Strident alarm bells blasted from every floor of the capital building, and strobe lights pulsed in magenta and white.

"Damn! They're lookin' for me!" He straightened up, addressing the cart. "I know it hurts, pal, but we gotta *run*."

The cart's axles were bent, preventing the four wheels

from touching the ground at the same time. When Webrid pushed, it didn't really roll, but did a painful jig, jumping forward and back and side to side. As a kind of shock absorption, Webrid mimicked the motions of his cart. The two partners continued their freakish, high-speed dance along the road, shimmying as fast as they could wobble.

Every third or fourth repetition of the lurching pattern, Webrid sneaked a look behind to see how many cop-bots were after them. He never saw a single one. For the first eight blocks, he was sure he was being pursued by some new type of bot that could blend in with city dwellers, or maybe camouflage as a storefront or something. By the ninth block, when he still hadn't been forced onto the ground by a circle of Vox enforcement goons, he finally started to relax.

He was downtown now. The gritty, greasy city smells stuck to Webrid's soul like a favorite song.

"Good to be home," he said to his cart, which bumped up and down worrisomely along the alleys. "We'll fix you up, and you'll be good as new." He added in a sing-song, "Good as old, which is better than gold."

Unconsciously, Webrid had begun walking the more dangerous of his carting routes, the one he used for distributing bootleg booze, not jamboro cakes.

"Where am I going, anyhow?" he asked, pausing near a Vernibec oaf passed out across a generator box. He was surprised to hear a loud, nasal response.

"Down the road to perdition, sweetheart."

The Vernibec hadn't moved any of his mouths.

"Who said that?" Webrid demanded.

A little yellow creature, barely reaching Webrid's knee, stepped from behind the generator.

"You sure ask a lot of questions for a psychic," he said.

Webrid bent down for a closer look. "Who says I'm a psychic?"

The little fellow pointed to his own hat with a rashy tendril. "You got one of them scarlet seeing caps, don't you? It's got the sparkly jewel in the center. Or did you swipe that?"

"What?" Webrid reached up and opened his palm in front of his forehead. The laser, shining through the scarf, made a small glowing circle on his hand. An image of the dissolving skull of his attacker on Cheed played back in his mind. He sure didn't need that to happen again.

"Say, friend," he started.

Eyes slanted with suspicion, the little fellow interrupted, "Whatever it is, brother, it's gonna cost you."

"But of course." With deft fingers, Webrid pulled a dendiac note from the stash in his pocket. Then he said something he'd never dreamed would pass his lips. "I need to find an Akardian."

Just the thought of one of those earlobe-wreathed sales slugs usually gave Webrid the severe heebie-jeebies. But he also understood that sometimes only a top-flight expert would do. Nobody could acquire exotic contraband as efficiently as an Akardian.

Webrid needn't have wasted his dendiac. The little fellow directed him to Reekol's Pub, which Webrid already knew to be crawling with Akardians and other of Bargival's undesirable but essential types.

"Sheesh, I've only been off the planet a couple days, and I'm already acting like a tourist in my own city."

What disturbed him more, though, was that he simply could not piece together exactly how many days it had been since his nightmare began.

"This laser thing's giving me brain damage, you bet," he grumbled. He'd reached Reekol's, and pushed his cart right into the pub.

"Hey, man, watch it with that thing," an irate customer

grumbled. "You ran over my toes."

"Sorry, gotta keep it with me." Webrid had lost the key to lock the wheels, so he couldn't leave his cart safely on the street. And he certainly wasn't going to be separated again from his beloved business partner and confidant.

There were plenty of Akardians in Reekol's. Not having a contact among them, Webrid reasoned that one was as good as the next. He chose the closest one. She was female; he knew because her many earlobes were more maroon than brown.

"Buy you a drink, sweetness?" Webrid oozed.

"Sexist bastard," she said. "But I'll take the drink anyhow."

Webrid, impressed by her forthrightness and practicality, obliged with a goblet of Yellow Cloud. He got himself his usual Val-Hundred. As he peeled more notes from his pocket, he longed to have a close look at his cash supply. The middle of this joint, though, was not the place.

"So," the Akardian said, "you're lonely. I can hook you up with somebody nice at a good price. Or do you just want to take something that makes you feel like you've got company?"

Webrid marveled at how she'd already completed two sales pitches before she'd taken as many sips of her drink.

"I need a different kind of merchandise," he said, not denying that he really was lonely. "It might be a special order."

"Lay it on me, boss. There's nothing I can't get my hands on."

"Okay, then." He leaned in toward her, unsure how dangerous this conversation was. "I need a bnarli."

"Say again?"

He did so, but she still looked blank.

Webrid tried to give some hints. "I got one off a colleague of yours a few days ago."

"Which colleague would that be?"

"Well, I don't know his name, but I thought you might..."

The Akardian stood up in a huff. "What, you think we all know each other?" She pounded down her drink in one gulp. "I guess we all look the same to you?" Her fillet of facial lobes wobbled with indignation.

Webrid stood, too, desperate to keep the peace. "No, no, I just don't know his name. I remember he had, um..." He clawed at his memory. "He had particularly long teeth. Very blue teeth, not gray like yours. He was working in the Central Spaceport."

The Akardian sat back down, clearly curious. "Long blue teeth?"

"That's right."

"Exactly where in the spaceport was he?"

Although it embarrassed him, Webrid answered truthfully. "In the, you know, the men's room." He was about to apologize, but the saleslady whooped with delight.

"You mean Kardistac?"

"Um..."

"Yeah, that's gonna be Kardi. He's my bro-in-law. Always works the guys' john." She stood and waved across the room. "Hey, Kardi! Got a customer."

Webrid was in equal parts relieved at his good luck and mortified to have this attention drawn to himself. But Reekol's attracted a mainly coarse-mannered clientele, so a little shouting garnered only a few brief glances.

A tall Akardian lurched across to the bar. To his surprise, Webrid really *could* tell them apart. This was unmistakably the pusher from the Spaceport restroom.

Kardi took one look at Webrid's laser-lit turban and chuckled knowingly. "Had a bit of bother?"

"You could say that, yeah," Webrid admitted, dreading how deeply he was about to get scalped.

Pretending to consider, Kardi said, "They ain't easy to get."

"Uh-huh." Webrid worked hard not to sound desperate. "But I bet you've got another one."

"Maybe. You got two hundred D?"

Webrid sputtered out a laugh in admiration for Kardi's raw chutzpah. "Seriously, man? Twice the price?"

They haggled the price down to a hundred and thirty-five D. As they shook on it, all Webrid could do was pray he still had that much cash.

He did, but only just. Kardi told him to meet him in the men's room. (What was it with this guy and restrooms?) Webrid made his way back to the facilities, and the Akardian showed up a few minutes later, having procured a bnarli from somewhere. It didn't look especially clean, and Webrid's stomach acids rose to imagine the fate of whoever had worn it last. Nevertheless, he put it on.

Kardi bought the red scarf from him for a couple dendiacs. That money would assure Webrid a warm dinner. But he was still a fugitive, and after dinner he'd be completely broke. Webrid bumped his cart out onto the street and thought about his next move.

hat Webrid wanted more than anything was to go home to his tenement apartment. He could think of nothing more enticing than to sniff its mildewed bouquet.

"Couple problems with that idea, though," he muttered at his cart, now parked next to a bench outside Sandwich Sensations.

Webrid enumerated those problems as he chewed his spicy jantz roll. "There's the ID situation. The ID card is my door key. And it's, you know, on another planet."

He took a large bite. "Now, I could get around that via the landlord. Old Ratchor Miggs was so impressed that I paid in advance, he'd probably fall for a line." He looked at his cart for encouragement. It just listened, reserving judgment.

"See, I could tell him my card was damaged. That another one was coming in a few hours, and couldn't he just let me in? He'd go for it."

Refocusing on the injured cart, Webrid recalled how many times its—and his—life had been endangered over the past few days. With an affectionate pat on the cart's handles, he assured it, "We won't go home now. That's exactly where they're expecting us to go." Webrid wiped his mouth with his sleeve. "There's gotta be someplace else we can crash for a couple nights. At least until things die down."

Sleepy and cold, huddling on the bench, Webrid's mind scrolled through his list of so-called friends. There were ex-lovers (none of whom would speak to him now), carting clients (none of whom would risk their reputations to help him), his aged mother (whose visitors were monitored by convalescence center security). And then there was Abna Stravin.

Stravin was an occasional drinking buddy. Officially, he made a little money as an engineer on city projects. Unofficially, he made mountains of money inventing mechanisms to assist various criminal endeavors. Although Webrid primarily needed a bed for the night, it would be an added bonus if Stravin could throw some free advice his way. Nobody knew more than Stravin about living below the Vox's radar.

Forcing his aching bones and mangled cart ten blocks to what he thought was Stravin's neighborhood, he asked around until he found the right house. Stravin was at home, and although he seemed thoroughly surprised, he welcomed his battle-battered friend.

"Oh, you must tell me every little thing," Stravin insisted, shaking his white, feathery skin as he often did when he was intrigued.

Webrid tried to breeze past his troubles. "I just need a place to stay." He was suddenly bashful about barging into the private life of a pub pal.

"You're most welcome. The latest love of my life just dumped me, so there's even extra space around here. And I could sure do with a sympathetic ear."

"My ear is your ear." Webrid started to relax, amused by a sudden image of Reekol's bar packed with hundred-lobed Akardians. "Hey, anyplace safe I could put this?" He indicated his cart, hoping he wouldn't be forced to leave it outside.

"Park it in the front hall, next to the Moti-Moto."

"Thanks, I appreciate it. Great-lookin' scooter, that Moti." Webrid admired the vehicle's shiny white finish. He thought about running a hand over the pliable burgundy seat, but his natural machismo objected.

The little machine was a jet propulsion scooter, very expensive. "It's the only civilized way to get around town," said Stravin. "Like to take it for a spin tomorrow?"

"Would I!" He pictured the come-hither looks he'd get from babes all over town. That wasn't something he often got to experience.

Stravin invited Webrid into the house and got him comfortable in a soft chair with a drink and a snack.

"Now," he said, adjusting the volume of the schmaltzy pop music he'd put on. "Spill."

Webrid made one brief attempt at feigning ordinary troubles. "Just a damned deal gone wrong, you know. Gotta lay low for a while."

Stravin draped his arms over the back of his chair. It was a disconcertingly feminine move. "Tell me *everything*. I love a good thriller."

Webrid was good at telling little lies quickly to get out of scrapes, but he had no skills at upholding a layered fictional narrative. Anyhow, Stravin had probably lived through any scenario Webrid's meager imagination could cook up. It would have to be the truth.

"Could you ask the Vox about the weather?" Webrid said.

Stravin's eyes gleamed. He knew that old trick. "Let's step outside and check for ourselves," he replied.

They didn't go outside, but into a small room with galvanized velancium walls and ceiling.

"No Vox here," said Stravin, "but do speak quietly. You just never know."

Webrid cleared his throat and wondered how to describe his last few days in a way that didn't seem ridiculous.

Stravin sprayed drinks from a siphon in the wall. "Direct line to a barrel of Yellow Cloud," he said with a wink.

"Right, thanks," said Webrid. He took a big drink and a big breath. "I have a secret government data laser implanted in my skull."

Stravin shook his skin so fervently, it looked like a sirocco was ripping through his down. "Oh, *please* go on."

And so, Webrid did. He told his friend everything he could remember, sometimes backtracking a bit when he'd missed a detail. Letting it all pour out was quite a relief. Then he chuckled, suddenly aware that Stravin was pacing the floor nervously.

"Sorry, man. I'm sure I'm boring you. And you can't possibly believe any of this crazy..."

"Boring me? Not *believe* you?" Stravin stopped pacing and drilled his gaze into Webrid, as if he had his own laser. "Darling, I'm designing a plan to *save* you."

Impressed, Webrid said, "Again, my ears are your ears."

Stravin refilled their drinks and dug a bag of fried shintal chips out of a trunk. "I'm set for any emergency," he said, winking again.

Webrid was not in the mood for coyness. "Do you really think you can help me? I gotta warn you, I don't have access to all that money anymore."

Wagging a finger, Stravain rebuked him. "Silly man. Silly, hairy man. I don't want your money."

"You don't?" Webrid drew an arc with his arm to show that he knew velancium walls were not cheap.

"No, no, noooo..." Letting the last utterance trail off, Stravin came very close to Webrid and whispered, "I just want an adventure."

When Webrid didn't respond immediately, Stravin rolled his eyes and said, "I want you to let me go with you, silly man."

Webrid squirmed at a number of things in that sentence. First, he wasn't attracted to males and feared Stravin had misconstrued their relationship. Second, he doubted their friendship had a strong enough foundation for trust in the midst of peril.

His third concern was the only one he voiced. "What do you mean, 'go'? Where am I going?"

Stravin's laugh was like the cascade of chimes you heard in the countryside on the first day of the straliem harvest. "Well, for one thing, my dear, you won't find the solution to your problems inside this house. And..."

"Oh," said a relieved Webrid, "you just meant..."

"And *second*," Stravin said forcefully, clearly a man not used to being interrupted, "you'll surely have to return to Cheed."

"No freaking way." Cheed had brought him nothing but misery. "Can't I deal with this in Bargival? I mean, it *is* the capital, and we know the government is in on the situation somehow."

Stravin walked past Webrid without meeting his gaze. Unsealing the door of the protective room, he said as he stepped out, "You may stay here. I can help you do it your way, for which I will charge you on account. Or I can help you do it the right way, no charge."

He turned to look at Webrid, and his eyes softened. "You're tired. Get some rest, and you'll make a better decision in the morning. The couch in the next room is quite comfortable."

It truly was a comfortable couch. Webrid awoke well rested, and sure he'd made up his mind. He asked a bleary Stravin to join him in the metal room.

"What would you charge to help me go off the grid?" he asked once they were soundproofed.

Stravin set a clod of jamboro cake in front of him. "Off the grid is not what you want."

"Yes, it is. I'm not going back to Cheed."

"Fine, fine. What I'm saying is, you want grid concealment, not to go off the grid."

"What's the difference?" asked Webrid.

"How's your cake, dear?"

Webrid nearly lashed out impatiently about wasting time, but he realized the jamboro was, in fact, delicious. It wasn't related to those rock-hard things he carted for Joffl Mar at Briziu Bakery.

"The cake is great. Really great. But I..."

Stravin shushed him. "Off the grid means living in a forest, in a thatched hut with no amenities, hunting and gathering your food, and giving up the ghost when you get sick. These exquisite cakes were a gift from someone I have concealed *inside* the grid. This person has an income, access to their money, housing, and healthcare. Yet the Vox couldn't tell you the first thing about them."

Webrid's heart raced with hope. "How's that possible?"

"I'm hooked into a network dealing in temporary IDs. The street name for them is 'loopholes' because they're made possible by a logic gap in the Vox program."

"Sweet!"

"So, the client must keep switching official identities within a certain class that doesn't attract scrutiny from the security system."

Even if this wasn't too good to be true, Webrid knew it was too good to be affordable.

Laughing in defeat, he asked, "What's the tab?"

"Just your firstborn child."

"No sweat," said Webrid. "I've got no paternal instincts anyhow."

They had a good chuckle, but soon got down to real numbers. The price was astronomical, and it was obvious to Webrid that he would spend his entire life paying it off, even with the money this Rempener Dras person or company or thing had put in his account.

"I just don't know," he admitted.

Stravin waved a downy arm. "Let me know tomorrow. Today, let's go have some fun. My treat."

They bar-hopped their way through their favorite neighborhoods, bragging and swaggering in drunken glee. And they each chatted up whoever seemed pretty enough, although that came to a disappointing nothing for both of them. It occurred to Webrid once or twice that he shouldn't be so visible, what with the cops being after him. But he was sure none of the denizens of these places would turn him in. The list of their own secrets was too long.

Sloshed and happy, Webrid and Stravin rolled back home in the wee hours. Without even brushing his teeth, Webrid slammed face-first onto the couch and fell asleep instantly. It was not, however, a restful and restorative night.

"Boy-oooo!" he heard a voice call from the depths of his consciousness. "Boy-oooo!"

Webrid sat up, or perhaps dreamed that he sat up. "Grandpa?"

"It's me, boy-o." Indeed, his grandfather's furry brown face hung like a film in his mind's eye. He'd been dead for decades.

"Gee, Gramps. What are you doing here?"

"I'm ashamed, boy-o."

"Ashamed of me? What did I do?"

"What did you do? What did you dooooooooo?" The specter cackled. "It ain't what you done, boy-o. It's what you ain't done."

Webrid reached out, but his hand went through the image. "What ain't I done, Gramps?"

"Such a pathetic oaf, you. Did your momma raise you to be a no-good? Tell me she didn't raise no no-good!"

"What do you mean, Gramps?"

"The job, boy-o. You got a job, and you ain't finished it yet. What kind of a carter are you?"

"The laser?"

"Whatever it is. Who cares what it is? Ain't your job to care. It's your job to cart."

"But I'd have to go all the way to Cheed and I don't want..."

"So it's lazy is what you is, eh? Eh?"

"No, I'm not lazy, I just..."

"If you ain't lazy, then do the job you got. There's so many people in the galaxy got no work, and you too good to do the job you been handed. You bring me shame, boy-o. You don't deserve to push my cart."

By now, Webrid was in tears. "I'm sorry, Grandpa. Don't be mad, Gramps. And don't take the cart away. Please, please, *please*. I'll deliver the laser. I will. I'll go to Cheed. Just please, you gotta be proud of me..." He was bawling openly.

"Webrid?" The sound of his name seeped through his blubbering. "Webrid, wake up." That wasn't his grandfather's voice. "Hey, silly man. You're dreaming."

The carter felt Stravin's soft, feathered hand on his forehead and pried open his eyelids to look into Stravin's black eyes. "Hey," he said.

"Tough night, huh?" said Stravin sympathetically. "That Val-Hundred will get you every time. You should switch to something lighter."

"Stravin?" Webrid fought back a waking onslaught of tears. "Stravin?"

"Yes, my dear?"

"Let's go to Cheed."

ou're not bringing this."

Packing for the trip was not going well. Stravin stood between Webrid and his cart, not realizing what a perilous place that was.

"I have to take my cart." Webrid was trying to decide at which joint he could most efficiently snap this feathered moron in two. Breathing deeply to control his anger, he tried a practical argument instead. "We can carry stuff in it. Clothes. Food. Water. If one of us gets injured, he can ride in the cart. If we get shot at, we can duck behind it. I just need my axle fixed, man. Anyhow, I'm not going without it."

Stravin remained firm and argued on the side of fashion. "It's old. It's broken. It's dreadful. We'll look like vagabonds."

"So? That's a great disguise."

"Speak for yourself, you tough-hided Yeril." Stravin stroked his own downy neck. "No one would believe it of me."

Deciding that a homicide rap would mess up his life even worse, Webrid tried logic. "But I'm a carter. And I'm going to Cheed working as a carter."

Stravin sighed. "But what you're carting isn't in this cart."

He pointed to Webrid's bnarli. "I'm not suggesting you leave your head behind, dear."

Webrid had zero taste for that flavor of condescension. Unable to stop himself, he grasped Stravin's soft, slender shoulders in his clawed hands. He spoke in a growl. "This cart has been in my family for generations." His breath made Stravin's silky facial feathers ripple. "Leaving it behind would be turning my back on my people."

"Well, why didn't you say so?" Stravin, obviously unafraid, wriggled free. "I'll make you a deal. You can bring your cart if I can bring that." He pointed at his Moti-Moto power scooter. "I abhor walking, especially in a strange place. It makes me feel such a... such a tourist, you know?"

Webrid agreed completely that bringing the scooter was a good idea, but admitting it seemed somehow like caving in. Trying to sound reluctant, he drawled, "Well, I guess that's fair enough."

"Splendid! Now, we've got things to do. I know people who can hook us up with some transport. And my friend Dremba can put a new axle on that thing." He raised his eyebrows and looked sideways at the cart. He then turned the same disapproving look toward Webrid's attire. "And you clearly lost all your decent clothes in the trash bin."

Too ashamed to admit that all his favorite shirts and pants had still been in his suitcase when he found it, Webrid simply said, "I can't access my money now, so..."

"Shhh! Not another word. New clothes are on me. I sense a better adventure coming than this screwny bag o' bones has had in two Raralt decades. The least I can do is sponsor the fun."

Stravin strode to the far wall of the metal room and dislodged a panel. After digging around in the wall for a few seconds, he pulled out a pouch of woven gareften fibers, an indestructible fabric used by the military and sun-hoppers.

Webrid was impressed. He'd heard of this ultra-rare fabric, and recognized it now by the telltale swirling rainbow sheen over its gray color.

With a wink and a warning to keep quiet, Stravin drew out a thick block of Universal Dendiacs from the pouch. U.D. notes were good not only on any of the four planets in the Raralt Circle, but also on space tours and on the Fregnis outer colonial planets. They were worth more than normal dendiacs, and were used mainly by top governmental officials, lawyers, and business moguls. Webrid was dying to "ooh" and "aah" like a schoolboy, but he bit both of his tongues.

"This should do us," said Stravin.

Webrid estimated his friend was holding enough for a carter of modest needs to live for three years.

"I'll pay you back," Webrid offered pointlessly.

Stravin gave Webrid an affectionate nudge. "Just remember, I'm buying an adventure."

"I don't think you'll be disappointed, then. I just hope you live to enjoy the memories."

"Really, my dear." Stravin beamed a smile. "I find I accumulate better memories if I live assuming I won't get to remember them."

Opening a small door on the back of the scooter, Stravin pulled out a towing hook. This he latched to the cart's push-bar. Then he patted the cart and climbed onto the Moti-Moto. "Come on. Let's go do something completely mad."

They rode slowly into town, with Webrid worrying about his cart at every corner they turned. The cart never capsized, but it teetered plenty. After ages of wending through Bargival's alleys, Stravin stopped in front of a garage door. Someone peeked her head out a window, then stepped out from a smaller door set within the large one.

"Darling!" cried Stravin.

"Darling!" cried a shiny, coal-black Zinna woman dressed in a tight-fitting, grease-smeared laborer's suit.

"Dremba, meet my friend Webrid."

After Stravin gave a quick explanation of what they needed, Dremba got them set up on her work floor. She inspected Webrid's cart while Webrid inspected her chassis. Happily, Dremba had as much skill as she did hips. It didn't take long for her to replace the axle.

"I owe this fella big-time," she said, indicating Stravin, who sat on a stool with his knees drawn up, apparently trying not to get dirty. "You want I should throw in some new wheels? X-Bindag Super-Molec synth, military-grade. You could roll over a mine field with these."

"Uh, yeah, thanks," said Webrid. As he watched her attach these wheels, shiny and tar-black as her beautiful skin, he silently wondered what the point was. Why have mine-proof wheels on his cart when the carter could be blown up just like any poor schmuck? Instead of asking that, he admired her quick, confident work. "Fantastic. Looks forever solid."

"That's my middle name." She bared her nubby teeth. "You guys want some lunch? Veer's up in the house and I think he was fixing some..."

The police pulse-net paralyzed her mid-sentence.

"Freeze!" grated the amplified voice of a cop-bot.

There were suddenly twenty of the multi-limbed, gun-toting machines, coming in through the windows and doors. Their engine screams and siren wails swirled around Webrid like an arsonist's blaze.

Webrid thought he'd been struck by the pulse-net, too, since he couldn't seem to move. Not quite true: He could blink in terror. He squeezed his eyes closed once, opening them to find Stravin gone from his stool. He closed his eyes again, and felt himself being hoisted and dumped. At the very moment his poor brain was figuring out that he was inside his cart, and that the cart was again attached to the scooter, the Moti-Moto roared forward at heart-squashing speed. Webrid had just lifted his head to get his bearings when the jolt of motion brought the cart lid down on his skull. Everything went black.

The carted carter awoke to the pain of two hundred bruises and the mother of all hangovers. Wherever he was, it was dark, hot, loud, and vibrating bumpily. He might never have remembered what had happened, but seeing and smelling the pinpoint of green laser light singe the corner of Stravin's designer suitcase did the trick. Webrid fumbled to adjust the bnarli, dousing the caustic light.

It took several Yeril-sized heaves to force the cart lid up far enough to see outside. Through the eye-width opening under the lid, he could see how his ancient cart was tearing past ramshackle abodes at the pace of a double-engine loping car vying for the finish line. Determining that there was nothing he could do about this, he nestled back down amid the suitcases and fell asleep.

During a vivid dream about warm janz rolls dripping with sauce, Webrid felt a cool spring breeze tickle his cheek. Then he felt feathers tickle his ear. "Stop it," he giggled to the sandwich vendor in his dream.

"Wakey wakey."

"I'm still hungry," Webrid moaned.

"There's some food on the boat. C'mon. Get up." The sandwich man's gentle voice morphed into the harsh rasp of an impatient Stravin, and the wispy feathers turned into poking fingers.

"Huh?" Finally awake, Webrid used the suitcases to haul himself to a sitting position.

Stravin was talking at high speed and low volume, while a murky green blob of a creature paced behind him with a squish-squish-squish along the swampy ground.

"I don't see how they could home in on your laser with that bnarli on you," Stravin was saying. "Must have found you from spy intel. Had to get the hell out of there. Good thing we brought the Moti, eh? And good thing I'd souped it up so it can go twice as fast as any crap police craft." Stravin paused for a satisfied, knowing laugh, which he shared with the squishy green guy.

The green guy said something like, "Xal teeja reeostril," and let out a gurgly snort.

"So true, my dear," Stravin said with a slow nod, and laughed again.

Webrid, disoriented and left out of the joke, felt small, naïve, and distinctly uncool. He was also becoming aware of a stomach-churning stench all around them. Before he could mention it, Stravin towed the cart—with Webrid still in it—onto the green guy's boat. They set off quickly from shore.

The air was hot as an Entra lady's navel, and Webrid couldn't bear to sit still. With the other two occupied at the helm, he climbed out of the cart and peeked over the edge of the boat. They were floating on a sea of something thick and cloudy that kept changing color. Then Webrid heard a deep, sucking sound below him. He leaned farther forward to investigate. Fortunately, the huge green guy yanked Webrid back by the shoulders just as a giant flame shot upward.

"Zharnikl!" He pointed over the side as he reproached

Webrid, who was trembling. "Zharnikl tabooshik!"

Webrid tried to thank the guy and introduce himself, but the green blob ignored him and slopped back to the control panel.

"What's that noise?" Webrid asked from the dead center of the deck, far from the shooting flames. He could hear the sounds of hovercraft and light scooters in the distance.

Stravin joined him. "The cops are still after us. You know, maybe we should cut off your head. Or maybe just do a little lobotomy. Lose that pesky laser of yours." He gave a tinny laugh.

Once again, Webrid missed the humor. "Look. If you need to ditch me, just do it. No reason for you to risk…"

"Don't even say it, darling. I'm in for the whole adventure. It's what I paid for, remember?"

Now Webrid knew why they had come to this particular point in the middle of nowhere. This must be the Drejeean Fireswamp. Cop craft would be destroyed by the super-heated flames that were belching up around them, but somehow this boat could withstand it all. In the distance, Webrid could hear choking engines, roaring fire, and exploding vehicles.

Stravin must have seen the look of concern on Webrid's face. "Don't worry, my dear. It's just cop-bots getting blown up. Not people."

That was a huge relief. After a few minutes, they could hear no pursuers, and the boat turned onto a tributary of calmer, cooler gases. Webrid almost felt hope.

"Can I ask a stupid question?"

"There are no stupid questions," said Stravin. "Only stupid people." He and the green guy guffawed.

"Oh, har har har," Webrid clucked. This feathered jerk was really gnawing at his nerve endings. "My question is, where are we going?"

"To Cheed."

"No, seriously. On a gas cruiser?"

The green guy snorted. Apparently there really were stupid questions after all.

"Of course not, silly man," said Stravin. "We're going to see another friend. She has a spacecraft."

"Uh-huh. You have a friend with her own spacecraft." *And I've got a nice plot of land to sell you on Rada-2,* Webrid added silently.

Stravin put too much effort into looking blasé. "Of course, dear. It's got the smallest space-safe engine in the known universe. And she owes me a ride."

"Really? What did you do for her?"

"Well..." Stravin turned and smiled coyly. "I designed the engine for the spacecraft." And he had to add, "On very short notice."

All Webrid could do was sigh. As usual, things were out of his hands.

Stravin went below deck to use a Vox-proof communicator (which he had also designed, of course), and the green guy settled in by the controls with a box of cookies that he did not offer to share.

Webrid rummaged through the food box and settled on a vacuum-pack of janz jerky and a bottle of straliem juice. Unhappily, there was no booze aboard. Probably would've caught fire in the gaseous atmosphere, he reasoned with a sigh. Safety first.

As Webrid chewed and the boat bumped over the semi-liquid river, he mulled over his choice to complete his mission, despite its clear peril and murky provenance. Could this, he wondered, be one of those moral quandaries he'd heard about?

Never before had he harbored doubts about his job. He'd always just picked up his cargo, delivered it, and collected his pay, as one thing naturally follows the next. There had never been anything to think about. He was a carter, not a philosopher. So why start now?

What did he care about government splinter groups? What did he care about resistance movements? Anyway, he'd never even found out what they were resisting.

"Ugh. Shouldn't have thought about that," he said aloud. Remembering the resistance group on the *S.R.S. Draspar* back on Cheed brought to mind the lean and luscious Leshi.

Webrid realized that he was facing no moral quandary. He couldn't care less about what he was carrying, or for whom. And, although he did want to complete the job for which he'd been hired, his work ethic was only part of what drove him in this suicidal mission.

The other part was love.

t was dark by the time they reached the docks adjoining a private airfield. The green guy hugged Stravin farewell, but didn't even acknowledge Webrid. No loss there, he figured.

Although Stravin offered to tow him in the cart, Webrid decided it was more dignified to ride on the Moti-Moto's rear seat instead.

"Hang on tight," Stravin said.

"I'm pretty beat, so maybe not light speed, okay?" Webrid requested.

"Right you are, dear. Slow and steady."

There was a rocket standing upright in the center of the field, and next to it was someone who waved as they approached. Stravin got all huggy again.

"Hi, I'm Zatell," said a creature who was apparently female. She had a head in the center of her body, ringed by long, thin arms (or were they legs?) like rays of a sun. She walked on several of them and waved with a few more. And sometimes she rolled, putting her limbs down two at a time.

She smiled warmly at Webrid. "You must be the laserman.

I hear you need a ride."

It was nice to be addressed in a friendly manner for a change. And "laserman" was a kickin' nickname. Webrid shook one of her hands, being careful not to cut the delicate extremity with his claws.

"Can you do this thing for us?" Stravin asked, looking ghostlike in the inky night.

"You got dendiacs for fuel?"

Out came the indestructible money pouch, and a sheaf of notes changed hands.

"So, I can drop you there," Zatell said, "but I gotta come right back. I got business here."

Webrid was about to object strenuously to being stranded on Cheed, but Stravin waved his hand to show it didn't matter. So that was that, then.

After some dinner, Zatell helped them pull clear air-pressure suits over their clothes. "Maybe I can come pick you up in a half-moon."

To Webrid, a half-moon in an uncharted section of a strange planet seemed like half a lifetime.

Stravin was still unconcerned. "A half-moon? Oh, that's much too far ahead to plan," he said. "By that time, we could either be dead or the newly appointed co-presidents of Cheed. In either case, we'll have no need of a ride back to Bexilla."

It was all so ridiculous, Webrid just shrugged and laughed. He sincerely hoped Grandpa could see the mess he'd talked him into.

"Well, let's get set up." Zatell seemed raring to go, clapping a few pairs of hands together.

The inside of the rocket was even smaller than Webrid had expected. It took some serious strength and coordination for the three of them to secure the scooter and cart onto platforms in the rocket's top portion. They then strapped themselves in, with Stravin at the top, Webrid in the middle, and Zatell on the bottom. In Webrid's opinion, this tin can of a vessel could not have had less to do with commercial flight, or with anything a sane person would try.

The driver's seat at the control panel was designed for Zatell's species to scooch back into, letting her push her limbs forward. She was the consummate multi-tasker, apparently gifted with the mental adroitness to control the many tasks her arms might simultaneously attempt.

Webrid tried several times to count her limbs, but she was always moving them so much that it was hopeless. Somehow it seemed rude to just ask her, or even ask what her species was called. Webrid was sure he'd never seen one of her kind before; he would have remembered seeing someone like her on a crowded street in Bargival. She was basically a ball of limbs, but by lifting the upper ones and pulling the lower ones together, she could become sort of cylindrical. This explained the shape of the rocket, which was less than ideal for most species.

Turning his head to inspect the cramped space, Webrid reached out his arms and was able to touch the walls to either side. He realized to his horror that, although this was his third interplanetary voyage, it would be his first while conscious.

"Anybody got anything to get drunk on?" he asked.

Nobody answered, so he tried another tack. "Are we gonna die?"

Zatell's melodic laugh drew a fine counterpoint against Stravin's descending scales of mirth. Charmingly symphonic, but not the reassurance Webrid was hoping for.

"It just seems kinda...kinda..." He paused, rejecting words like "junky," "rickety," "unfinished," and "lethal." He settled on saying, "It seems kinda close quarters in here."

While Zatell laughed again, Stravin said, "Don't worry,

dear. I'm very soft when I land on you. Ask anyone."

Fountains of laughter sprang anew from Zatell, who was tinkering with a tiny metal box.

"Looks like a shoebox," Webrid said, pointing downward from the seat where he was strapped.

"Shoes of the gods, then, dear," Stravin sighed dreamily. "There's never been an engine like this."

"Definitely," agreed Zantell, entering some codes.

Something didn't make sense. Well, several things. But the issue foremost on Webrid's mind was the first to come out of his mouth. "How come you didn't sell this amazing engine to the government, or to the military? You'da been set for life."

The roaring of the engine drowned out more peals of laughter. Stravin looked down from his seat and mouthed, "Too good for them," favoring Webrid with a wink.

The take-off commenced. It bumped, it ground, it rattled, it rolled. Webrid thought all the rivets in his cart would become dislodged, not to mention the tendons holding his own limbs in place. The pain of the laser jiggling in his skull blurred his vision with a shower of green light. During the upward thrust against gravity, he was sure he'd lose his lunch. He then decided for certain that they would die within seconds.

Reaching that determination was oddly calming. Not only was Webrid no longer afraid, he didn't really care one way or the other. It was fate. A group of governmental radicals had chosen him. The resistance movement had chosen him. The government's establishment had chosen him. Somebody or something named Rempener Dras had chosen him. Even Stravin had chosen him as a means to an adventure. And here, through no choice of his own, was Ganpril Webrid, a carter and his cart, about to be atomized by a massive change in pressurization, a malfunctioning micro-engine, or the whim of the gods. What did any of it matter?

And then there was silence, silence so deep that Webrid assumed it was the corridor to eternity. He breathed in its welcome and let his mind float.

Hearing Zatell's voice surprised him deeply. "We're between atmospheres," she said, "just for a minute."

He could see Stravin at an odd angle from below, but even the dandy was still for once, perhaps awed by the sanctity of space. Webrid loved his friend for that. And his heart, jump-started by love, was grateful to be beating. He hadn't wanted to die after all.

The floating silence didn't last. Soon the rattling and rumpus rose again. The descent was a war zone of lurching, cracking, slamming, lung-squeezing, burning, artery-cutting, tooth-grinding agony. It was probably short, but you could have fooled Webrid. When they hit water, his head snapped forward so fast that he thought he'd broken his neck. No such luck. His day was just getting started.

"Um, guys?" It's never good when a pilot says that. Zatell did not sound happy. "Um, shit. There's a problem."

The rocket was on its belly now, in a body of water or other liquid sea, presumably on Cheed. Webrid could not even imagine what could be described as "a problem" that would not kill them almost immediately.

"A big problem."

Nice.

Stravin sounded offended. "*Not* with the engine," he announced as fact.

"No, no. Engine's fine," Zatell said.

Webrid thought that seemed like good news. Less likely they'd blow up.

"What's up, then?"

"Sorry, Strav," said Zatell. "Even a pristine engine designed by you won't fly a ship with broken thrusters." She used several arm-legs to unbuckle herself and turn back toward Webrid. "This rocket ain't going nowhere."

They crawled out the rocket's side door, which was now facing upward, out of the water. Webrid was impressed how Zatell's limbs provided perfect swimming propulsion. She back-flopped into the lake and paddled toward the bank with the speed and precision of a motorboat.

"Hey, Webrid, give us a hand," Stravin called from inside the rocket.

"What do you need?" Webrid struggled to keep his balance on the rounded metal sheeting.

Stravin poked his head out the door. "Let's get my Moti out."

"And my cart," Webrid said firmly. It worried him that Stravin didn't respond. Webrid knew he had the strength to pull his cart out by himself, but he was not at all sure he knew how to swim. He lowered himself back into the rocket.

"You pull." Stravin had unstrapped the Moti-Moto and was trying to lift it with his spindly feathered arms.

"Amateur," Webrid mumbled. Stretching out his arms, he grabbed the scooter, yanking it out with one heave.

What he hadn't thought through was the theory of kinetic motion as it applied to this show of strength. As he and the scooter emerged from the rocket, they just kept on going, right into the lake.

Still holding tight to the front scooter seat, Webrid was engulfed in reddish water. He was just admiring some sort of glowing, spiky fish when two huge airbags exploded from the sides of the Moti. The scooter, and Webrid with it, popped up onto the surface, where the carter's drippy, bleary eyes made out a smiling Stravin.

"Welcome back, dear," he said, waving a couple of fingers. "Have a nice dip?" He went on before Webrid could clear his lungs. "Let's hook this up."

Stravin reached out and steadied the bobbing Moti. Following his orders, Webrid helped hook the towing line to the rocket cone. With Stravin in the driver's seat, darned if that little scooter didn't tow the big rocket, ancestral cart and all, safely to shore.

Webrid, panting, felt the stinging spray of the water—or whatever it was. He also felt Zatell staring at him from the glistening weeds. The Moti bumped hard against land, and Webrid was thrust forward, knocking Zatell backwards.

"'Scuse me," he mumbled. He had to admit it. She was hot in a weird way, with all those limbs. But, man, she was stand-offish at the moment.

"This is all your fault," she whined.

Bluntness. Always a fine quality in a woman. Who had time for prevarication and games? Certainly not Webrid.

He shot back, "Did I break the rocket? Did I?"

"Kind of."

Stravin snickered, tipping Webrid's fragile mood squarely into foul territory.

Webrid stood, wobbled, steadied himself, and spoke. "How could I have broken your rocket? I didn't touch..."

"Look at yourself," Zatell said, using four hands to show him to the world, a circus freak you didn't want to miss. "You're huge."

Webrid was just deciding to take that as a compliment to his masculinity, but Zatell wasn't finished. "Your gross, massive bulk and your big, ugly metal cart skewed the balance when we landed. I should never have agreed to... rrrr." Zatell, apparently too frustrated to continue, rolled away, placing each limb down hard so she somehow trudged as she spun.

Webrid was as deeply mired in guilt as he was in pond weeds. It was stiflingly humid and stinky in the swamp, and they were stranded and probably lost. For a few seconds, he really believed it was his fault. But then he changed his mind.

"No!" he shouted.

Freezing mid-trudge, Zatell turned toward him with eyes wide. A droopy lavender bug flopped out of a tree and landed on her nose. She blew it off with a whistle. "You got somethin' you want to say, ugly?"

Webrid was raring for a fight. "You're the pilot. You should have refused the job if it wasn't gonna work."

"Yeah? Well…" Her face looked swollen around her pursed lips. Webrid was not the only one feeling guilty, it would seem. "Maybe not. So, I screwed up. So, hell with it. Just…just…" She waved several arms to shoo Webrid away. "Just go. Both of you. Scram. Leave me with this mess."

Stravin bent his willowy form toward her. "But, my dear, whatever shall you do if we leave?"

She shed a purple tear. Webrid got suspicious, as he usually did when a woman cried.

"I guess I'll just stay here, see if I can call for help," she sniffed.

Now Webrid was sure Zatell was doing the martyr act. He recognized it from playing the role himself a few times with his landlord and the traffic judges. The "poor me" refrain never struck a sympathetic chord, though.

But Stravin fell for it. "No, you can't call, darling. The Vox will pick up your comm. Big trouble for you since we didn't have a permit to come here."

"I know, I know, I know." The limbs above her eyes straggled like a bad hair day. "I'll use a secure frequency." She puckered her lips into Webrid assumed was supposed to be a coy pout.

Stravin's parental side was shining through. "This will not do. You won't be safe here with the rocket. Its metals alone some brigands would consider worth killing for."

Webrid had had enough. "Okay, stop it. Can we skip this act and cut to the chase? Stravin?" He turned to his feathered friend. "She wants to come with us. She's angling to be invited. You don't suppose she's planned the whole thing?"

From behind him, Zatell objected, "I would never..." An upward sweep of Webrid's clawed hand warned her to hush, and she got the message.

"Now," Webrid continued, still facing Stravin, "can we trust her?"

Stravin's eyes hardened. "Why, my dear, how could you even..."

"Can. We. Trust. Her? Will you guarantee on your life that she's not a spy? That she won't sell us out?"

Webrid knew his voice was shaking. Despite his rough exterior, he never badmouthed women. And he'd sure never accused anyone of being a traitor. Frankly, he was scared.

Stravin, on the other hand, seemed to have recovered his confident attitude as he stepped toward Webrid. He looked taller. "I'll have you know," he began in the swooping pitches of haughtiness, "Miss Zatell is not only one of my oldest friends, but also a long-time denizen of that world of thieves and assorted bastards in which I proudly claim membership myself."

Webrid missed part of the next sentence because he was still parsing the grammar of the first one.

"...with my life," Stravin was saying. "Furthermore, if you distrust her, then you distrust me. In which case, it is with regret that I inform you that you must undertake your quest without our able assistance."

A mighty streak of annoyance steadied Webrid's voice. "Oh, come off it, Stravin. By all the gods' chest-hairs, I'm just trying to be, you know..." What was the word? "Responsible."

Not a term that often left his lips.

Finally, Webrid turned and spoke to Zatell. He lowered his big head near the flower's center that was her face. "No offence meant," he said, fully aware how ridiculous that sounded. "You can come along if you can keep up."

Three of her limbs shot out, and Webrid was supine in the muck with a stinging midriff. Stravin stood over him, laughing.

11

on't worry, toots," Zatell said, helping Stravin pull Webrid back to his feet. The Yeril was too big for either of them to handle alone. "I'll just stay until I can get myself a ride back. I'm sure there's an underworld here on Cheed that can offer me its illicit services."

Webrid's vision was clouded by memories of nearly being killed at Stim's Diner by Eshalo's flunkies. "Yup, definitely an underworld on Cheed," he assured her gloomily.

"Still," she said, winking one eye and curling a hundred fingers, "I hope I don't find them too soon. You're pretty cute for an oaf."

Nothing could have made Webrid more uncomfortable. After a lifetime of chasing tarts around Bargival, now he was getting the come-on from two intelligent, professional women in one week. Was it the air on this planet? These classy dames were way above his pay grade, and he longed for the tawdry familiarity of Joolo's Skinny Dip Club.

Stravin had pranced onto the rocket's side. "Don't mean to break up a mating ritual, my dearest darlings, but we have things to do. Webrid, help me get your awful cart out of here before the whole mess sinks."

The thought of losing his ancestral cart spurred Webrid into frenzied action.

"I got it," he said, and with a few strong heaves had the cart up on shore. Its wheels sank into the muck up to the axles, but at least it was clear of the water.

Emerging from the rocket door, Stravin held up a black box. "Engine, kiddies. Maybe we can use this. Anyway, it's priceless. It could buy our trip home, or buy off some pretty high-powered creeps if need be."

"Good thinking, Strav," Zatell said, offering a few hands to steady her friend as his foot squished into the embankment. "So, what's the plan?"

She was answered only by the hushed sounds of the marshland fauna. None of the sentient beings had a plan, apparently.

The great thing about being a big galoot like Webrid was not being conscious of his low rung on the mental ladder. "Why did we come here again?" he asked without shame.

Stravin had started the Moti's motor and was hooking up the cart to its towing line. He shook his feathered head. "Seriously, my dear, how do you get dressed in the morning?"

"Huh?"

"This is your life. Can't you even keep track of your own life?"

"Not really, no." It seemed like a reasonable question to Webrid, who didn't detect the reek of sarcasm.

"Well, hop on, my little pretties, and I'll explain while we ride. That rocket must have attracted the Vox's attention, and I have no wish to greet the cop-bots when they arrive."

They packed themselves in. Webrid did the gentlemanly thing and let Zatell take the back passenger seat on the Moti. That left him riding in his cart again, but he flipped the top open so he could feel included. As they rolled through the swamplands and eventually onto a meager road, Stravin recounted what he knew of the situation.

After listening for a while, Zatell asked, "So, we're looking for some government outpost?"

"That's right, dear. It's somewhere in the Northern Territories on Cheed."

"The uncharted Northern Territories?"

"Yes, dear."

"And we're going in without a map?" she asked.

"Well, there isn't one, dear, is there? That's why it's called *uncharted*."

While Zatell swatted Stravin in the back with a few limbs, Webrid tried to catch up with the conversation, which he could barely hear.

"So, these guys put the thing in my head?" he shouted over the engine. "And we're going to... Why are we going to see them?"

It was Zatell who answered, much to Webrid's annoyance. She was the newest on the scene, so she shouldn't understand things better than he did.

"Maybe they can read the laser. Maybe they can take it out of your head."

The mission's true purpose came flooding back. "I'm carting it!" he shouted. "They paid for me to bring it to them, so that's why I'm here."

He noticed Stravin and Zatell exchanging looks. But they weren't carters, so what did they know of that sort of professional pride?

The road opened up into a field. It was a relief to be out of the humid swamp. Knowing exactly where they were or where they were heading would have been nice, but they were safe for the moment and had a mighty fast scooter to flee on if need be.

The tan flatness of the terrain made Webrid's mind

wander. He had long, lean thoughts of fleshy Leshi. Where was she now, he wondered? Had her revolution succeeded? Had it even really begun? What were she and her brother revolting against, anyway? He never had found out.

An urgent thought occurred to Webrid. "Um, guys?"

"Yes, dear?" shouted Stravin. The wind carried his voice back to the cart.

"What about the *Draspar*? The rebel ship?"

"What about it, dear?"

Webrid was feeling uncommonly clever. "Well, they tracked me down before. Why not now?"

"You didn't have your bnarli on, dear."

"Yes, I did."

"No, you didn't."

Webrid thought very hard. He thought as hard as a Yeril can possibly think. And he was sure.

"I had it on," he yelled. "I didn't lose it until the government ship took me off the *Draspar* and tried that surgery in the capital building. I know I had it on until then."

Zatell was laughing so hard it took two limbs to wipe away her tears and several others to hold her in her seat.

"What's so funny?" Webrid wasn't about to let this limb-fringed butterball disrespect him. "This is serious. I had this thing on and they found me anyway."

"My dear, it's not possible," Stravin was saying. He seemed to be trying not to laugh, too. "Nobody can read signals through a bnarli. That's the whole point. Who could possibly have the technology to circumvent a bnarli?"

Webrid was looking at a growing gray speck in the sky. It couldn't be, could it?

"Honestly, tell me," Stravin said, "who in the universe could home in on your laser while you were wearing a bnarli?"

Still watching the sky without blinking, Webrid saw the

S.R.S. Draspar come into focus.

"The guy who invented the bnarli could probably do it," he answered in a monotone.

Wind and flying dust scraped Webric's eyeballs as the vast ship lowered its landing gear. Stravin had stopped the scooter, and he and Zatell stared at the *Draspar* with mouths agape.

Webrid felt nothing. Perhaps the events of the previous few days had burned out his capacity for surprise, like an overloaded circuit that shuts down to prevent an explosion.

The enormous gusts of air that ripped outward from the *Draspar* forced Zatell and Stravin to climb off the scooter and retreat, arms over their faces. Webrid, though, hardly noticed the wind. This all seemed an inevitable and divine visit, portentous, not to be missed even for a blink-length. If he turned away, how could he tell his grandchildren about this great moment?

A door under the ship's outer rim, slanting forty-five degrees toward the ground, opened on hinges, and a staircase unfolded into the scrubby grass. With his friends huddling behind his cart, Webrid awaited the emergence of the all-powerful rebel gods. Sure enough, down came Leshi's brother Debley, that slender and handsome specimen, even handsomer than Webrid had remembered.

Webrid jumped when Stravin dug his silky fingers into his shoulder. "Who *is* that?" Stravin demanded. "What manner of creature, do you know?"

Webrid was no longer awed. Now he was smug. He knew something Stravin didn't, had an in where Stravin desperately wanted one. Pride overtook reason and Webrid crawled out of the cart. He had no idea how the rebels would treat him after his apparent escape. How did kidnappers feel when their prisoner was kidnapped out from under their noses? For all Webrid knew, they'd restrain him in an electromagnetic cell this time, or even kill him and take the laser.

But it didn't matter. The smugness was addictive and milking it was worth any risk.

"That," Webrid bragged to a drooling Stravin, "is my old friend General Feklari Debley." He strode forward, waving. "Halloo, Debley! How've you been? How's that delightful sister of yours?"

Webrid longed to turn around and see the wonder on Stravin's and Zatell's faces, but he feared it might ruin the nonchalant effect.

Debley did not return the friendly greeting. Instead he drew a weapon longer and thicker than Webrid's arm, and pointed its fluorescent nozzle at his chest.

Assuming he was about to die anyway, Webrid was determined to go out with blazing coolness. He raised both hands high in the air but kept up his loud, manic patter. "Ooh! You got me. I tell ya, Debs, you are such a kidder. Careful that thing doesn't go off. Your sister would never forgive you. My friends here have been dying to meet you. Get it? Dying?" He pointed a trembling finger at the glowing gun. "I told 'em all about your fantastic ship. Floating office building and control room and whatnot."

Webrid was a stone's throw from the weapon now. A child could have aimed well enough to blow his head off from that distance. He could see the sinews twisting in Debley's skinless muscles. That scared him; one twitch could easily be transferred to the man's trigger finger. But Webrid could also see confusion on Debley's face, not anger. Maybe he was changing his mind about blasting a tunnel through Webrid's ticker.

Or maybe not. Debley suddenly stepped down the last few stairs and strode toward Webrid, who froze with his arms in the air. The weapon was all he could see as it sped toward him with each motion of Debley's absurdly long legs. In seconds, it was shoved into his ribcage and Debley had his fingers buried in the hair on Webrid's upper arm.

"Don't you talk about my sister," he said in his low double-reed voice. "Did you think you could get away from us?"

He tried to push Webrid down but couldn't budge that Yeril bulk. This struck Webrid as hilarious when he remembered how easily little Zatell had flattened him earlier that day. His amusement gave him enough confidence to lower his arms.

"I don't think you'll shoot me," he said quietly, not quite brave enough to make eye contact.

"What makes you so sure?" Debley forced the barrel of the gun deeper against Webrid's liver.

Not being skilled in the art of witty repartee, Webrid couldn't think of any words to defuse the tension. Fortunately, relief came in the form of two glistening magenta feet that appeared on the exit stairs of the *SRS Draspar*.

"Leshi?" said Webrid, his voice choked.

"Ganpril Webrid." She said his name solemnly.

The unsettled air pulled her scent of oil and coal dust toward him. Her brother didn't smell like that. Webrid wondered whether it was a perfume, or maybe her species' female hormones. Whatever it was, it stirred Webrid's lust.

Leshi had her hands on the business end of Debley's weapon. She wasn't afraid of him.

"Put it down," she commanded. "Let him go."

Webrid tried not to whimper with relief when the gun was removed from his upper G.I. region.

"So, how've you been?" he asked, his voice a major sixth higher than normal.

"Pretty good," she said. Shyly? Coyly? Webrid wasn't sure.

"Introduce us, Webbo!" A shout from behind him at

waist level made Webrid spin around.

It was Zatell. Stravin hung back a bit, looking on with keen interest. What had been a near-death experience turned into the mundane introduction of one set of friends to another, the sort of thing that happened on routine bar crawls back home.

"Okay, yeah." Webrid cleared his throat, feeling ridiculous. "Um, Leshi, that's Zatell there. And that fella is called Stravin. They're both from Bexilla. And, um," he indicated the man who'd nearly disemboweled him a minute before, "this here's my friend Debley, Leshi's brother." He still couldn't look him in the eye.

Neither could Stravin, he noticed. The usually glib and elegant wit proffered a hand. He gasped audibly when Debley's equally long and slender fingers enmeshed with his.

Webrid and Leshi looked away, embarrassed. Zatell started to giggle. That was apparently how she got through all emotionally fraught situations in life. There was something admirable in that, it seemed to Webrid.

He whispered to Leshi, "You know I didn't run away. I didn't escape. Somebody took me. The government. Or part of the government. I'm still figuring it out. But I didn't run away."

There was no point in his whispering, since everyone could hear him perfectly. Yet it made him feel he was speaking intimately and directly to Leshi. "I don't know about being in your revolution and all," he went on, "but I really didn't want to..." He knew it sounded like a line from a cheesy daytime visi-story, but he said it anyway: "I didn't want to leave you."

Now it was Debley's turn to laugh. Webrid's stomach acids curdled as he fought the urge to claw his ear off.

Leshi grabbed her brother by the throat and pulled his face nose to nose with hers. "I believe him," she said. And that was that.

She turned to Webrid, her face relaxed and her eyes revealing nothing. "Why don't you and your friends come inside?" She spoke as if it were an invitation to a housewarming rather than entrance to an anti-government HQ. "We'll have lunch."

Debley groaned.

Zatell said, "No thanks, we're busy."

Stravin said, "We'd love to."

Webrid's was the deciding vote. "I could definitely go for a janz roll," he said.

hey'd been properly fed. There'd been a tour of the main floor and control room of the *Draspar*. The niceties were over, and now they were all seated in Debley's office.

"So, you're headed north?" Stravin asked as a fuzzy Zenivar placed a hot beverage in front of him. "To the uncharted..."

"I wish people would stop calling Northern Cheed 'uncharted,'" Debley broke in. "*I've* charted it." He sighed and snapped his head back dramatically.

Webrid thought it a pity that this poser lacked a head of long hair to toss around.

Stravin didn't seem put off by Sir Pompous. "Oh, you don't say." He said it...respectfully? Had Stravin actually addressed someone respectfully? "How *did* you manage it?" He leaned forward, showing keen interest and giving Debley a full view of his chest feathers.

"Unh." That noise came from Leshi. She looked at Webrid and crossed her eyes. Webrid thrilled at this intimate sarcasm. He crossed his eyes back at her and flicked his tongues out one at a time, a Yeril sign of ennui.

Debley had launched into a well-rehearsed adventure tale that his sister had clearly heard a thousand times. "I built a little plane," Debley said, pacing. "A silent, sneaky plane armed with the best geographical cameras ever made." He paused for effect.

Stravin made a high-pitched "ooh." Webrid took the opportunity to burp.

"Since I'd already invented a beam-shield to detect and block the Vox presence," Debley continued, waving his arms widely to indicate the Vox-free *Draspar*, "I used it first to find the extent of Vox surveillance in the North."

He went to a plain white metal rectangle on the wall and placed his palm against it. "Wall Map 16A," he said.

The wall behind Webrid groaned. It was not the solid stuff it seemed to be; its surface crumpled and puckered until it was a relief map showing hills, mountains, valleys, and rivers.

"Add projection layer one," Debley said.

Colored lines, squiggles, and shading appeared on the map.

"Those green areas are covered by the Vox," he explained. "Once I'd done the painstaking work of mapping those outlines—" His sister snorted. "—it was no trouble to make approximately fifty recon flights to get topographical images and measurements of the whole northern hemisphere." He sidled up to Stravin as if adding a tidbit just for him. "The initial Vox map allowed me to avoid detection."

"Fascinating," Stravin gushed.

Zatell finally spoke up. "So, where exactly are we headed? Where's that government gang holed up?"

With the annoyed grimace of a man whose afternoon lovemaking has been interrupted by the housekeeper's knock, Debley left Stravin's side and marched to the wall map. He smashed his long index finger hard into the center of the largest patch of green shading, far to the north.

"There," he said. "I'm sure they're there."

Webrid looked at the placement of that finger. "There? Really?" He burst out with great guffaws from deep in his great chest. "Wait!" he roared, fighting for breath. "Just hang on a sec."

"So ill-mannered," said Stravin. "What's your problem?"

Webrid truly had something important to say, but he couldn't stop laughing long enough to talk. It didn't help that Zatell, so susceptible to the giggles, was whooping uncontrollably across the table.

Debley looked nonplussed, Stravin looked angry, and Leshi wore a mysterious smirk.

Webrid calmed his breathing with a mighty effort. Walking over to Debley, whose hand was now splayed over the largest green section of the map, Webrid poked a claw through the map's surface between two of Debley's fingers.

"Here?" Webrid said. "You think they're right here? In the green area?"

Debley drew himself up in an intimidating manner. Although he was slender, he was taller than Webrid. And he didn't seem used to being questioned.

"Yes," he answered sharply. "Have you an argument against that theory?"

With his claw still in the wall, the carter raised his eyebrows as he spoke. "You don't know what's here."

"How do you mean?"

"You couldn't map the green parts, right? Because of the Vox?"

"But I *did* map the green parts. That's why they're on the map, you..."

"No!" Webrid cut in. "You said the green shows where the Vox signal is. Those are the places where you couldn't get pictures of the, of the..." Webrid's vocabulary failed.

Zatell called out, "The topography." Lowering herself from her chair to the floor, she rolled over to the wall. "The hairball has a point for once. So, even if the government outpost really is there, there's a ton we don't know. Like, is it a valley? A mountain range? Desert? Forest? An island in the middle of a lake? A sub-oceanic cavern?" She erupted in giggles again.

Stravin got up and stood next to Debley. He lifted his arm gracefully and, hesitating only a moment, dropped his hand onto Debley's shiny shoulder. The feathered man spoke quietly, patiently, to his new friend. "Do you know the terrain of the Vox area?"

It was Leshi who answered, in a strange, dreamy tone, like someone possessed. "It's forest. All those beautiful trees." She rested her chin in her hand, staring more through the map than at it. "Trees, trees, trees." She could have been an adolescent repeating the word "kiss." Webrid didn't know what to make of it.

Debley seemed a bit embarrassed. "Yes, I think it's forest."

"But you're not sure," Webrid wheedled.

"Not exactly, no." Debley glared at Webrid for a moment before turning tenderly back to Stravin. "But forest makes sense, since that's what's in the areas I *could* map in detail. And I'm pretty sure all there's a waterway running straight through." He ran his finger from the bottom of the green section up to Webrid's claw.

Leshi joined them by the map. "That's actually not a bad theory, bro. They'd want the Vox to protect the only reasonable access to the outpost, so it's got to be either a road or a river. I agree that a river's much more likely. Requires little or no maintenance. And with all the lush forest up there, there has to be a major water supply."

Webrid's heart sank to hear Leshi re-team with her

brother. Also, his claw was stuck fast in the wall. His arm was getting tired, but he couldn't free it without looking like the buffoon he already knew he was.

"Fine, it's a river," he growled. "How does that help us? You couldn't go in the green area to make the map, so how can we get in there now?"

Stravin rushed to defend Debley. "But this vessel blocks the Vox, so it can be done, right?" He looked wide-eyed at Debley, as if expecting great wisdom.

"My brother's not *quite* that clever," said Leshi. "The Vox can't hear inside most of the *Draspar*, but it's aware of the ship's presence. We let a small amount of audio out so nobody gets suspicious." She focused on Webrid. "Like I explained when you were here before, the Vox thinks we're an office building." She batted her eyelash-less lids. Webrid found it surprisingly appealing.

"Yeah, I have to admit," Debley said, "I haven't been able to take the beam-shield anti-Vox that one last step. I can't make us invisible to the Vox. I can only get us in if we look like something else."

Zatell piped up from the floor. "So, what kind of ship should we be?"

"That's really the biggest problem," said Debley. "Practically no vehicles are allowed into the Northern Territories. I mean, there have to be some that bring supplies, but we don't know what they are."

"Stake-out," said Webrid.

They all looked at him.

"We should do a stake-out. At the border. Watch who is allowed to come and go. Then we'll know what we should pretend to be. So maybe Stravin and I could...What? What?"

Webrid noticed that the siblings were sharing a meaningful glance. They both raised their forehead muscles where their eyebrows should have been.

"What'd I say?"

Leshi wrapped her hand around Webrid's against the wall map. "That was our plan," she said.

"Lesh, don't." Debley's voice contained a note of warning.

"We might as well tell him. Webrid, when we first took you on the *Draspar,* our plan, if you can call it that, was to go up near the border and wait."

"Wait for what?" Webrid noticed that Leshi was squeezing his fingers awfully tightly.

"Wait and watch, so we could try to get through in the right kind of vessel. We'd tried before, but hadn't gotten close enough to see anything."

"So, you really didn't have a plan. You just took me. Kept me prisoner." He tried to look at her, but she was behind him and he was pinned in place by his claw. "Who knows how long you would've kept me. Is that about right?"

He felt her gently, slowly pulse and pressure her hand back and forth against his. It was distractingly sexual until he realized what she was doing: she'd bored a larger hole with his claw, and now he could get free. Very smooth.

"Can you forgive us?" she asked, pulling his hand down with hers. "Can you forgive me?"

He tried not to show his pleasure. "I suppose you meant well."

Webrid had been hoping for a deep, heartfelt look into each other's eyes. Instead, Leshi craned her neck to look past him. "Uh-oh," she said.

The magical moment dissipated. Webrid sighed, disappointed. "What's wrong?" He followed her gaze to a far corner, where Debley and Stravin were whispering intently.

Leshi called to them. "Hey! What are you two up to?"

They turned, all smiles.

"Strav?" asked Zatell. "What have you gotten us mixed up in now?"

Debley answered. "Your friend Stravin, by which I mean your incredibly brilliant friend Stravin, thinks he can cloak us from the Vox."

Zatell let loose peals of laughter. "If anybody can, he can," she said.

Stravin was beaming, and had finally regained his bravado. "I'm sure I can do it, my dears."

While Webrid honestly didn't doubt his friend's unsurpassed gift for invention, he was too proud to let Stravin swoop in and save the day without a fight.

"Oh, please," he scoffed. "In his own house, he has to hide from the Vox in a galvanized cave. How's he ever gonna…"

"With Debley's beam-shield technology as a springboard, darling. Why are you being so recalcitrant?"

Webrid didn't know that word, but he did know that Stravin would probably succeed. He looked over at them, ready to admit this. But, wait, were they holding hands? There was no point in trying to talk to them now. Time to get scarce and let the two scientists set about experimenting. Webrid released a long combination burp-yawn and addressed Zatell and Leshi with a deep bow.

"Ladies? Either of you care to join me for a brimming bowl of Valestin?"

"Really?" Zatell sneered. "Oaf like you's gonna stand us a round? Like a gentleman?"

Ignoring her, Webrid turned to Leshi and tried to will his coarse facial hairs into a heroic sheet. "Your Zenivar attendant told me there's no booze on board." His tongues clicked out his sultry mating rhythm. "I don't believe her."

With an enigmatic smile, Leshi led them to an elevator. Its doors opened up to reveal a remarkably posh lounge.

"It's intended for high-end business guests," she explained when Zatell remarked on the hand-sculpted furniture.

"These are made of trees, aren't they?" Zatell rubbed

several hands over the surface of a throne-like chair. "I haven't seen wooden furniture in years."

Leshi placed both hands on a wooden table and, to Webrid's amazement, knelt in front of it and seemed to whisper a prayer. When she stood up, there were tears in her eyes. Webrid coughed and tried to continue the conversation as if nothing bizarre had just happened.

"Er, my grandpa had a wooden table." Webrid remembered the cracked, gouged table with fondness. "He left it to me."

"Oh, really? You own a wooden table?" Leshi's face was taut, her voice strained. She might have been asking whether he kept a slave.

Webrid, feeling inexplicably guilty, answered defensively, "Well, only technically. Like I said, Gramps left it to me. I didn't, you know, buy it." He glanced at Zatell, who was examining Leshi with a puzzled expression.

After an uncomfortable silence, they settled down, each in the chair that suited him or her best, for the seats came in all different sizes and shapes. Leshi took in a deep breath and looked at the floor as she spoke. Webrid got the sense that she was trying to sound unemotional. "We think the forest is one reason the government has cut off access to the Northern Territories," she said as a Zenivar brought them their drinks. "It's the only surviving forest in the Raralt Planetary Circle. Wood is a luxury item. They could make serious dendiacs by controlling it."

Webrid gulped his Val-Hundred, trying not to show how let down he felt. He put his hand against the bnarli at his brow. Surely this wasn't just about a bunch of stupid trees. He had to believe that being ripped from his humble life and thrown into the jaws of peril was for something that really mattered.

But his head ached and he couldn't find the words to express what he was thinking. Instead, he did what he was good at: He chatted up the women and slurped down some powerful liquor.

Webrid awoke to the smell of Valestin, wood varnish, and dried Yeril spit. The brain-crunching hangover felt oddly welcome. He'd missed relaxing in bars and getting soused, so he didn't mind this kind of headache and blurriness. He did, however, wish that whoever was poking at his arm would stop.

"Shtobbit," he said into the tabletop.

"Wake up, you uncouth beast. Oh, heavens, you stink."

Ugh, he knew that voice. Feather Man.

"Whatchoo want, Shtrav'm?" he asked, without raising his head.

"What I want," said Stravin, over-punctuating every consonant, "is for you to sit up and rejoin the living."

"Why?"

"I beg your pardon?"

"Why should I rezh, rezh..." He tried again. "Why should I sit up?"

"Because, my dear," said Stravin, pulling Webrid's head upright, "we're about to leave for the Northern Territories."

Webrid thought very hard. Then he thought some more. He knew there was something wrong with this plan, but he couldn't send enough controlled impulses through his cerebral cortex to figure out what. The only comment he managed to construct was, "But we're in an office building."

travin smooched Webrid's forehead. "Silly, we're not going in the *Draspar*."

Blinking hard to shake the crust from his eyes, Webrid tried to follow the conversation. "Not the *Draspar*?"

"No, dear. I was up all night with Debley—" he sighed a most delicate sigh "—intensifying his beam-shield."

"Is that what they're calling it these days?" Webrid was now officially awake.

Stravin picked up a drinking bowl and tried to splash Webrid with the contents. Of course, it was empty. No self-respecting Yeril left booze in his bowl.

"Anyway," Stravin said with a great show of rolling his eyes, "we're calling it AVS, Anti-Vox Shadow. It seems we can block Vox visibility over a small area. Say, the size of my Moti-Moto."

"So we can take the scooter into the green zone, and the Vox won't be able to see us?"

Clearing his throat and snaking his silky fingers together, Stravin said, "About that. The scooter really only carries two."

Webrid might be awake, but he was still a bit thick.

"Yeah. You and me."

"Well, Debley really needs to get up there. I'm thinking he and I should take it for a test run."

"No freakin' way. You're bringing me." Webrid pointed to the bnarli. "I gotta get this taken care of. I'll be in the test run. I ain't waiting an extra day or who knows how long to get this thing out of my head."

Stravin looked impatient. "Yes, yes, I'm sure you feel that way, but Debley needs to come in case there's trouble with the AVS, and I don't know how we can all fit..."

"Tow my cart," said Webrid, sure he'd solved the problem. "I'll ride in the cart."

"Well, my dear, I really am not certain the Shadow will cover the cart..."

"Well, my dear," Webrid mocked him, "we'll be finding out. 'Cause I'm going in the cart."

Stravin paced around the table, gesticulating. "You and that cursed cart. My whole life would be easier if you didn't have that ugly thing. What's to stop me from drugging you with a barrel of Val and hurtling that cart into space?"

It didn't sound like a joke. More horrible to Webrid than the prospect of losing his ancestral pride was the realization that he was about to cry like a little kid. He took a huge breath to steady himself, but when he tried to speak, his lips wobbled as pathetically as his voice.

"Don't. Don't do that," he said, *con molto vibrato.*

"Hey, now, my dear." Stravin sat down next to Webrid and put a soft hand on his wrist. Webrid yanked his arm away.

"Hey, now," Stravin repeated. "We'll take the cart. I'll find a way."

A new voice said, "And what about us?"

Webrid looked around but couldn't see who had spoken. He finally found Zatell down by his knees, pointing up at Stravin.

"You got a plan to take us," she said, "or is that cart more important than a couple of brilliant women?"

Stravin smiled the grin of a man who's dug his own grave. "Wouldn't you like to ride in the cart, too?" he asked with a flourish of his arms, trying to make the idea appealing.

"With this stink-monster?" Zatell smacked Webrid's shin. "Next idea?"

"Leshi could ride with me," Webrid volunteered selflessly.

Harmonized peals of laughter cascaded from Stravin and Zatell.

"You guys talking about me?" Leshi, smiling, loped into the lounge.

Webrid suddenly wondered how long he'd been face-down on that table. All he remembered from the night before was the scarcity of wood in the Raralt Circle and the abundance of Val-Hundred on the *Draspar*.

Eyeing Leshi, who looked fresh and well rested, Webrid said, "Rrrff." This was Yeril slang for, "Apparently I didn't get lucky last night."

The transportation problem was solved once Leshi had the idea to make two AVS shields. The *Draspar* was equipped with an individual transport car, not as fast or cool as the Moti, but it could carry two people. By the following morning, the bushy-tailed Explorer's Club was ready for its foray into the unknown. Leshi and Zatell took the *Draspar* car, Stravin and Debley sat in the Moti-Moto, and Webrid, swallowing every last morsel of pride he possessed, lowered himself into his cart to be towed.

A team of furry Zenivars stuffed suitcases, water, and preserved foods all around Webrid, packing him in. To ease his shame, he insisted that they bring him a fresh janz roll to munch on the way. Soon enough they might be living on dried meats, so he wanted a nice sandwich to remember.

More accurately, soon enough they'd probably be dead. Webrid knew this journey had as much chance of ending happily as a Bargival tourist had of winning at street cards. And it annoyed him that he didn't really understand the plan. He was left out of the loop, as usual. As they revved their engines and started along the bumpy road, he asked, "What are we doing again? You know, once we get there?"

Nobody bothered to answer, which didn't surprise him. Webrid chewed thoughtfully, wondering what life would throw at him next.

It was a good thing they'd brought the funny bubble-shaped car from the *Draspar*. Although the Moti had a mapping system, it was calibrated for the planet Bargival, not Cheed, and Stravin didn't have the right data and codes to correct it. The plain plastic bubble car was fitted with state-of-the art mapping and pre-loaded with every registered business on Cheed.

"But it has no info for the north," Zatell pointed out when they stopped for a snack.

"We don't need it up there," Debley explained. "I loaded my northern maps into the Moti's computer. It's getting up to the border that's the challenge. The customs office should be on the car's mapping system."

Webrid knew a bad idea when he heard one. "We can't go to the customs office. Our visit won't be secret anymore."

He could tell by the way they all turned to stare at him that he'd said something dumb. Zatell laughed until all her limbs shook.

Leshi leaned over and whispered into the cart, "We need to know where the customs office is so that we can stay away from it."

It was the most obvious thing in the world, once she'd

said it.

The trip north wound through little towns of gray metal huts, a city with a dirty edge and a gleaming middle, and farmland protected from UV rays by massive purple filter nets. There were also stretches of nothing. The nothing tended to be swampland like they'd landed in or scrubland like they'd first driven through. Webrid had no use for nature, so he considered these areas to contain nothing.

Two boring, bumpy hours later, Stravin surprised them all by pulling into the parking structure of a shopping complex.

"Getting some new underwear?" Zatell cracked. "Do you even wear any?"

"Honestly, people," sighed Stravin. "We need a crowded place in which we can activate the AVS. If we had driven into a deserted area and then disappeared," he pointed upward at the Vox, "it might have been noticed. But there are thousands of vehicles in this lot, all expected to remain parked for ages while people shop. We'll put up the AVS and slide right on out of here."

"That's fantastically clever," said Leshi. Webrid gurgled with jealousy.

"Yes, I know," said Stravin. He and Debley opened the scooter's motor compartment and tinkered. There was a bit of arguing about which lever should go in which direction. This did not enhance Webrid's sense of confidence in the project.

"You sure it works?" he ventured.

They ignored him.

"Aha," said Stravin. "We have now set up the Moti's Anti-Vox Shadow." The pair of slender mechanics began work on the *Draspar* car. That's when things got sticky. They had attracted company.

"Spot of trouble?" A mall security robot had rolled over

to them. "May I assist you?"

Webrid had the presence of mind to leap out of the cart and hide behind a hover-van in the next parking aisle. He pressed both palms against the bnarli, praying that pressure might increase its effectiveness. The last time he'd seen a police bot, it had tried to paralyze him. The time before that, it had drilled a tiny hole in his skull.

"...checking the, the, the digital indicators," Debley was saying with an uncharacteristic stutter. Webrid was silently pleased that wonder-boy didn't know how to lie.

The security bot wasn't going away. "I am equipped with a vehicle-analysis kit compatible with seventeen thousand land- and air-motion models. Please stand aside and I will inspect your vehicle and repair any problems."

Leshi tried to resist. "No, thanks, sir. It's really not..."

"It is my prime directive to assist customers in distress."

"We're not in distress," Leshi assured him.

"You *are* in distress," the bot decided. "Stand aside. I must analyze your motor. Stand aside."

Webrid got an idea. The process of doing so instantly gave him a headache, but he shut his eyes to focus on it through the pain. It was just a germ at first, but he bared his teeth, squeezing his brain cells, forcing his idea to grow. Then he opened his eyes. Yes, yes, this might work.

Webrid started to run amid the vehicles while screaming, "AAAAAAAAAGH! Help! Security! I'm in distress!"

Peeking over his shoulder, he could see the security bot come to attention, scan the area, and roll in his direction. It seemed to be working.

"Help!" Webrid cried again.

Unfortunately, Webrid had forgotten that the fruition of ideas happened in stages. Screaming out his distress had distracted the bot. However, he had neglected to plan for the second phase, when the bot came after him.

On the positive side, he no longer had to pretend. With the bot chasing him, he really did feel that he was in distress, so his screams were quite convincing. All he could think to do was continue zig-zagging among the vehicles and hope that the bot never caught up to him. But he couldn't keep that up all day. His legs were already tiring.

"Webrid, over here!"

Oh, such a beautiful sound. It was Stravin waving from the Moti at the end of a parking aisle.

"Run for it. Jump in your cart as fast as you can," he ordered.

Webrid, completely out of either fully or partially realized ideas, was thrilled to comply. But the bot saw him dart from behind a four-doored swamp-coupe and high-tail it toward the Moti, and gave chase. Webrid was sure that no biological being could outrun a security bot. He was done for.

As a proud Yeril, Webrid was determined to die running away at tremendous speed. He lurched forward on his big hairy feet, claws smacking the non-skid plastic pavement, arms flailing about like a lottery winner's dance. The world slowed down. Debley and Stravin were waving and shouting as if underwater. He could see the *Draspar* car pulling out of the lot and wished Stravin would just go ahead and follow the women with his scooter. At least then, Webrid's cart would get away, even if Webrid himself had to be killed.

"Stop," the bot was saying in its metallic voice. "Stop. You are in distress. Stop."

It was right behind him now. Webrid had always heard that his life would pass before his eyes if he were ever in this situation. That's not what happened. As Webrid dove head-first into his cart and the scooter pulled away, something else passed before his eyes. A thousand lighted green numbers stacked into equations scrolled through his head. Then they were gone.

Surely that was just caused by stress, Webrid reasoned, although why a man who could sort of add and definitely not subtract would have such a vision, he couldn't explain.

He had more urgent matters to deal with anyway. The Moti was cranking away and Webrid wasn't quite in the cart. He'd landed on the suitcases and travel foods. Instinctively, he'd grabbed the first thing in front of him. That was a box of dried shebel strands, which were highly nutritious but almost weightless. No good as an anchor.

"Whoa!" he called out, not really meaning it. He certainly didn't want Stravin to slow down, since that bot could roll as fast as the scooter. But he also didn't want Stravin to switch to supersonic speed until he was safely inside.

"Whoa!" he cried again as Stravin turned the corner out of the parking lot. "Wha?" he cried next, when Stravin slowed down.

"Come on, dear. Get yourself settled," Stravin said as Webrid tried to pull his legs in and look behind him at the same time.

"But, but, but, the bot! Go, go, go!" He hadn't done all that fancy footwork through the parking lot just to get caught once he had a ride. "Floor it, why dontcha?"

Debley turned around and spoke to him in the tone of someone who can't believe he has to bother. "It's not chasing us anymore."

Webrid shoved suitcases aside as he argued. "Just because we're not in the parking structure? Are you nuts? It's connected to the whole security system. Trust me, I know about this stuff. It's contacted the Vox and before you know it every cop-bot on Cheed will be…Why are you guys laughing? Hey, where are we going?"

While Stravin and Debley chuckled at a secret joke, they'd pulled the Moti into a field. Webrid could see the *Draspar* car waiting there. Leshi leaned against its front grille. Several of Zatell's arms were waving out the window.

"What's going on?" Webrid asked urgently. "I tell you, they're gonna get us, so we'd better scram."

"Really, my dear," said Stravin when they'd stopped. "You're not much for science, are you? The whole point of the AVS is to block us from the Vox. As soon as we switched the AVS units on, both of these vehicles became invisible to that security bot. It's got nothing to report. Nobody knows we're here."

Everybody laughed. Definitely at Webrid, not with him.

Zatell climbed out of the car and rolled over to the cart. "Hey, handsome, I'm hungry. Toss me some dried shebel strands, would you?"

It took all Webrid's self-control not to use the damned shebel strands to poke all his friends in the eye.

14

Now that the Anti-Vox Shadow was functioning on both vehicles, the intrepid quintet made ready to cross the border into the north.

"Since we're cloaked," Debley said with grating confidence, "getting to the Northern Territories will be no trouble. The trouble will be..."

Leshi breathed in to finish her brother's sentence, but Stravin beat her to it.

"Avoiding visual detection once we near the government outpost," he said. "It's bound to be guarded by true-sight cameras and biologicals instead of just relying on the Vox for security."

"That's what I was going to say," Leshi told a rock she was massaging with her glistening fuchsia big toe. Webrid gave a barely audible snicker so she'd know he was on her side.

"It behooves us to do some recon," Debley pontificated. "Too bad we didn't bring any Zenivars. They have tremendous skill in the arts of espionage."

This surprised Webrid. "I thought they'd been genetically selected to be servants," he said.

"And who better to be the best spies, wouldn't you say?" Debley's tone was so condescending that what should have been fascinating info turned sour and distasteful. Webrid shut down the learning apparatus in his brain, just as he always had in school.

He felt a light slapping against his lower leg. It was Zatell, her limbs like rotating car-wash brushes.

"We'll do the recon," she announced. "Me and the whiskerpuss here. My brains and my brawn and his ridiculous height, there's nothing we can't do."

Webrid felt oddly gratified that weird little Zatell had chosen him. Maybe she wasn't so bad after all.

He looked at Leshi, who was gazing at her brother. That scene was hopeless, he decided right then and there. Tall, elegant, accomplished—it was the recipe for an inaccessible woman. All those encouraging hints he'd taken from her must have been in his imagination. Women like her simply weren't interested in carters.

As if in answer to that thought, Leshi left Webrid's side and bounded over to Debley. "So, where are the rest of us going?" she asked.

"We'll find a way to enter the Northern Territory," Debley said.

Webrid's confidence evaporated. He'd been included by one of the cool kids, only to be barred from joining the even cooler ones. He was determined to save face.

"Fine," he said. "Sounds good." He patted the bubble top of the *Draspar* car. "You three can take this. Zatell and I will take the scooter and my cart."

Three people talked at once.

Debley said, "I'd get claustrophobic in there."

Zatell said, "Can't we leave the cart back here?"

Stravin finished alone. "Nobody else drives my Moti. Nobody. Maybe if it were factory stock, dear. But, really, the work I put into the engine... Only I drive this baby. Got it?"

"I'll drive the *Draspar* car," Leshi volunteered. To her brother, she said, "You two take the scooter."

Debley moved toward the hitch at the Moti's rear. "I'll take off the cart." The next sound from him was "Ow!" because Webrid had his claws pressing into Debley's unprotected shoulder meat.

"No need for that," Stravin hurried to say. "Here's what we'll do. We'll all drive to a point closer to the customs compound. Then we'll drop you off and unhitch the cart so you can, um..." he seemed to weigh his words, "...look after it."

"That idea stinks," said Zatell. "I thought we'd have a vehicle. Like real spies."

With a snort and a distasteful smirk, Debley made it clear that he was sharing a silent joke with his sister.

Stravin hissed out a nervous laugh. "Nonsense, my dear," he said, slinking onto his scooter, "no spy would get near the compound in a car. On foot's the only way."

"And we can hide behind my cart." Webrid thought it was a generous offer, but everyone just gave him a wide-eyed glance and turned away. That was cold.

They drove off-road for a bit and stopped at an abandoned lot filled with massive, rusted-out metal tanks.

"Meet back here," Debley ordered. "Zatell, try to get up there." He pointed to a precipice that could be reached by a gradual incline. It was covered by an outcropping of rock. "Customs should be just below. You shouldn't be visible there from either below or above. See what you can see and report back."

Webrid noticed how he'd been left out of those instructions. But he was so pleased to have his cart safely in hand that he didn't mind so much.

"Wait." Zatell was hitting the cart with her lower limbs, as close as she could come to kicking it. "What about AVS protection?”

"You'll have to take a chance, dear," said Stravin. "Neither of you has a live Vox ID card on you, right?" Webrid shook his head and Zatell shook her whole body. Stravin beamed a shiny smile. "Shouldn't be a problem, then." He had the nerve to wink as he chirped, "Try to blend in."

Those words rang dissonantly in Webrid's head as he watched the scooter and *Draspar* car drive off across the dusty landscape. But there was nothing for him to do but push the cart behind Zatell's rolling body. Up they went along the rock levels. The cart got stuck only once, which Webrid chalked up to his long experience navigating the trash- and body-strewn gutters of Bargival. One of his grandfather's favorite maxims echoed through his memory: "You never know when your special skills might be called upon in life, boy-o."

At last they reached the plateau from which Debley had told them to gather intel on the customs compound. Sure enough, they could see it. But they had no idea what they were looking for.

"I guess we just sit and watch," said Zatell, lowering her middle into what she seemed to think of as a sitting position. Webrid folded his big body until he was down at her level. The ground was stony and unpleasant. For ages they sat there, observing guards and workers of various species as they walked across and around the compound. Watching bugs lay eggs in bread loaves would have been more exciting. And they didn't see a single vehicle pass over the border.

"You remember the days before the Vox?" Webrid said, just to pass the time. "Things used to be, you know, safer. Remember?" Webrid had heard about people who'd been "disappeared" after being overheard or seen doing something the authorities didn't like. But that sort of scary stuff had only started ten years before.

"Of course I remember." Zatell ran a few limbs lightly through the dirt, tracing curlicues. "When they started the Vox, all it did was talk when you asked it something."

"Hey, you're right." Webrid sat up straighter, thinking. "At first it just gave info. It was so helpful, and everything seemed a lot more organized. It was the greatest invention since sliced janz lunchmeat. Then it got all weird and it started…"

"…Listening. And watching."

"Yeah."

"Bummer."

Their conversation had petered out, so they sat without talking, watching the people at the compound go about their business and not do anything interesting.

"This is dumb," said Webrid.

"Yeah, maybe," Zatell agreed. "Let's stay just a little longer."

"They won't know we're here?" That question had really been bothering him.

"No. That's why Stravin asked about our ID cards. If we don't have them with us, the Vox might see us, but it can't tell who we are. So, hopefully, it won't pay any attention."

There was something wrong with Zatell's reasoning, but Webrid couldn't quite nail it down. So he let it go. The two sat in silence again. Webrid was beginning to drift into sleep when Zatell's voice startled him awake.

"So, did you ditch your ID card or what?" she asked.

Webrid had to think about that. So much had happened recently. "Yeah. I'm pretty sure I left it behind in some fancy hotel room in Ksacheel. How about you?"

"Me? Oh, please, I haven't had a legal ID in years."

It was an intriguing, romantic notion to Webrid. "Amazing. So how do you get food and money and stuff?"

Zatell reached up to her flower-center face with one of her hands and scratched her nose. "Well, my biz is cash-only, of course. As for food," she winked an eye framed by lashes as long as Webrid's front claws, "there are ways around that."

Webrid squirmed his rear to find a comfier seat on the rocks. "Like what?"

"Oh, you know, the loopholes. Forges and stiffs."

"I know what a forgery is. What's a...oh, you mean...?"

"Yup!" she said. "Dead guy's ID. Gotta get it quick, though, before the Vox knows he's dead." She held out one of the arms near her brow. It had a band around it. With another hand, she released a flap in the band and pulled out an ID card.

"This was my first one. It's been deactivated for years, but I carry it for luck."

Webrid read: "Dajem Roos." He looked at Zatell and then back at the card. The picture matched her, but something was wrong. "It says he's male," Webrid said, fearful of this turn in the conversation.

Zatell's little mouth burbled with laughter. "Yeah, how about that?" she practically squealed. "And no one ever called me on it. For some reason, store clerks don't think I'm all that feminine." To Webrid's horror, she propped herself up against his cart with several limbs and started making kissing sounds at him. "How 'bout you, big boy? Am I woman enough for you?"

Webrid's great, hairy mind chugged as fast as it could go, but he couldn't think of a thing to say that wouldn't cause an unpleasant backlash, not to mention a slug in his solar plexus. It was therefore a relief when he heard a mechanical voice screeching above them.

"Remain still! You are in a restricted area!"

Webrid and Zatell looked up to see a toy-sized cop-copter circling the outcropping. Webrid was amazed. "How did it see us? It must be that damned stiff's ID you're carrying." He tried to give Zatell a withering glare, but she was no longer near the cart. A scuttling sound made him turn, and there she went, hand over fist over foot, escaping into a gap between two rocks. The gap was much too small for a Yeril to squeeze through. The only other direction to run was out from under the rock shelf. Such an idiotic move would surely draw gunfire.

Webrid just stood there and sighed, missing the protective, if condescending, company of Stravin and the fleshy sibs. Now he would be captured, and the laser would be ripped from his skull and his carcass thrown away like a shamtibby sucked off its shell at a beach smoke. For the tenth time in just over a week, Webrid assumed he was about to die. He was getting used to the feeling, and by now it caused more of a dull disappointment than a panic.

Figuring he might as well speed up the process, Webrid stepped just to the edge of the outcropping.

"Remain still!" the cop-copter screeched.

"Got it," called Webrid. "I'll just wait here. Come on down." He put one hand on his cart handle to steady himself, body and soul.

Down came the toy flying machine, spouting, "Trespasser!" Far from his usual instinct (to respond, "But, you see, officer..."), Webrid nodded his head glumly. He tried not to flinch as the cop-copter wobbled toward him, apparently hitting some bumpy air on the way down. Webrid even smiled for its camera.

But then he got an idea. This had been happening to him a lot lately, and he kind of wished it would stop. All his ideas ever did was buy him time, putting off his execution one more day. Still, there was no real reason he should be captured and killed right at that moment.

With his smile still chiseled across his face and both tongues hanging out over his teeth, Webrid raised his left arm slowly. With the right he kept a tight hold on the cart, which he was preparing to crouch behind. Higher, higher went his left hand, toward his forehead.

With a lightning-fast flick of his claw, Webrid flipped back the bnarli. He scrunched his eyes closed and waited for his laser to blow up the cop-copter.

There was no explosion. He could still hear the cop-copter whirring. Had he missed? Opening one eye just enough to peek, Webrid was so startled by the cop-copter's proximity to his face that he popped open both eyes and gasped. That shock, however, was not nearly as great as the one that followed.

"Ganpril Webrid," said the cop-copter in a businesslike tone. "First State Universal Carter. Presence in restricted area approved." It angled its camera lens toward the cart, scanned it from front to back, then flew away.

Webrid's fingers had grown numb against the cart's handle. His breath was shallow. His knees gave out and his rear hit the hard ground. With his right hand extended above his head, still clinging to the cart, he just sat there, unable to move.

"Hey, kid, you okay?" Zatell was somehow next to Webrid, peering at his frozen face. "You hurt? How'd you get rid of that thing? Hey, what's on your forehead? Is that the laser? Did you blow up the chopper? I didn't hear it. Did you vaporize it or what? 'Cause I was just back there and I..."

"mmmmmmmnnnnnnaaaaAAAAAGH!" The sound from Webrid's throat started as a whimper but ended as a scream. It felt good, so he did a bit more screaming, still sitting on the ground with one hand clawing into the cart handle.

For a change, Zatell was silent. Webrid forgot she was there. He spoke to his cart and to the spirits of his carting ancestors. "No matter what I do, it makes no difference."

There was something he wanted to ask his ancestors about, some power he was lacking, a power he felt was his due as a living creature. But he couldn't express it.

ebrid hauled his bulk up from the ground with the cart as balance. His right palm was bleeding from his claws' grip on his livelihood. On shaking legs, Webrid padded to the edge of the precipice overlooking the customs compound.

"How come?" he called downward.

"Shh!" hissed Zatell.

"How come?" He didn't care who heard him, but he couldn't think of the rest of the question.

"Webrid," Zatell said, over-gently, as if to a slightly crazy person standing at the edge of a precipice, which described Webrid exactly. "Hey, pal, let's go see Stravin and those guys. Wouldn't you like to see your old friend Stravin?"

She reached up and grabbed his belt, guiding him away from the cliff. Webrid's mind was a fog. He trailed after Zatell on automatic, pushing his cart. He would have blindly followed her anywhere, even someplace terrifying—a police station, say, or a library—but she simply led him down the hillside to the abandoned tank yard.

When they reached their meeting place, Webrid

continued forward until his cart bumped into one of the huge round energy tanks. The lettering on them indicated that they had once held nephraceon gas, but that fossil fuel had been depleted a generation before. No chance anyone would be around. Webrid, feeling suddenly cold, pressed his back against the sun-heated metal tank. The comfort it brought him cleared his mind, and he thought of his question.

"How come," he whispered to the sun as he pushed the bnarli down tight against his forehead, "I don't ever get to choose for myself?"

"Choose what?" asked Zatell.

Webrid looked down at her and sighed. She didn't get him. He didn't have the energy to explain. He thought about Leshi. She would understand.

Zatell and Webrid sat in the shade of a tank for quite a while, sharing a bottle of water from the supplies in the cart. By the time they heard the Moti and the *Draspar* car approaching, the sun was getting low.

"We found a way in," Stravin announced. He showed no concern for his colleagues. "Let's get going before it's too dark."

Without a word, Leshi took a bottle from the cart and walked back to the *Draspar* car. She leaned on the hood while she drank. Webrid thought his eyes might catch fire from all that hotness.

But it was her brother who addressed Webrid. "I can hook you up," he said.

Webrid stared at him.

Debley spoke again. "Want me to hook you up?"

In his fragile state, Webrid simply could not understand. Hook him up with whom? "You got an Entra lady in your pack?" he quipped, getting a little excited at the idea, in fact.

"The cart, man," Debley said, taking a few steps back. "Hook up your cart. Damn!" Shaking his head as if to ward off any more weird Yeril vibes, Debley got to work attaching the cart to the scooter's hitch. Webrid prayed to be swallowed into the ground, but the gods didn't oblige him.

To his surprise, Leshi tossed her bottle between two tanks and loped toward the cart. She was the last person Webrid wanted to chat with in his current state of self-loathing. But he doubted he could out-lope her. Closing his eyes, he braced for the psychological impact of whatever Leshi had to say. At least she couldn't bring him down any lower.

It threw him literally off balance when Leshi wrapped her arms around his torso and whispered, "I'm glad you're safe." He was so startled that she had to hold him upright.

She was moist and warm, and her oily coal-dust scent made Webrid's guts shiver in an intriguing way. He couldn't send a nerve signal to his arms in time, though, so he didn't manage to hug back before she pulled away and began to talk to Zatell instead.

Now it was Stravin's turn to bother Webrid.

"Everything all right, my dear?" he crooned. "You look a little, um, well…"

"They knew who I was," Webrid blurted out. "They know I'm here."

Stravin's feathery brow shot up. "How is that possible?"

Fighting the urge to rip his claws through his friend's face, Webrid shouted, "How would I know? Seriously, tell me. How would I know?"

They were all looking at him. Again.

"All right, dear," said Stravin, holding out his hands, which Webrid did not take. "They know you're here and they didn't kill you or kidnap you. That's something, then, isn't it?"

"He's a liability," Debley said, just loudly enough to be heard.

Stravin turned to him and spoke clearly. "He is the

reason we're all here. Maybe we're the liability to him."

Touched by Stravin's show of solidarity, Webrid was sorry he'd considered ripping off his face. That Stravin fella was all right.

"If we're going," Zatell said, her mouth full of crackers, "we should go."

It was pure, simple wisdom that nobody could argue with. Stravin and Debley mounted the scooter. Zatell climbed up into the *Draspar* car and Leshi fitted herself down into it. Webrid the carter, naturally, settled into his cart.

As they rode northeast, Webrid noticed something strange on the horizon. "What is that scraggly stuff stretched across there? Is that a wall?" he shouted to anyone who could hear him.

Even over the roar of the two engines and the clatter of the cart's wheels, Debley's condescension rang through clearly. "They're trees," he said. "Trees. You know, as in a forest? You've heard of forests and trees, right?" What was he, Webrid's tutor now?

Conversation was pointless with all the ambient noise and offensive attitude, so Webrid sank low among the bags and boxes, propping his right elbow against Stravin's tiny rocket engine. He thought about trees. Trees. Why did people seem to care so much about trees? He couldn't imagine.

Then he saw two strange things. First he noticed that Leshi, driving the *Draspar* car next to the cart, was alternately pointing to the distant trees with her free hand, and brushing tears from her cheeks. The lady loved her trees, no question. But then he experienced another manner of sight. Green mist covered his vision, the way it had when his laser was first installed. And those particles of green coalesced into a shape he now recognized. It was the tree he'd seen on that first day.

"What the hell?"

As soon as he spoke, the image dissipated, and his vision cleared. He must have imagined it. He could see that Zatell was comforting Leshi in the car. What *was* it with trees?

After a while, the landscape started to change. There were scrubby bushes, more than Webrid had ever seen before. The bushes got progressively larger the farther they traveled. Eventually, they were driving among very tall bushes with long, thick stems. Trees, presumably. Real ones. And darkness was a problem because the tops of the big bushes were blocking out what little sunlight remained. The Moti and the *Draspar* car had headlights, of course, but there wasn't actually a road to drive on.

"Hey-ey-ey," bumped Webrid, worried as much about his cart's new axles as his own neck. "We should sto-wo-wop."

Pulling into a grove of thick, mossy trunks, the two vehicles parked and everyone piled out. The forest was disorienting to Webrid, who sniffed the dank, cold moisture in the air. Every noise they made, every cough and closing car door, was absorbed and diffused into the mist. It didn't sound anything like the city. And then there were the sounds of the forest itself, whoops and squeals and growls and cheeps, like a thousand secret creatures sniggering at them. Webrid would have welcomed the scream of a drug dealer being murdered, or even a police siren.

Stravin had left the Moti's mighty front lamp lit so they could see a bit while they unpacked some crackers and preserved fruits. Each jar opened with a *pop* that seemed to threaten the very ecosystem. More than any time in his life, Webrid felt like he didn't belong. He was an intruder. It wasn't the Vox or the government splinter group that he feared. He expected retribution from the forest itself.

After supper, stepping behind a tree trunk for a pee, Webrid found himself facing a demon. Three yellow-green lights drew near him in the slate-colored air. He couldn't even breathe out, let alone call for help.

"Wh...? Wha?" squeaked the big hairy Yeril. Those strange lights hovered before him, getting closer; they didn't seem to be attached to anything.

"Rrrrrrrrrrrrrrrrrmmmmm," answered the light spirit, *basso profundo*.

Webrid was not a religious man. He'd heard about the gods in fairytales from his youth and in curses from his adulthood, but he never put much stock in it all. He was a modern, urban creature who knew mortal wiles had as much power to shape and preserve a life as any deity. But in these enigmatic woods, with a mysterious laser implanted in his skull, on a planet not his own, Webrid was primed to believe in the supernatural. Maybe his laser had called forth this apparition.

"Is this your tree?" Webrid mumbled. "Did I piss on your tree?" His hand shook so hard, he could barely zip up.

The triangle of lights grew and tilted. Webrid thought of the speed with which his own laser had killed that gangster woman at Stim's Diner and wondered how many seconds he would live if he got shot by three at once. Sounded good and painless. That emboldened him. He hooked back into his familiar urban bravado.

"You gonna kill me for this?" he said a bit louder, although his syllables fell with a thud into the wet sod. "Is this tree, this one tree, really so special? Eh?"

"Rrrrrrrrrrrrrrrrrmmmmm, sssssnxxxx. ZCHOOO!"

It sneezed. The spirit sneezed. It also reeked of unwashed living creature. Although he'd never been in a forest before, Webrid had pulled enough all-nighters in bars to know the scent of a guy who really needs a bath.

"ZCHOO!" The sneeze was followed by a head, fat and shaggy, with long upper lips hanging downward and glistening with drool in the scooter's headlight. The creature had three eyes. There weren't any lasers, and there wasn't any tree spirit.

"Gods, I'm an idiot," said Webrid, trying to push the curious snout away from his chest. "Now shoo!"

"ZCHOO! Rrrrrrrrrmmmmmmm."

Near his feet, Webrid heard Zatell's voice. "Aw, how sweet! What is he?"

"Do I look like a, like a...?" Webrid couldn't think of what an animal specialist might be called, so he just stomped back to the grove and sat next to his cart.

"What's going on?" said Stravin.

"Some animal," said Webrid.

"Oh, heavens, not an animal. I can't abide nature."

"You said it," agreed Webrid, city-born carter.

Debley and Leshi had been murmuring together on the far side of the *Draspar* car for some time. At last they broke up their tête-à-tête. Debley sat on a suitcase next to Stravin, who shared the bottle of juice he was drinking. Leshi joined Webrid.

"I wanted to..."

"Before you start, just tell me," Webrid interrupted. "Do you mean 'I' or really 'we'?"

"I don't see..."

"Whatever it is you're about to tell me, are you speaking for Leshi, or for The Great Revolution, or whatever you call it?"

Leshi pulled her facial sinews back to form a smile. "Let's put it this way: It's me, Leshi, who wants to tell you about The Great Revolution."

"Huh."

"So? May I?"

"Yeah. Go ahead. Does this really have to do with trees?

Are these trees really so great?"

Leshi pulled in a few heaves of laughter. Then she became very calm, even solemn. When she looked at Webrid, he could see a certain pride reflected in her eyes. Or perhaps it was a trick of the headlights.

"We're called the Swarattan Resistance Force," she began, "and trees are symbolic of the many issues that concern us."

This was starting to feel like school. Webrid swallowed his anxiety. "What kind of resistance force did you say?"

"Swarattan. After Heesha Swaratt."

"Who?"

"You've never heard of Heesha Swaratt? She's a famous historical figure. Every child knows…"

Again with the condescension. "This child didn't know. So sue me." It came out too loudly, and Webrid was embarrassed. He continued barely above a mumble. "It's just that I never, you know, paid too much attention in class."

"Oh. Right."

Webrid shook his head. He was out of patience with himself, with Leshi, with the whole damned world. "Forget it. Just tell me about her."

"Well, she's the reason there's a Raralt Planetary Circle. She was instrumental in designing and founding the joint government with Cheed, Bexilla, Prellga, and Rada-2."

"Wow." Designing and founding a government were not activities that a lowly carter could really picture, but he knew he should be impressed. "So she's kind of your hero."

"Totally my hero." Leshi's voice had an energy and richness now that Webrid hadn't heard in it before.

"Nice. So, what is the, um, the mission or whatever of your Swattan, Swartan…"

"Swarattan Resistance Force," Leshi said patiently, and smiled again. "Our mission is to return the government of the Raralt Circle to Swaratt's founding principles."

She looked at Webrid with such hope and significance that he felt awful about having to ask the next question.

"And those principles would be what, now?"

She gave an enthusiastic recitation. "Peace, Prosperity, Fairness, Justice, Community, Individuality, and Forestation."

"Seriously?" More proof that civics class was a total crock. Webrid could barely keep from laughing. Sucking in air and wiping away a tear that was about to escape, he asked without looking at her, "You're saying those are the principles of the Raralt planets? Peace? Prosperity? What was it...forests?"

"I'm saying," she steamed, "that's what the principles were supposed to be. Obviously—" she overemphasized the word, "—it's not that way now. It's all police state and corruption and evil. Hence the need for the resistance movement, to return things to a Swarattan path."

"Uh-huh," said Webrid. He was trying to figure out what to say next, when the green-lit image of a tree glowed for a second before his eyes. "Huh!"

"Is that all you have to say?" Leshi sounded hurt.

"Did you see that?"

"See what? Were you even listening?" Leshi flashed him a lethal glower and stalked away.

It was just as well that Zatell chose that moment to start yelping from behind a tree. "Get off. Hey! Stop! I said cut it out, you ugly mudsticker!"

Webrid heard the light slap-slap-slap of multiple limbs, then the "Rrrrnt!" of a wild beast and rapid hoof-falls growing dimmer through the brush.

Stravin and Webrid reached her first. "What happened, my darling?" Stravin asked, kneeling to Zatell's height. "Are you injured? What did that awful creature do to you?"

"Nothin'," she grumbled, and rolled with a huff out into the clearing.

Webrid followed. "That three-eyed critter was crazy big. You sure you're not hurt?"

"I'm not hurt, okay?" she shouted. The forest responded with a burst of caws, whirs, and rustles. Zatell looked up at Webrid and whispered, "I think it wanted to mate with me."

ebrid spent a fitful night inside his cart. He wanted to close the lid over himself to keep out all the three-eyed, long-lipped, hooved animals and whatever else might be out there. But between the fear of suffocation and the fear that his friends might abandon him, he chose to let the tree branches and night sky be his roof.

It was impossible to lose himself to sleep in the unfamiliar world of the forest. Every crackle and drip, every musky scent riding on a breath of breeze, startled him to wide-eyed wakefulness.

His companions seemed to be having similar problems. The only one getting any proper rest was Zatell, who had claimed the *Draspar* car as her bedroom. Starlight revealed how the car's bubble top was fogged by her deep breathing.

Leshi was stretched out on the bare ground, unafraid of the squirming universe of creepy-crawlies that surely traversed the forest floor. Still, despite having two blankets (Zatell had given hers up in payment for an indoor berth), Leshi tossed and shivered all night. Webrid thrilled each time she whimpered.

Stravin had made a show of being unwilling to sleep on the ground. He'd pulled three suitcases out of Webrid's cart and laid them flat, end to end, as a bed. The lowest one he placed next to the Moti so he could rest his feet on its floorboard. Obviously, this was his way of protecting the Moto from the sneaky hands of prospective new owners. Webrid marked this sign of distrust of Stravin's fellow creatures, and heartily approved of it. Good to see some urban paranoia amongst all this verdant wholesomeness.

During the night, Stravin rolled from side to side, making the plastic suitcases squeak. At one point, he did a full turn and his upper body shifted onto the ground. Awakening with a sharp exhale, he brushed himself off manically for longer than could have been helpful, then stretched out again on the cases with a sigh.

Debley sat upright all night, leaning against the front right wheel of the car with a blanket draped over his lap. He remained still with his eyes closed, although Webrid doubted that he was getting much real sleep in that position. His head never lolled forward or to the side.

The night seemed to last forever. Webrid considered counting his heartbeats to fall asleep, as his mother used to tell him to do. But the forest had its own complex polyrhythms, which distracted his focus. At one point a leathery thing, about the size of Webrid's thumb, crawled across his face. He grabbed it, scraping his own skin with his claws. Without trying to see what he'd caught, he hurled the tickly ball into the dark and heard it splat against a tree trunk. Satisfied, he lay back and let his cheek sting.

As it happened, the hours of discomfort and sleeplessness bore a magnificent prize. When dawn finally came, the new sun poured thin beams of pink, orange, and lavender through the leaves, dappling the campers with splotches of colors that Webrid had never seen before. The side of his cart, catching the chromatic light, shimmered like a stripper's dress. The sounds had changed, too, probably because some creatures had gone to bed and others gotten up. This kind of calm was entirely new to Webrid, and he struggled to maintain his sardonic edge. It was hopeless; the world was just too beautiful.

Webrid was trying to decide whether to awaken his friends when a loud rustle in the underbrush did the job for him. Everyone stirred and muttered "good morning," and the spell was broken. It was just another day on a suicide mission.

"So, are we in Northern Cheed?" Zatell asked as they folded their blankets and rubbed their eyes.

"Yup," said Debley.

"That was easy," said Webrid. He was suspicious of anything easy. "Why was it so easy?"

"Because, my dear," said Stravin, arranging his arm feathers into rows, "there's nothing here, so there's no guarded border. We're in the Vox-free zone, uncharted. Except by our Debley, of course."

Webrid looked around. "It's kinda nice. Can we just stay here?"

Leshi spoke from behind a tree. "Like live here?"

"No," said Webrid. "Just keep driving in here. That way the Vox can't see us."

Debley stood and stretched. He didn't even look at Webrid when he said, "Why do you suppose we put all that effort into making the Anti-Vox Shadow? The woods are impassable for vehicles. We've got to enter the Vox zone, as planned, both because it will be easier to travel, and because the government splinter group has to be in the Vox zone."

Webrid opened his mouth, but before he could ask his question, Stravin answered it. "Even a splinter group needs the Vox to get info and provide protection."

"So, why won't the Vox protect them from us?" Webrid asked. The whole group looked at him. He could swear Leshi sighed.

"The AVS," Zatell and Debley said together.

But Webrid was getting more confused. "Don't we want to talk to them? About my..." he pointed to the bnarli, "... problem?"

"We don't want a conversation," Debley said. "We want the laser reader."

"Wouldn't it be easier to just have them read it?"

"No. They wouldn't tell us what it said."

"So what's the plan?"

Leshi opened a package of crackers. "We're going to steal the laser reader. And if we can't, we'll sneak in and use it without their knowledge."

Webrid now had his first policy disagreement with his fellow explorers. Politics mattered nothing to him. Neither, frankly, did knowing exactly what was on his laser implant. Granted, lifting a priceless machine owned by the government sounded like good fun. Webrid's current objection was grounded in his work ethic. He believed the government splinter group had hired him. This Rempener Dras who'd paid him all that money must be their accountant. He wanted to deliver the laser to them. Mostly, he wanted the next step: for them to remove the thing. Surely their fancy machine could do that if you punched in the right code. Why invent such a specialized item if it only did half the job?

As his companions finished their dried breakfast foods and situated themselves in their vehicles, Webrid started forming an alternative plan. It didn't rate high for logic, but it was better than nothing. The supposed plan went something like this:

He would let his brainy, nimble colleagues find the place

where these outlaws—or rather, his clients—were hiding. They could figure out how to break in and also locate the laser reader. Then Webrid would burst into action.

"What's that expression?" he asked aloud while being bumped along the tree roots and rocks behind the Moti. "Oh, yeah. I'll 'make myself known.' Yeah, that's it." He was as pleased with his phraseology as he was with the plan. "I'll sound the alarm. I'll find the government guys, and I'll offer them..."

He almost said "offer them my head," but realized that he needed to be quiet so he wouldn't give away his plan. The irony and perhaps literal peril of those words bounced out of his mind with the cart's jerking motion. He ignored the nagging half-thought niggling at him. Something about safety, his own and his friends'. Something about a slow, tortured death.

The scooter and car made slow progress for a while until the sun grew brighter through the trees. As they came to a stop, Webrid could hear water rushing, but couldn't see its source.

Leshi's head emerged when the car's bubble top opened. "River, right?"

"Sure seems like it," said her brother. And he had to add, "Just like I told you."

Webrid let out a wet snort.

"How far, do you think?" Stravin said, leaning sideways to peer between the trees.

"Our mapping doesn't give us that info. We can't be precise until we're in the Vox zone, which begins, presumably, at the river itself."

Zatell said something from inside the car.

"No way," answered Leshi, looking down at her passenger.

A few more muffled syllables came from Zatell.

"Seriously, no," said Leshi.

"What does she want?" asked Debley.

Leshi rolled her eyeballs so far up that the irises disappeared. In her skinless face, it made her look like something you might find by the side of the road after a village had been ransacked by drunken Edjenels.

"She wants to drive," Leshi said.

Debley had himself a good hearty laugh. Webrid wanted to defend Zatell, but then he pictured all those tiny limbs pawing at the steering levers, and he laughed, too.

Stravin didn't hesitate. He chose sides in a way that really impressed Webrid. "This woman is a rocket scientist, my dear," he said, nose to nose with Debley. "I don't use that term poetically. She is *actually* a rocket scientist and astronaut. If she can pilot a rocket from planet to planet, how could she be unable to drive this silly toy car? Honestly, darling." Stravin gave Debley the gentlest graze of a punch along his jawline. But Webrid could see in his eyes that he would put some real force behind it if his old friend Zatell didn't get some respect, and quickly.

Apparently Debley picked up this vibe, too. The tone of his laugh changed, like it came from the place in his gut where he usually kept fear. As he spoke, he never broke eye contact with Stravin. "Okay, then. Lesh, let's see what your pal can do. I bet you could use a break, anyway."

"Well, all right!" Zatell could be heard to shout. She wedged herself in next to Leshi's skinny legs, in front of the control panel. Leshi pulled herself free and slid over to the other seat, her lip upturned as if she were wading through a cesspool. She sank down into her seat and lowered her head just in time to avoid getting it caught in the closing clear bubble.

Webrid, conflicted, decided he was glad Zatell had a chance to drive. But he was way too much of a Yeril not to expect it all to end in tears.

Zatell took off like a wild forest creature. The *Draspar* car choked and whirred, zigging around trees, becoming briefly airborne, then landing hard.

Stravin, trying to keep up on the scooter, kept shouting, "Hey! Hey!" Webrid wasn't sure if he was calling to Zatell or just responding to the growing excitement. Debley, on the scooter's passenger seat, clung on with all he had. Webrid could see the tension in his shoulders and hands.

As for Webrid, he got that old, familiar feeling of imminent demise. He dug his claws so hard into the cart's frame that he could feel the metal denting. The axles, he knew, hadn't a prayer, so he prayed that his organs might stay in his body as he was bounced from root to root. One by one, the suitcases, boxes, and bags jumped from the cart. Some of them sprang upward only to find their way down via Webrid's skull.

The sunshine was getting brighter as they neared the edge of the forest. During a blessed respite from his pummeling, Webrid wondered how long it would take them to drive from the forest edge to the river, and whether it would be a nice, flat surface, or maybe even a paved road.

Then a big black animal jumped in front of the *Draspar* car. It moved like a shadow, and in later discussions they would find that nobody saw it well. Webrid was sure it had scales, black on black, and a belly's worth of red dots. In any case, it was three times the size of the *Draspar* car, and directly in its path.

Zatell swerved right, which put her en route to a perpendicular meeting with the Moti. Webrid could see how fast her little arms moved on the levers and knobs on the dashboard. The car turned left just before making contact with the scooter.

Leshi was pressing her palms tightly against the left side of the bubble wall, and rocking. For a second, Webrid assumed she was panicking and trying to escape. Then he saw what was happening.

The car was now heading into a tree. Leshi's motions swung the little car sideways, its two right wheels up in the air. It looked like the car was trying to climb the tree before it straightened out on the other side of the trunk.

This acrobatic move slowed the car just enough that the Moti could finally get ahead of it and turn to block its path. Webrid just had time to wonder whether the flotation balloons worked on dry land.

As it turned out, the point was moot. Once Zatell righted the car, she tore off at top speed. Perhaps she hit the wrong knob, but in any case, she lost control. As she flew past the Moti, the car caught the scooter's front wheel casing, dragging the Moti behind it through the last bit of forest. The cart, flailing along as the caboose on a train to hell, got wedged between two trees, snapping loose from its hitch.

Webrid flew forward and wound up on his belly, skidding forward through pungent soil. But when he stopped, he was hanging over water and a great amount of air.

The forest, in fact, had ended abruptly and become river. The river was artificially made, or at least enhanced, so its banks were sudden, steep, smooth plastic. Webrid could see this when he landed, but he couldn't process it fast enough to shout a warning in time. Not that it would have helped. Once the two vehicles careened out of the forest, there was nothing under their wheels.

The scooter did two spirals in the air, by Webrid's reckoning, shaking Debley loose into the current. Stravin held on like a daredevil, his hands on the handlebars but the rest of him waving loosely behind like a white feathery flag. Fortunately, he had the sense to let go before his beloved souped-up Moti-Moto struck the water upside down. To Webrid's great relief, he saw Stravin splashing madly toward the bank.

During this experience, Webrid learned that the *Draspar* car was equipped with an emergency eject system. At the moment of impact with the far bank, the car's bubble top split open and its two passengers flew out. Zatell, her arms a blur as she twirled past, was catapulted into a treetop. Leshi's body shape and angle of trajectory made her a torpedo shot deep into the woods.

Despite his pain and shock, Webrid had a gleeful thought. His much-maligned cart, which had broken free of the Moti hitch, was now the only one of the wheeled contraptions that could probably still roll.

ebrid lay on the ground, watching a million green math equations flash behind his eyes. When at last the numbers faded and his shiv of a headache dulled, he tested out the rest of his body. Although his ribs were a bit bruised and his left elbow was scraped, Webrid was able to get up on his feet. He then faced the decision of which friend to help first.

Debley and Stravin were in the water on opposite sides of the river, clearly furious but apparently safe. Stravin, on the far side, had a grip on one of the gray plastic notches that poked out from the artificial bank at regular intervals. Debley was on the near side, moving hand over hand toward some sort of dock made of the same gray plastic.

Looking behind him into the forest, Webrid couldn't see Leshi. He wanted to run around searching for her, but urgent shouting from above demanded his attention.

"In the tree," squealed Zatell. "I'm up here, in the damn tree!"

Webrid craned his neck. "Can't see you. Which tree?"

"This one."

"Which one?"

"How the hell do I know which tree this is? It's the tree with me in it, you stralem-brained hoongofl."

Webrid wasn't sure what a hoongofl was. He figured that was for the best. "I'll get you down," he said, trying to sound comforting.

"Hurry up."

"Yeah, yeah. Just let me look from over here."

As he spoke, Webrid backed up with his chin in the air, trying to see into the tree branches. After a few steps, he tripped on a root and fell backwards, his rear landing hard in the dirt. He could hear Zatell's familiar laugh falling on him like seed pods. At least he now knew which tree she was in. Its branches shook with her giggles. What he'd taken for a bird's nest was Zatell's many limbs. Webrid had practically no experience with birds' nests, so it was an understandable mistake.

"Okay," he called wearily, hauling himself up. "Now I see you. Just stay put."

"What are you gonna do?"

"Come up and get you."

She laughed again, pushing words out between whoops. "You don't really look like a climber."

Webrid realized she was right.

"Fine," he snapped. "What do you think I should do?"

"Stand still and put out your arms."

Webrid was just forming the word "What?" when Zatell came crashing down, splintering tree branches as she fell. Webrid didn't exactly catch her. It was more like he broke her fall. Down he went again into the dirt, this time with a dozen squishy little hands paddling his face.

"You're not that soft for such a hairy guy," Zatell said as she rolled off him.

"Oh, thanks," Webrid countered, trying to sit up and

pick the leaves out of his ears. "Well, you ain't such a good driver for a rocket scientist."

At that, the paddling limbs turned into striking weapons, and Webrid scrambled to protect his eyes from Zatell's angry blows.

Suddenly someone else was laughing nearby, a more complex, appealing laugh than Zatell's.

"Leshi!" Webrid cried.

Zatell stopped her thrashing. The carrier pushed her off him and found the strength to stand. "Leshi, are you okay? I tried to ... I couldn't see you..."

"It's fine," she said, her magenta flesh a deeper purple in the forest's shade. "I'm fine."

"You didn't get hurt? You really went flying out of that..." Webrid stopped, sensing Leshi's embarrassment.

"We, um, we Fekli..."

"That's your people?" Zatell asked, rolling herself forward through a pile of leaves.

Webrid shivered. He'd never thought to ask Leshi's species before, and hearing its name made him feel closer to her.

"Yes." Leshi shrugged. "We Fekli heal ourselves."

"Wow," Webrid said.

"I mean, if it's really serious, we can't handle it on our own. But cuts and bruises, you know?" She kicked at some dried leaves. "We don't talk about it. It's a social thing. Bad manners, since most folks, you know..."

"Need doctors," Zatell finished kindly.

"Wow," Webrid said again. He couldn't believe how badly he wanted to kiss her.

Zatell tugged at his pants leg. "Um, weren't there five of us before?"

They looked at each other for an instant before taking off toward the river in a burst of profanity.

"There they are," cried Leshi as they reached the top of

the steep bank.

By squinting into the white glare of sunshine, Webrid could see that Stravin and Debley were in no need of rescuing. The two slender men, one gleaming red, the other fluffy white, were stretched out side by side on the deck Debley had been clinging to before. They appeared to be sunning themselves.

Over the river's rushing, Zatell shouted, "Hey! Get your lazy asses up!"

Webrid, equally offended by their sloth, kicked a chunk of dirt down the sloping bank. It wasn't a direct hit, but it got Stravin sitting up, desperately preening his feathers with his fingertips.

Debley waved. "Come on down."

Leshi neared the forest edge as if to slide down the bank, but Webrid grabbed her arm.

"You come up here," he shouted down at the sunbabies.

"You lost your mind, dear?" Stravin called back.

"My cart's up here."

Debley let out a single, artificial "Ha!" before starting, "We don't need that stupid…" But he stopped short.

Webrid grinned, triumphant. They needed the cart, and everyone knew it.

Because both men on the pier were tall but light, it didn't take much effort to pull them up the raked bank.

"Now what?" asked Stravin.

All of them, even the arrogant Debley, looked at Webrid.

"Well, the cart's stuck over there."

With two of them pushing and two pulling, and Zatell acting as project foreman, the cart was freed with only a few minor injuries. Debley cut his finger, which he promptly healed. Stravin's shin got in the way as the cart sprang loose. A knot rose up under his feathers, but the bone didn't seem to be broken.

The worst wounds were to the cart itself. Its sides were badly scratched and one of the lid's hinges had been pried loose. But even as Webrid grieved to see his ancestry mangled, he was thrilled that the axles and all four of the new military-grade wheels were intact and functional.

It was a ragtag band that limped along the edge of the forest, following the river north. Webrid pushed his cart with Stravin riding in it, both to rest his sore leg and to babysit the engine from Zatell's rocket, which he had confidently predicted would save them. He never said what it might save them from, and everyone was either afraid to ask or too tired to care.

At Debley's insistence, they stayed close enough to the river to keep it in sight. "We have to protect ourselves, see the enemy approach," he said.

Webrid thought the enemy, whoever that might be, would be more likely to sneak up on them from the forest side, but he kept his mouth shut and stuck to doing what he knew: He pushed his cart. He pushed it for so long, with the others trudging silently around him, that he forgot where he was.

The uneven ground reminded him of one summer as a kid he'd spent hawking frozen zheg-jellies at the Tenpilla Beach south of Bargival. He had figured out pretty quickly that he'd have one leg shorter than the other if he always went in the same direction, so he'd designed a pattern that snaked back and forth along the beach. He wasn't allowed on the flat parts because you needed to buy a special license. Very few carters had had the chutzpah to sell on the slant, and it got him quite a reputation, not to mention a nice little pocketful of dendiacs to spend.

Zatell's voice shook him from his pleasant memories.

"Lookit! Lookit down there!" She was pointing a good forty of her fingers, so it was easy to see where to look in the river.

"It's a raft," said Leshi. "Seems like it has a motor."

"Let's grab it, darlings," said Stravin. "This present form of transport is most undignified."

Webrid growled.

"And I'm tired of all this hiking," said Zatell, blowing on several limbs.

The raft, made of a solid floating plastic, was moored to one of the vertical notches on their side of the bank. Zatell slid down first. Once she hit the water, she was surprisingly buoyant, and had to struggle to grab the raft as she rode past on the current. She busied herself with getting the motor started.

Everyone else stayed up top until they could make a plan to get the cart down to the water safely. They decided to work in pairs. Webrid and Stravin scooched down the bank on their rears and lowered themselves into the water near the raft. Then the long-torsoed siblings, lying on their bellies, shepherded the cart as it rolled down by holding its back axle until they couldn't stretch any farther. It only had to roll free for a second before Webrid and Stravin stopped its front wheels.

The bigger strategic challenge was getting the cart onto the raft. Webrid spent much of this process pressed underwater by the cart's weight, so he didn't get to observe the details. But once he emerged, sputtering and spitting, he saw that his cart was safely aboard. It took all four of his comrades to drag the heavy, wet Yeril onboard behind it. Shivering in the sun, he wished he were on Tenpilla Beach instead of with these clowns.

"Motor's dead," Zatell announced as Webrid tried to

drain his ears of river water. "There's no fixing it."

"Would this help, my dear?" Stravin said, reaching into the cart. He pulled out his compact rocket engine. There was much rejoicing.

Stravin and Zatell puttered with the engine for ages. Webrid would have liked to spend the time talking to Leshi, but the plain fact was, he couldn't stay awake. The next thing he knew, Zatell was pawing his shoulder and saying, "Hang on, hairball!"

Stravin wrapped himself around the hybrid motor. The other four each grabbed a cart wheel with one hand and any nearby part of the raft with the other (or others, in Zatell's case). When Stravin started up the engine, it might have been the gods sawing the planet Cheed in twain. The volume of the roar was matched only by the velocity of their takeoff.

A raft, of course, is not aerodynamic, not meant to travel at high speed. This big square of plastic cut through the water with all the grace of a spatula, forcing up a huge wall of water on either side. At one point, Webrid swore they scraped bottom. He also knew that he was screaming the whole way, although he couldn't hear himself over the din their rocket-raft was making.

Finally they stopped. Webrid, numb in every limb, was also temporarily deaf. He lay still until the sounds of the world began to break through. When he finally lifted his head, he saw the others fighting through similar sluggishness.

"Anyone hurt?" he said. Or maybe he shouted. He couldn't tell.

They all shook their heads, looking stunned.

Debley crawled over to Stravin's side. 'Why did we stop, babe?"

As Stravin turned to address them, Webrid could see bare patches on his arms where feathers had been torn off as he held onto the motor. Yet Stravin was smiling.

"Behold," he said, waving a balding arm dramatically up and to the right. "The government splinter group's outpost."

Everyone turned to see an imposing building rising from the upper banks. It was covered in round tiles made of a black metal that gleamed blindingly in the afternoon sun.

"It's a fortress," said Leshi.

Webrid agreed that that was the right word. This building seemed impenetrable.

"Well, my loves," said Stravin in a lilting tone. "Shall we go a-visiting?"

Zatell's laugh rang out across the water.

"Any brilliant ideas?" Debley asked.

Webrid imagined that Debley avoided looking at him when he said that, but made eye contact with all the other, smarter explorers. This brought out his sardonic side. "I say we waltz on up to the front door."

Then he remembered his Alternate Plan, how he'd wanted the fringe group to know he was there. Wanted them to remove the laser, no matter how secretive and thieving the others tried to be. Webrid felt the urge to bolt up the bank to the fortress and ring the doorbell.

But there was a major hurdle in the way. At this spot in the river, and as far back as they could see, there was no sloping bank, and no place to tie up the raft. There was a vertical wall of clay running alongside the fortress, taller than three Yerils laid end to end. And that was mighty tall.

Webrid felt Leshi's slender fingers on his upper arm.

"You know we'll never get the cart up there," she whispered. "I'm so sorry."

oots," announced Debley, pointing toward the riverbank.

Stravin squinted at the shore. "What roots?"

"Those rope-like things coming out of the clay. Tree roots."

Webrid saw them. "Those aren't roots," he said. Having bumped and tripped over hundreds of tree roots over the past few hours, he fancied himself an expert.

"Trust me," said Debley, "they're roots, held deep in the soil. And they're so strong that they'll take our weight."

Leshi bounded up to her brother's side and kissed him. "And that's how we'll climb up there. Brilliant, bro!"

Webrid swallowed the queasiness that rose at this show of sibling love. "And how do you think we can get close enough to them so-called roots to grab hold? You might've noticed, we can't exactly control this raft. And what're you gonna tie it to, anyway?"

Zatell spoke up. "Is that clay soft, you think?" She didn't wait for an answer. "Let's go find out."

Using their hands as oars, they paddled closer to the side

of the river. Stravin pressed at the clay with his fingers and declared it fairly soft.

"Great," said Zatell. "Everyone hang on like you did earlier." She shooed them to their corners, but took Stravin's place at the engine. "I'm driving."

Webrid objected. "Last time you drove, we crashed." Then he remembered the rocket landing and added, "In fact, the last two times you drove, we crashed."

She took it well. "Yeah, but this time, that's the point."

As the other four were positioning themselves, Zatell asked them to paddle backwards a little. Then, suddenly, she shouted, "Okay, that's good. Hang on!" The command was so urgent that Webrid squeezed his eyes shut, clawed at his cart's wheel and the raft, and braced for impact.

The rocket engine fired up, and seconds later there was a violent jerk and a muffled thud.

"Whoo! There ya go!" Zatell shouted.

Webrid's back muscles were still vibrating, but he managed to look around him. He had to hand it to Zatell for her cleverness. One corner of the plastic raft was now jammed into the clay bank. This gave them a stable base from which to climb onto the roots.

"Last one up's a hairy hoongofl," said Zatell. She zipped up the embankment like she was weightless. She could grab many roots at a time, at any angle.

"An advantage to her shape," said Stravin. "Surprising, eh?"

"And the raft will be waiting for us later. That's a comfort," Leshi said, standing. She took a deep breath as she stood on tiptoe and got a hand grip to pull herself up. Zatell was already at the top.

Debley crawled up after his sister. Their Fekli limbs were awkward and gangly compared to Zatell's controlled, compact climb. But they got up all right.

Stravin regarded Webrid, then the cart. "Right. Well. See you up there." Stravin scaled the embankment. He got stuck once when his bruised leg gave out, but Debley reached down and hauled him up.

Webrid thought about staying behind on the raft with his cart. As in, forever. Probably he could live on river algae and the odd fish. It was a mesmerizing fantasy. Zatell's patient encouragement nudged him back to his senses.

"Shift your lazy haunches, Webber!"

This was it. Webrid turned to his trusty cart. "I'll be back soon," was all he said.

Yerils were a muscular people and the tree roots formed ample loops for feet and hands. Before Webrid knew it, Leshi and Stravin were pulling him over the lip of the clay wall and onto the grass.

Webrid allowed himself one glance down at his old friend. It looked pathetic down there, all dented and scratched. Still, what struck him most was how, despite the rushing current, the raft was not bobbing around, stuck fast as it was in the clay. That fact gave him just enough hope, just the tiniest glimmer, that he'd see his cart again.

The five of them headed north toward the mysterious black fortress. They tried to run stealthily through the brush like a team of commandos, but Webrid couldn't manage anything more graceful than a galumph. They would, he was sure, be caught at any moment. He tried to listen for the sound of cop-copters, but all he could hear was his own heart pumping and the twigs breaking under his big feet.

Soon they had reached the cleared ground where the fortress stood. Everyone stopped at the edge of the woods.

"Should we all hide behind a tree?" Zatell asked. "We could each take our own tree for cover." Webrid thought it seemed reasonable.

"Don't bother," said Debley. "If they're going to see us,

they're going to see us. Hiding won't help."

Webrid snorted. "Deep, man. Very deep." Suddenly he was thoroughly fed up with his companions, and not at all afraid. Looking straight ahead, he bid them a friendly "Nice knowing ya," and strode into the open air.

Ganpril Webrid, first-state universal carter, hoped his death would be swift. He'd had it with hiding, not to mention being kidnapped and threatened and generally pushed around.

"It's been a good life," he said aloud, hoping it was loud enough for the Vox to hear him. "Wish I had my cart with me, though. Wanted to die next to my cart." At those words, a mist of green light clouded his vision for a few seconds. "What, no pretty picture of a tree this time?"

He was nearing the spiked black wall, and there was still no sign of a security force, either biological or robotic. How long were they going to tease him?

"Come on and get me, foxy Voxy. Hey, I'm right here!" He shouted this upward while waving his arms around. As he looked up at the top of the fortress, he was surprised to see, not razor wire or soldiers with guns trained on him, but whorls of spectacular flowering ivy.

"Something ain't right about this," Webrid said more quietly, lowering his arms. He could now reach out and touch the conical wall spikes. He did touch one, hoping it would set off an alarm.

Nothing. Webrid tried again, touching two spikes at once, poking their tips and caressing their sides. He was startled by Stravin's voice behind him.

"Deserted, it would seem." The others were with him.

Leshi said, "It's like everyone packed up and left."

"Must've known we were coming," said Debley.

Webrid was startled to hear Zatell's squealing laughter at his knees. "Honestly, Debbers," she said, gasping for air, "why would whoever lives in this big, scary place care that we were coming? I mean, look at us. Talk about a sorry bunch."

"So they left a while ago, maybe," said Leshi.

"Um, wait, wait. No, wait." Webrid shook his head. It couldn't be true that nobody was inside. "They have to be here. They have to."

"Why, dear?" asked Stravin.

He pointed to the bnarli. If nobody was home, nobody could remove the blasted laser. This trip would have been for naught. "They just *have* to be."

"Now, now," Stravin said, putting his arm around him. "I would recommend that we all stop jumping to conclusions."

"Fine," said Debley. "So what should we be doing?"

"Well," Stravin said with a flourish of his arm, "we might start by finding a door."

Nobody could argue with that. Scanning the wall they were facing, Webrid was mesmerized by the thousands of spikes at regular intervals. There was no obvious door on this side. To the right was the deep forest. To the left was the river.

"That's gotta be the front," said Webrid, taking off to the left. The sun was getting lower behind them, covering the wall with hashmarked shadows cutting across the rows of spikes.

At the corner of the building, a breeze blowing along the river stirred Webrid's arm hair and Stravin's feathers. Webrid felt a bit calmer, in spite of himself.

"Guys, over here!" It was Zatell, halfway down the building's façade. She must have really hustled to roll there so fast. "This looks promising."

The four long-legged folks joined little Zatell in front of the largest pair of doors Webrid had ever seen.

"Who *are* these government people?" he said. "A race of giants?"

"I never voted for any giants," said Zatell.

"Me neither," said Leshi. She pushed tentatively at the black metal slabs, which did not move. There were no door handles, or any visible lock.

"As I understand it," said Stravin, taking a step back and looking up at the formidable entranceway, "this is the headquarters of people who were not elected." He turned to Webrid. "Wouldn't you say?"

"I wouldn't know," said the carter. "I ain't much of a voter." He didn't want to chat. His nerves jangled with a new anxiety, as if all his old anxieties weren't enough. "Can we get in there, or what?"

Debley had his eye against the crack between the doors.

"See any way to open it, darling?" Stravin asked.

"Nothing obvious, and lacking any equipment..."

"Let me," said Leshi, pushing her brother aside. After examining the door and its perimeter, she stepped away. "Nope. No idea how this thing works."

"Is there a doorbell?" Zatell asked. "If there is, one of you will have to reach it." She giggled.

"Don't see anything like a doorbell," said Stravin, taking her seriously.

Webrid had been brooding, just at the river's edge. Now his nerves were ready to pop. "Enough!" he roared. "Outta the way. I'm going in!" He lowered his head and pawed the ground with his foot claws. Mixing a whine with a growl, he lunged forward with all his considerable strength.

His four friends threw themselves in his path as he neared the door. They all landed in a heap.

"What the hell's the matter with you?" squawked Zatell.

Leshi was more understanding. "Oh, Webrid, I know you're frustrated, but you could have split your head open."

"Not likely with his thick skull," Debley sniped.

A rush of Yeril pride pulled Webrid to his feet. "Why?"

he asked the heavens. "Why are you doing this to me? What's the meaning of this? Of *this*?" He yanked off the bnarli, as if to remind the gods about the laser they'd implanted and forgotten. "Why do you keep stopping me from figuring this out?"

Webrid stared hard at the gigantic doors. A tiny green light appeared halfway up the join between them, skittering across the carbon-colored metal. There was a deep click, then another. Something whirred. The two doors opened slowly inward.

"How did you do that?" asked Debley, uncharacteristically impressed.

"Don't point that thing at me," said Zatell, who flopped two hands over her face.

"Are you all right?" Leshi asked gently. She took one of his arms, and Stravin took the other.

"Here you are, dear. Better put this back on, eh?" Stravin said as Leshi stretched the cord of the bnarli around Webrid's big head. He let her fit it over the laser without complaint.

Webrid allowed himself to be led inside the dark hallway. He was preoccupied with the thought that he might have killed someone by removing the bnarli, so he didn't pay much attention to his surroundings.

"Er, hello? Is anyone at home?" Stravin called in a small voice, as if he did not really want to be heard. Nobody answered.

In two jittery clumps—Leshi, Webrid, and Stravin arm in arm up front, and Zatell clinging to Debley's leg behind them—they inched forward. There was just enough light to see by, but there was nothing much to see. The walls were metallic and smooth, interrupted occasionally by doors. These doors were normal in size, and the few they tried led to nondescript rooms with no furniture. The explorers began to walk with more courage, although their footfalls rang through the empty corridors. Every once in a while one of them would call out, but no one ever got an answer.

As Leshi and Stravin released Webrid's arms, his senses woke up. Carters had to learn to trust their instincts for direction; following his, Webrid took a turn in the hallway maze that he was sure would lead them to the center of the fortress.

Yerils also had keen noses, a pretty comical trait for a people who tended to live in overcrowded cities. Webrid's nose explored the rooms they passed. They smelled empty of living beings.

Yet something was bothering him and his nose. Something wasn't right. Something was there that didn't belong.

In the middle of a deserted fortress in the middle of an uncharted forest, Webrid smelled freshly heated janz meat. He would have staked his life on it.

smell lunch," said Webrid, realizing with a hopeless sigh just how hungry he was. He couldn't even calculate how long ago he'd eaten that handful of dried whatever and some tasteless crackers. Health food never hit the spot.

The others were still sneaking down the dark hallway, poking their noses around corners. But Webrid had a better use for his nose. He let it guide him to a succulent snack. A few turns, a few opened doors, and he was standing in front of a smorgasbord of cold cuts, rolls, fatty zempra salad, and deep-fried pa-chips.

"They knew I was coming," he said, his eyes filling with tears of gluttony.

"Oh, you're crazy," said Zatell as the rest of the crew found their way in behind her. "Must have been for the guys who work here."

Leshi stepped up to the table and stabbed at the shaved lunchmeat with a fork. "I agree with Zatell. Something must have happened. Some emergency. And everyone left all at once."

"I'm telling you," Debley said, "it's us they're afraid of.

They saw us on the Vox and made a run for it."

The arguing continued, but Webrid ignored the finer points and tucked into a janz roll. For as long as his tongues and gums gnashed against the spongy bread and gelatinous gobbets of meat, so long as his teeth released its bitter juiciness, nothing could disturb him. Webrid was contented. Maybe not in control, but contented.

He was starting on his third sandwich when he noticed Zatell waving something in front of his waist, something small, pinched between two fingers.

"What?" he asked her through half-masticated meat.

"You dropped this, your Grossness."

Webrid swallowed and bent down for a closer look, but he still couldn't make out what it was. "Just put it in my hand." When she dropped the small, gray object into his palm, Webrid had a choking fit as he gasped in a fragment of sandwich. Without question, he was looking at a Yeril claw.

"Webber is molting! Webber is molting!" Zatell sang to a freakish melody as she spun around the room.

"Ew," Stravin opined.

"It's not mine." He looked at Leshi, feeling somehow that it was important she understand. "This can't be mine. It's not my time of the year." Yerils molted their claws annually. Ages ago, it had been a communal event for a whole tribe. In these latter days of civilization, every Yeril had his own molting schedule.

"There's another Yeril here?" Leshi seemed a little too excited by that prospect.

"Can't be," said Webrid testily. "Yerils never go anywhere. We all just stay on Bexilla."

There was that look again, everyone staring at him like he'd just shaved off all his fur. "What?"

Zatell pointed several fingers at him. "What about you? You're a Yeril. *You're* not on Bexilla."

This honestly had not occurred to Webrid. And the thought somehow made him squeamish. "I'm telling you, there can't be another Yeril here." But he said it without conviction while shoving a huge bite of sandwich into his mouth for comfort. His vision misted green again.

Stravin stepped forward and flicked the hollow claw from Webrid's hand. "This is all fascinating, but we are trespassing. Whoever molted that claw is bound to return soon. They may well have called for reinforcements. Army, that sort of thing. So, my dear, perhaps you could tear yourself away from this gourmet repast and help us search for the laser reader."

Webrid had forgotten about the laser reader. "Oh, damn. Yeah!" He gave the others a confused glance and started out one of the room's two doors, still clutching his sandwich.

"We already went that way," Zatell said. "We just came from there."

"Well, *pah*-don me all over the place," said Webrid, spinning around and bending low so he could talk right into her face. "What do you experts say I should do?" He punctuated the question with a burp that made Zatell stagger backwards and set the other three snickering.

"Debley and I already looked in there, too," Leshi said, indicating the other door.

Zatell pointed upward with ten or so limbs. "How about that way?" She ripped out a few giggles.

Webrid was not in the mood. He bit off an oversized chunk of janz roll and spoke with a defiantly full mouth. "So, where the hell should I go?" was what he meant to say, although he was aware that it didn't sound like much of anything. He swallowed and looked up. "You're not serious about going up there, right?"

As the words left his lips, the floor gave way beneath him. Again. Sinking to a lower level was becoming his signature move.

This time, the large floor tile became an elevator, reminding Webrid of—which time was it? Ah, yes, when he'd been kidnapped off the *Draspar* by the government and taken to the capital building. Wait, was it the main government or the splinter group? Webrid couldn't remember, and he couldn't care less.

The trip down was slow and controlled, but Webrid kept his eyes shut anyway. Once he felt the tile stop moving, he opened them, but doing so didn't have the expected result. He saw blackness at first, then numbers, millions of numbers, hazy and green, floating and scrolling and crawling and flashing at every angle of his vision.

"Stravin?" He barely moved his jaw, as if sudden pressure might break his skull open. "Um, guys?"

He could hear the others speaking, but their voices were muffled, their words only occasionally clear. "What are you doing...supposed to get down...Hang on, we'll...Webrid, can you..."

Webrid didn't dare move in any direction, although he figured his friends needed him to get out of the way so they could climb down. "Hurry up," he squeaked. "Can't see. Gonna barf."

The voices above him continued, something about "down" and "ladder" and "aw, crap!" Soon the voices were near him, surrounding him, and he could feel gentle but urgent hands guiding him to a chair. Sitting made him feel safer and more relaxed. The numbers seemed less intense. Now he could see fuzzy outlines of his friends with pale green numbers projected in front of them. His hearing was returning to normal, too.

"What in heaven's name happened?" Stravin appeared to Webrid as interconnected feathered ropes. He could feel his feathered fingers tickling his arm.

"I see math," whimpered Webrid. He fought to keep down his oversized lunch.

"You see math? You mean numbers?" Stravin's voice was a comfort.

"They're fading now."

Leshi put an arm around Webrid and he breathed in her silty scent. The scary green numbers disappeared as she spoke. "It must be from the laser. You guys look around for the reader, and I'll stay here with Webrid."

"This does look like a lab," said Zatell, rolling hand-over-hand toward a brace of sleek silver machines. Webrid thought their starbursts of glowing wires were terrifying, but Zatell approached them like an old friend. Stravin and Debley each strolled up to strange computers and devices with a similar serene curiosity. For the first time, Webrid was truly grateful to be surrounded by scientists.

He was also suspicious. In his normal daily life, he did not keep company with the geeky-brainy type. What were the odds that, just as he came to be host to a cranial laser implant, he should attract class valedictorians like an Entra whore attracted clients? It was a vague, unfounded suspicion, harmlessly irritating, a stale food smell in the upholstery of his mind. Webrid didn't bother to mention it.

He was distracted by Debley waving his fleshy arms. "Think I've found something here, folks."

With Leshi's strong left hand at his waist, Webrid hobbled to join the others around a reclining chair bolted between two complex control boards.

"That looks pretty comfy, actually," said Webrid, suddenly craving a nap.

"Maybe you shouldn't..." Zatell stopped when Webrid plopped himself down and adjusted his rear in the soft seat.

The clamps were around his ankles, wrists, and neck before he knew it. Apparently it was time to get nearly killed again. Webrid sighed.

Stravin seemed unconcerned. "That's a good sign."

"A good sign?" Webrid tried to glare daggers at him, but he couldn't turn his head.

"Well, sure. The restraints are a sign that this really is the laser-reading apparatus." Stravin clapped his hands like a nerd about to play with a new tech toy, which is exactly what he was. "Okay, Debley, my sweet, let's crank this thing up. Girls, you see what you can learn from the other board."

A scientific battle of the sexes commenced, with Webrid lying bound in the middle. Each pair tried to one-up the other with their analysis of the wires, knobs, slides, readouts, and chips before them. Webrid couldn't understand a word. He just wanted to be back on Bexilla, selling clods of jamboro cake to rude businessmen in the dirty Bargival heat. He closed his eyes and thought fondly of his non-literate hometown squalor.

"Righty-o!" Zatell chirped. She had climbed up the side of Webrid's chair and yanked the bnarli out from under the metal head restraint. And she had a hose in her hand.

Webrid's eyes snapped open. "Get off me. What is that thing?"

Zatell screwed the end of a tube into the center of the headband, just where the laser was implanted. It was uncomfortable, just this side of painful. Webrid squirmed.

"Stay still," said Leshi. She laid her hand on his arm and smiled, which calmed him immediately. "We think we know…"

"We *do* know what we're doing," Stravin broke in. His breeziness sounded forced. "Don't you worry at all."

"No, sure, what's to worry about?" Webrid said helplessly. "You're gonna suck out the laser and half my brain. Then I'll be dead. No worries."

Leshi lifted a long, magenta leg and straddled Webrid at

the waist so she could look deeply into his eyes. She spoke in an earnest whisper. "I swear to you, the tube we just attached contains only wires. It has no mechanism for removing anything, either the laser or anything else. We don't know how to remove the laser. All we're trying to do here is read it. Okay? Will you trust me?"

With a routine like that, she could have cut off his arm without anesthetic. "Here's the deal," he said, fighting for breath. "You all can do what you need to, but Leshi stays right there on my lap." There had to be some perks to all this suffering.

Debley started, "No way, you perv..."

"Yes," she said. "I'll stay right here." Leshi turned to Zatell. "Commence the extraction sequence." And to Stravin on her other side she said, "Prepare the collection file." Finally she looked straight at Webrid. "Just relax."

The procedure was very fast, and Webrid experienced no pain, only a strange visual phenomenon in which ribbons of green light snaked into the infinite distance. He heard several mechanical clicks, then felt Leshi's wet lips on his forehead.

"The restraints are off, Webrid. Can you hear me? How do you feel?"

Since he felt pretty much the same as he had for days, he didn't bother answering. Only one thing mattered to him. "Is that damned laser still in my head?"

Stravin helped him sit up. "As Leshi explained, this machine can only..."

"I don't care. Get it out of me." He stood up suddenly, which made him feel more crazy than dizzy. He roared. "Cut off my head if you have to. I can't take it anymore." He lurched across the room toward a particularly expensive-looking gadget, a large silver box covered by a rainbow of translucent panels. "Can this machine take out the laser?"

Zatell was at his knees. "No, that's just a..."

"Then we don't need it." Webrid attacked the machine's faceplate with a long, strong arc of his Yeril claws. The floor was littered with rainbow shards of translucent panels.

"Hey, buddy, why don't you sit down?" Zatell's squashed smile looked fake, which made him even angrier.

"You don't know," he said, dragging his claws through another delicate lab instrument, which collapsed at his touch. "You don't know what this is like." He set his sights on the control boards on either side of the chair where he'd just been restrained. "This stuff is all garbage. This place is a junkyard. None of it matters if I can't get this thing out of my head."

It took all four of them to tackle and subdue him. Webrid struggled for a while, but suddenly became terribly tired.

"Zatell and I will hold him," said Stravin to the siblings. "You two see if you can read the data we collected." To Webrid, he just said, "Ssshhhh."

Webrid could see Debley rolling his eyes in a face pinched with displeasure. It did Webrid good to know he'd made Debley uncomfortable.

From her position on his chest, Zatell spoke. "Maybe there's an infirmary. You should lie down."

"I am lying down." Webrid was fascinated by this close view of her face, which was covered in a million tiny pink puckers, like flower petals. She was adorable, in a hideous sort of way.

"What are you lookin' at?" Zatell crossed her eyes and laughed. "You gonna be good? Can I let you up?"

"Yeah, yeah. I'm too tired to break anything else." Zatell slipped the bnarli back on his brow and crawled off his ribcage. She and Stravin joined the others as Webrid lay there on the floor. The nonsensical scientific chatter lulled him to sleep. He woke up to Debley's whine.

"Folks, we have a problem."

Webrid struggled to sit up. "No, that's great. We needed a problem."

"It's serious. There's nothing in this data. Ran it through the program three times, and the computer insists that it's random. These aren't any kind of recognizable equations or algorithms. They're not in code. Nothing. Just random."

And the old laser headache started up again. Webrid lay back down quickly, smacking his skull on the floor. It actually helped a bit. "Now what do we do?"

Sometimes the heavens listen in and provide an answer to the more profound queries of life. This was one such time. A gruff voice called from the hole in the ceiling.

"Raise your hands above your heads. Any sudden moves, and the big hairy one dies."

It was a biological voice, and Webrid prepared to face law enforcement. Therefore he was surprised when a Gemfessl oozed down toward him from the ceiling. Webrid knew this mucus-coated species from Bargival, where they usually kept at least one of their fingers—or rather, their arm stumps—in crime. Despite being digitally and mentally challenged, they always kept company with the Raralt Circle's top criminal minds. Apparently the Gemfessl schmoozed as well as they oozed.

"How are you holding a gun?" He couldn't help it; he had to ask.

Dripping along Webrid's upheld arms, the Gemfessl spoke through bubbling saliva. "What makes you think I have a gun?"

Stravin sniffed. "Seriously, my dear, you're holding us up with no gun?" Zatell spewed out a fountain of laughs.

"Who said there was no gun?" the Gemfessl gurgled, now imprisoning Webrid's arms in a viscous embrace.

"So, where is it?"

"I've got it, feather-head," said a creature built like a

dozen white toothpicks glued together. It was stepping into the lab through a door they hadn't noticed in the back wall.

Debley exclaimed, "Oh, gods, it's a Slof-Borogin."

"And female," added his sister. "Damn."

Webrid had heard of these creatures. The females carried a paralyzing poison in their hollow limbs, all of which ended in a point for easy injection. The Slof *was* the gun.

"Is that the guy?" she said in her flute-like voice, pointing one arm at Webrid.

"I'll check." The Gemfessl flipped up Webrid's bnarli. "Yup."

"Do we need these others?"

"Nope."

"Okey-dokey."

As the Slof aimed her hand against Leshi's heart, Webrid looked at his precious skinless maiden. Then he looked back at the Slof. There had to be something he could do, and instinct told him that he would have a better chance of helping if he could make eye contact. So he focused his gaze squarely into the assassin's face. His intention was to plead with the Slof for Leshi's life. To bargain for her. Something noble or something illegal, didn't matter.

Instead, his laser melted the Slof's skull. He had forgotten that the Gemfessl had raised the bnarli.

"I didn't mean to. Oh, gods, not again." To Leshi he said, "Run!"

She did.

There's nothing more distracting than the congested scream of a Gemfessl. Webrid was so startled by the sound that he gave his living chestband a puzzled look. He seared those stumpy limbs into a puddle of boiled snot.

All that killing had made Webrid disoriented. Someone was pulling at his arms, but he didn't really want to go anywhere. More pulling. Some dragging. He finally came to himself in a tunnel. He found that he was running, or rather falling furiously from one foot to another.

"Cover that thing," Stravin called back, pointing to his forehead.

Webrid pushed down the bnarli, and was overcome with the memory of his melting spree. Nausea turned into a cramp, but Leshi and Debley wouldn't let him stop.

"Do we know where this tunnel goes?" Leshi asked.

"Not a clue," said Debley, "but it's taking us away from whoever those guys were."

"Who were they, do you think?" Webrid puffed, breathing every two words.

The siblings both said, "Government."

"This," Webrid wheezed as they neared a ladder that led into what appeared to be daylight, "is why I don't bother voting."

It took Stravin pulling and Leshi and Debley pushing to get Webrid up that ladder. Finally they were all up and looking around to figure out where they'd emerged. They were outside, and behind them was the black, cone-covered wall of the fortress.

"Put your hands in the air," said a seriously ugly purple fellow with a seriously big gun. Waiting behind him at the edge of the woods was a hovervan, decorated with the purple triangle of the Eshalo gang. The purple guy and the driver, who looked like he might have some Yeril blood, pushed the four of them into the back of the van.

The four of them. There had once been five.

Zatell wasn't with them. The blood around Webrid's heart felt like it had crystallized. He hissed, "Where's Za..."

"Shhhhhh!" hissed the other three.

But it was too late. The purple pimply gangster was now interested. He heaved his sour-smelling face near Webrid. "Where's who?"

Nobody can out-stink a Yeril who's just had lunch. And nobody can out-craft a cornered carter. Webrid blew out a breath from deep in his belly. The guard staggered back as Webrid spoke. "I said, 'Where's my Zegg bug?' Haven't seen it in a while."

Zegg bugs, being instantly lethal to every known species, were not something you wanted crawling around your hovervan. If he'd thought for a second, the purple thug would have realized that nobody kept Zegg bugs as pets. But people like him aren't paid to think. So, to the amusement of all his prisoners, this fearless captor danced around the back of the van like a Mdrekoo bride crossing the Chemicals of Fertility.

As he looked into the faces of his three friends, Webrid's mirth faded. They all seemed worried. Webrid told himself that Zatell's absence was surely a good thing. For all she was short and impulsive, she was also smart and courageous. She would come through for them. On the other hand, maybe she'd just high-tailed it out of the region like any sensible person would do.

"Wish I had my cart," he said voicelessly. He'd have felt safer with his claws on its handle.

They rode for quite a while, and the whir and gentle bump of the air under the van made Webrid drift into a light sleep. When the vehicle stopped and its back doors were opened, he was surprised to find that it was dark out.

The purple guy had been pouting in the corner since realizing there was no Zegg bug on the loose. His pimply arms hugged his big, scary weapon, which he'd clearly been ordered not to use. When the hovervan stopped, he herded the four prisoners out as roughly as he could without actually harming them. Whoever had had them kidnapped was also protecting them.

Stravin was pushed out first. He looked around and

whistled low as Webrid joined him on a walkway. "Look at that spread, my dear. Nice to see some real taste exhibited. Classy, you know?"

Webrid squinted at the building in the distance. His vision hadn't been quite right since he'd had his laser read at the fortress lab. The green mist was back, and the building was fluorescent. It looked positively toxic. "What's that building made of?"

"That, my dear, is wood." Stravin breathed in deeply. "A whole house made out of trees. Isn't it magnificent?"

Webrid blinked a few times, and his vision cleared. The building's outer walls now appeared to be several shades of beige and brown.

Debley was steadying his sister's descent from the van. He snorted. "A house made of wood? That's disgusting. What a waste of rare living things."

To Webrid's surprise, Leshi seemed to be holding back tears. "I hate it," she whispered, "I just hate it. It's a crime to kill trees for this. It's murder."

Stravin smoothed his arm feathers. "You must admit that it's beautiful."

Webrid noticed the meaningful glance that Debley shared with his sister before answering. "How it looks is immaterial."

"Immaterial?" Stravin sputtered, "That's preposterous." He side-stepped on the walkway, moving closer to Webrid. The four were now facing each other as two pairs, the Fekli sibs versus the Bargival dirty duo. Webrid was pleased that Stravin had chosen him as his partner. Anything that cut arrogant Debley down a peg was top-notch with him.

Without warning, the walkway began to churn forward, causing Webrid's knees to buckle. Their two-against-two standoff ended when his three friends joined together to push him back to his feet. The moving walkway drew them quickly through thick forest toward the floodlit wooden structure.

As he got closer, Webrid couldn't pull his eyes away from the building. It was a far cry from the cingy metal boxes crammed along the streets of Bargival. "Building" didn't even seem like the right word for this palace. Its façade was made of slats fitted neatly together, slightly porous, and marked with vague swirls. Unlike the great spiky metal fortress they'd just come from, this place seemed to grow from the forest floor and extend outward above them into the trees' canopy.

"Nice," said Webrid. It really was nice.

"I'm gratified that you like the house." It seemed like the building itself was speaking to them. "Do come in. The interior is worth seeing."

"Show yourself," Leshi called into the twilight. Webrid admired her moxie.

"All in good time," said the voice. "Brulo-Gee, bring them in."

Apparently Brulo-Gee was the purple thug with the low IQ and matching self-esteem. Webrid had lost track of him, but now he felt his massive weapon against his back.

"Move. All of yous."

"Here we go," sighed Webrid.

"Indeed," sighed Stravin.

The walkway ended flush against a wooden door that opened inward. Its motion stopped sudcenly, sending the prisoners stumbling inside.

The same voice greeted them, now tuned to a more intimate volume. "We'll talk in my study."

The brute Brulo-Gee pushed Webrid hard in his back, making him fall against the other three. A second door opened, swallowing them into another room, then closed behind them. Webrid took a breath to start planning with his colleagues, but he let it out again once he got a look at his surroundings. The others were staring too, mouths open.

"Is that wood?" Webrid squinted at the walls, decorated floor to ceiling in a three-dimensional geometrical mosaic of small rectangles colored in shades ranging from deep red-brown to pale yellow. Just for an instant, everything turned that noxious, glowing green, like there was a filter over Webrid's eyes. But then the room reverted to its natural colors.

Leshi slipped her hand into the crook of his elbow. "I think so, but I've only read about stuff like this. Wow."

Stravin had his arm around Debley's waist. "Tell me truly, sweetness, that you do not find this beautiful." Debley nodded his head, wide-eyed.

"Spectacular, no?" It was the same voice, unamplified. Webrid scanned the room for the person speaking, but saw no one. "Look a little harder, Ganpril Webrid." The voice came from somewhere near a wide wooden desk at one end of the room.

All Webrid could see now was the familiar green outline of a tree projected in front of him, flashing this time like a danger signal.

"There he is," said Leshi. "Look carefully at the wall behind the desk."

Webrid looked so hard through the flashing tree icon that he thought he would pop a blood vessel. Finally his vision cleared. He still couldn't make out who was speaking, though, until a head, which he'd taken to be a sculpture, pulled away from the wall, taking part of the wall with it.

"Great heavens, what a gorgeous dress!" Stravin had a hand over his heart.

"What dress?" Webrid was very confused. "What's going on?"

Debley sneered. "It's an optical illusion. That man's robes

are made to look just like the design on the walls. Very cute."

The head was smiling. Webrid finally saw that it had the good sense to be attached to a body draped in an intricately embroidered gown.

For some reason, this enraged Webrid. "Why the hell would anybody want clothes that look just like their walls? That's insane. Stravin, he's insane, right?"

His friends were shushing him urgently, but the strange man in the funny dress laughed heartily, shaking his haute couture. "Oh, priceless." He wiped a leathery gray cheek with a leathery gray hand. The mirth was contagious, making Webrid chuckle at his own folly. The others were laughing, too.

But suddenly the man strode forward, his hand outstretched. With his fingers splayed, he pressed his palm against Webrid's forehead, sending a charge of pain clear down the carter's spine.

"I believe," the leathery man said, "you have something that I want."

The fraud alarm pulsed again in some ancestral crevice of Webrid's brain. This was not the client. This was not the party he was supposed to delivery the goods to, and not the one who'd paid him. Realizing that made him cocky. He looked straight into the yellow eyes of this charlatan. "You with the government, or what?"

The gray leather around the threatening mouth once more creased into a grin. "No, by the gods, although the government has been known to contract my services." Webrid watched a tiny red worm crawling across the man's teeth as he spoke.

"Who are you, then?" Stravin asked. After a beat he added, "If I might inquire, sir?"

"I...." The man took a step back. "I am Eshalo." He slapped his hands against his chest. "Eshalo. Eshalo." Over and over he slapped his chest slowly, repeating his name in a crescendo that rose all the way to screaming. "ESHALO. ESHALO. ESHALO."

Webrid decided that he'd been correct in his first analysis: This guy was crazy.

ebrid spent the night alone in a cell. Stravin, Leshi, and Debley had been dragged off somewhere else. Still no sign of Zatell. In Webrid's heart, there was no trace of the proud Yeril who didn't need anyone but himself. He slouched in the corner of a wood-walled bare room, so lonely and depressed that he gave up any hope for his friends.

"They're dead by now. Goners, every one of 'em," he said periodically through the night. "Probably chopped up for fertilizer for all these damn trees."

As for Zatell, when he thought of how she'd abandoned their mission, he lashed out in the darkness. "Oh, you just know she's back on Bexilla with a wad of dendiacs from whoever she sold us out to. Bet there never was anything wrong with that rocket when we landed."

The sun, its rays diffused by the room's thick skylight, had just begun to brighten the world when the thugs came for Webrid. The chains they locked around his hands and feet surprised him. He wasn't about to go gently, though. As he shuffled between them, he muttered, "This place had better not be run by the government if they treat you like a mass murderer before you've even got a lawyer." He said more loudly, "Don't I have some rights?"

The purple guy—what was his name? Webrid had forgotten—answered by tripping Webrid. He fell hard onto his knees.

The other guard, a scaly, four-legged Derapa by the looks of him, hissed out a laugh. "Yeah, you got rights. The right to stand up, you clumsy Yeril bastard."

"Real comedian, you…" His sentence was cut short when the purple one kicked him in the face.

"Where is the carter, Brulo-Gee?" asked the ceiling. Webrid hadn't thought it possible to be grateful for Eshalo's voice. The guards scrambled to drag Webrid to his feet. At least now it would be over soon.

They entered a lab. Webrid sighed. Yet another lab. He'd had enough of labs. So what if this one was tastefully and expensively decorated with wood-mosaic walls? It was still a lab. Webrid didn't bother resisting as they brought him to another damned reclining chair. They unlocked his chains, only to re-cuff his legs and arms to the chair. They left his head free, but Webrid knew that was temporary.

"Just cut off my whole noggin with a laser knife, would ya?" he said to the Zenivar lab worker, who ignored him. "Where's my crazy-ass host? I want some entertainment before I die."

A mechanical whirring filled the room, making Webrid's chair vibrate. The whirring was accompanied by a metallic groan as a large square area of the floor in front of him began to rise. Beneath it was a clear case, a transparent elevator car pulled up by the rising floor. It contained Eshalo himself, his arms outstretched. His flowing raiments this morning were ember-orange, tightly pleated, and dotted with sparkly bits that Webrid assumed were precious stones.

When the clear elevator doors opened, Eshalo took a single step out and struck a pose. The elevator disappeared back into the floor.

Webrid snorted. "Now those are some spiffy duds. You got a whole closet of stuff like that?"

This was, it would seem, not the right thing to say. Eshalo widened his glistening yellow eyes to the size of Webrid's fists and wobbled them in his direction. Webrid had never seen such big eyes in such a small, dry, gray head. The effect made his stomach acids spray up and hit the back of his tongues.

"I want your laser." Eshalo turned to an assistant. "Remove the bnarli."

This was perfect! With the laser exposed, Webrid could go all homicidal. He'd whack Eshalo and disable his employees, maybe just melting their arms. And the machinery. He should destroy a lot of that, burning holes in it and making its electricals go *boom*. That would be satisfying.

Webrid hatched this dramatic plan as the Zenivar, now wearing a blue apron, pulled the bnarli off his head. Realizing just in time that he had no wish to harm a sweet, furry Zenivar, Webrid whipped his head sharply to the side.

"No, no. Look at me." Eshalo swooped in close and pulled Webrid's face toward his.

The opportunity was too good to be true. Over and over, with his whole being, Webrid thought the word "Kill," while being vaguely aware that he was roaring. He forced his eyes to stay open so he could have the pleasure of watching Eshalo's skull melt.

No such luck. The gangster's face remained as intact as it was revolting.

"Oh, hush now," Eshalo said to the astonished, hoarse, impotent Webrid, who snapped his jaw shut to stop his roaring.

There was nothing he could do, however, to stop his tears. He cried and cried at the utter unfairness of it all. Here he was, with a lethal weapon he couldn't even use when his own life was in danger. At least it was fun to watch Eshalo blow his cork at all this weeping.

"Cut it out! Stop it. Stop it!" Eshalo paced back and forth in front of Webrid's chair, his red-orange garment fanning the floor in his wake. "Just stop it." The gangster slapped his hands together and addressed his minions. "Hook him up. *Shut* him up."

So, now he was going to die. But wait! Through the waterfall of his lamenting, Webrid recognized the equipment around him. This was like the hose from the fortress lab, the one Leshi had sworn could only pull data from his laser, not pull out the laser itself. There was still time left for old Ganpril Webrid.

They performed the same procedure he'd been through the day before in the other lab. Again, he saw the ribbons of green light. Again, it was over quickly.

"Was that good for you, too, sweetheart?' he slurred when they'd finished.

"Numbers, numbers, numbers," Eshalo whined, poring over a monitor. "What are all these numbers?" He spoke into an intercom. "Bring the other prisoners."

Other prisoners? His companions weren't dead yet! Webrid found himself flooded with hope, ridiculous as it might be. What could he hope for? That they should all be executed together? How sweet.

His three lanky companions, one feathery and the others shimmery, were led in. They looked tired but uninjured. Webrid wished fervently to embrace them, although he didn't normally go in for that sort of thing. The snuggling urge dissipated into envy when he noticed that they were not chained or cuffed, as he had been. Granted, there were armed guards with them, but still.

Eshalo was pressing Debley's head down toward the monitor, rasping at him. "What are these numbers? Explain them!"

It was a surprise to hear Stravin answer instead. "What, you can't read them either?"

Stravin dodged artfully as Eshalo took a swing at his jaw, releasing Debley's head in the process. Debley and his sister looked at each other with grave concern.

"Mister Eshalo?" Leshi spoke without looking away from her brother. Webrid couldn't imagine what she had to say.

Eshalo walked over to her, the yellows in his orange robes making her flesh look blueish. "Yes? Can you tell me about these numbers?"

"No."

He grabbed her shoulders with both hands. Webrid figured he must be standing on tiptoe to manage it. "You *will* tell me."

"But I can't. Seriously, you can't read these either?"

He let her go. "What do you mean?"

"You don't know what's on Webrid's laser? Because we sure don't know."

"That's true," Debley offered.

Eshalo sputtered, "But she told me it was the records for..."

Webrid strained to hear, but Eshalo apparently realized that he was about to spill classified info, so he clamped his crusty mouth shut.

Meanwhile, Stravin was making good use of the time by unlocking the restraints on Webrid's chair. Nobody stopped him. In fact, Eshalo was oddly silent as he stepped back and surveyed all his prisoners. "You say you can't read these numbers?" He sounded thoughtful.

Leshi, Debley, and Stravin all shook their heads.

To the Zenivar lab assistant, Eshalo said, "You work on deciphering them now."

"Yes, sir." Before busying herself at the monitor, the Zenivar looked deeply, meaningfully, into Webrid's eyes. The look was gone in an instant, but it had definitely happened. Webrid wondered whether it meant anything more than, "So long, sucker."

But he didn't have much time to ruminate because Eshalo said something rather important to his guards.

"Kill them."

Leshi instigated the heroics by walloping Eshalo with an uppercut that felled him. This, it seemed to Webrid, was a waste of time and energy. Regardless of their employer's state of consciousness, he'd already given the kill order, and the armed guards would doubtless carry it out.

Webrid lunged at the scaly Derapa guard who was aiming a gun at Stravin. His shot went wide, hitting a metal box behind Stravin's shoulder, and Stravin whooped like a little girl when it exploded into polychrome flames.

"Watch it, Webrid." Darned if it wasn't Debley, trying to save Webrid despite their prickly past. Debley tackled the purple guard, first dodging his fire and then kicking him in the head.

On Webrid's other side, Leshi spun into a high-velocity kick that sent a third guard sailing across the lab. There were advantages to being tall and lithe, Webrid realized.

That left only one more armed man, and he had Webrid, Leshi, and Debley all within easy range of his gun. Webrid put up his hands in a futile attempt to surrender and make this guy forget that kill order. Webrid's thoughts were a mixed tornado of final prayers and the threads of a brilliant plan to blackmail the guard.

He also longed to turn toward Leshi and say something to her. "Nice working with you," maybe, or "Sorry we never got to have sex." But he could not tear his gaze away from his impending doom.

Just as well. He would always be grateful to have witnessed what happened next.

The guard had failed to notice that only three of the four prisoners were visible. There was still hope. Unfortunately, Webrid realized that the missing party was Stravin, a paragon of physical self-pampering. Stravin was about as likely to risk getting maimed as an Akardian was to sell you something below wholesale.

But Webrid had not given Stravin proper credit for all his dealings with criminals in the toughest city in the Raralt Circle. Stravin was smart. Stravin was cunning.

Stravin bent low and lunged forward, coming at the guard at knee-level from behind. Poor sod never knew what hit him. He toppled backward head-first into the machine that his colleague had recently totaled. His body jerked while a rainbow of sparks spewed out of his skull.

Straightening, up, Stravin primped his arm feathers. "Shall we get out of here, my dears?"

"What about..." Webrid looked around at the lab technician, cowering at her computer. "Never mind. Let's go."

From the floor, Eshalo cackled deeply. He pulled a small device from somewhere in his robes and spoke into it. "Squadron Three. Kill all the prisoners."

"That's not good," Webrid said.

Eshalo was trying to crawl toward the door, but Leshi and Debley held him still. Webrid kicked the device from his hand and enjoyed watching Stravin bring a chair down on Eshalo's head.

"Let's make sure he's the only one here when Squadron Three shows up."

Squadron Three turned out to be a quartet of armed chopper-bots that immediately came in through an entrance in the ceiling.

"We're gonna die!" Webrid screamed, taking cover under a computer desk. It wasn't manly, but it was probably accurate. There was a hailstorm of laser shots. One hit the unconscious Eshalo, and his dress caught on fire.

"The whole place is gonna blow," called Leshi from wherever she'd taken shelter.

"But we can't get to the door. We'll never make it." Debley was the frantic voice of doom. "Not with four of them shooting at us."

And suddenly there was silence. All four chopper-bots simultaneously fell to the floor. Just like that.

"Eh?" Webrid couldn't think of any better question. Then he felt something very soft against his arm.

"I turned off their power." It was the furry little Zenivar, still in her fetching blue apron. She began spraying Eshalo with a fire extinguisher.

Stravin narrowed his eyes and brushed himself off. "Well, thanks, love. Truly swell of you. But how does a nice, obedient lab technician have access to the security software?"

"We don't have time for questions. May I please help you escape now?"

They stood there gawping at this sweet little fuzzball servant who, it seemed, was a spy under deep cover. She walked toward Webrid and offered him his bnarli, which she'd been keeping in her apron pocket. He put it on.

Debley was the first to speak. "Who do you work for?"

She just smiled that pleasant customer-service smile. "We truly don't have time for questions. Please follow me."

Webrid was numb and shaky as he and his friends tromped behind their diminutive guide. But he did notice that she wasn't heading to the door. "The exit is that way," he said, pointing.

"No. We will be killed if we are seen."

Clear and concise. Webrid admired that.

"Hey, what's your name?" It came out with a slight "Do you come here often?" slur, but if she noticed, she didn't let on.

"Azhanda," she said. "Please enter the floor now. Please do not talk. Please do not cough."

One by one they crawled down into an opening left by a metal plate Azhanda had removed. She wasn't kidding about the coughing. The ventilation shaft was nasty with dust and dried insects. Webrid's tear ducts protested the needles of pain in his lungs by flooding his vision. He could see nothing, so he just inched forward, following the scrape of his companions' knees and hands, and the echoes of their wheezes in the metal shaft.

"Exit is here," Azhanda said.

There was more scraping, and heavier breathing, and Webrid could make out the blurred glow of a flashlight.

"Exit is locked." Azhanda still sounded like she was offering drinks on a plane. "We are trapped."

et me try. Shine that light here." Stravin wriggled past the others to join Azhanda at the end of the shaft, at what must have been an outer wall. Webrid could just see that there was a metal grating between them and freedom.

Stravin messed with the grate for a while, with Leshi and Debley pushing their heads in to help. There were murmurs about "stuck" and "hopeless" and "we're screwed."

Webrid stayed out of it, resting on the five points of his knees, his forearms, and the top of his head. Sucking in the spicy, familiar stench of old metal and his own unwashed body made him miss his cart and his home. Enough with this nonsense. He gave a short farewell speech. "Okay, then. I'm just going to head back the way we came so I can get shot with my limbs extended."

"Don't be such a hoongofl."

It was a disembodied voice. Webrid knew only one person who used that word. Impossible. Could that be Zatell? He really had gone around the bend. But he heard it again.

"I've been looking for you guys."

Yup, it was her.

All five of them shoved each other to have a peek through the outer grate.

"What do you think, I'm suction-cupped to the outside of the building like some creepy Entra?"

Webrid was the first to figure it out. "You're above us?"

"Give that guy a janz roll."

Leshi looked up. "You can see us?"

"Just barely," Zatell said. "There's another layer of ducts above you guys, and I'm looking through a slit between two sheets of metal." A sliver of light appeared for a second. "See that? That's my flashlight."

"Oh, Zatell, dearest," Stravin gushed. Webrid was moved by how he placed his feathery fingers against the top of the shaft where the light had been. "We're stuck here, darling."

"Funny you should say that. I can get you out."

There was much congratulatory hand-slapping, which resulted in much banging of elbows on the metal shaft. Only Azhanda the Zenivar remained focused.

"How might we assist you, ma'am?"

Zatell drew in a sharp breath. "Who the hell is that?"

"Our tour guide," said Webrid. "She's cute, but I think on my next vacation I'll splurge on the tour where you get to stand up straight and not get killed."

Zatell's pealing laughter echoed in a disturbing way through the chamber above them.

"Shouldn't we be quiet?" Debley said curtly.

This only made the laughter increase. "Everybody's left the building, dopey. They're all out looking for you, I guess."

Leshi wasn't laughing. "How many are there?"

"I only saw six or so. I was scoping this place out all night, and I think it's really under-staffed."

"That is correct," said Azhanda.

Webrid tried to sound gruff, but a wobble slipped into

his voice. "You've been watching over us, Zatell?" His spleen burned with guilt over his uncharitable thoughts from the night before. But how could he have known?

Leshi asked, "How many chopper-bots do you think there are, Zatell?"

Again it was Azhanda who answered. "None. I've disabled them permanently."

Employee of the month, that one. Webrid kissed one of her plush cheeks while Stravin kissed the other.

"Now," Zatell called down to them, "are we just gonna chat about it, or do you really want out of here?"

"What's the plan, babe?" Stravin asked.

"The plan is, you guys back up."

Slowly, clumsily, they did so. There was no space to turn around, and Webrid found crawling backwards to be a significant coordinational challenge. He let the others slither past him, and then Leshi pulled him backwards by the waist. It was weirdly erotic.

When they were all back to what they hoped was a safe distance, Azhanda said, "What is the lady attempting to do?"

Stravin chuckled. "Knowing her, she's got a blowtorch."

She did, in fact, have a blowtorch. The glowing red square appearing on the shaft's upper surface made Webrid jealous. He passed his fingers over the bnarli and considered the useless laser in his forehead. He should have been the hero, using his lethal green ray to sear an escape hatch in the outer wall. But, no. Not *his* laser. He had a dud.

A rough-cut square of metal crashed into the shaft, arm's length from Webrid, jolting him out of his self-pity. When his ears stopped ringing, he could hear Zatell above him and the others behind him urging him with varying levels of politeness to put his sorry ass in gear and move forward.

He did, burning his hand in the process. It was a great relief to poke his head up through the hole, allowing his back to straighten. He even enjoyed the gentle paddling of his face when Zatell wrapped herself around his upper body in a squealy hug.

"You big, ugly hairball!" She kissed him, and he returned the favor. "Now, let's move."

The upper shaft was a lot roomier, so Webrid was keen to pull himself through. He singed himself a few more times, but he didn't care. Zatell had already burned a hole in the outer wooden wall, and Webrid took in a great lungful of cool forest air tinged with smoky char before helping his friends up.

After a quick round of hugs and handshakes, they were ready to escape onto the grounds.

Zatell lowered a rope down the outer wall.

"Where'd you get a rope?" asked Webrid.

"Presumably the same place she got a blowtorch," Stravin answered. Zatell just laughed and laughed.

Acrobatic Leshi and Debley went first, and they held the rope for Azhanda and Stravin. The four of them caught Webrid as he came skidding down. He was blowing on his raw fingers as he watched Zatell dance down effortlessly, a blowtorch half her size clutched in a few of her limbs.

They ran through the lightly forested grounds with Zatell in the lead. Webrid was impressed with her all over again. That woman could really roll. At last they reached the wall surrounding Eshalo's compound.

Debley leaned in closely to inspect it. "Wood, obviously," he said.

Zatell wielded her blowtorch menacingly. "Super flammable!" She moved one hand to the on/off switch.

Webrid watched in horror as the sweet little Zenivar lunged in front of Zatell and grasped the nozzle of the flame machine. "Watch it, Azhanda. You'd better stand back." He could just imagine what would happen to the fool who stood between a blowtorch and something Zatell wanted to set on fire.

Azhanda didn't look worried. "Please desist, ma'am."

Zatell moved the blowtorch down and around, pulling the nozzle out of Azhanda's grasp and pointing it at her heart. "You tellin' me what to do?"

In a voice flatter than a Revlampik's rear end, Azhanda said, "The wood in this fence is run through with heat-activated sensor wire. If you turn on this blowtorch, there will be many explosions. We will most likely be dismembered."

"Let's not do that, then," said Stravin, with a high-pitched laugh. Bending down, he took the weapon away from Zatell, much to Webrid's gratitude. No one else would have risked it. Zatell was making a creaking sound and her face was scrunched so tightly that her eyes were hidden in the folds of flesh. She looked like a child pouting after a parent takes away a dangerous toy. Webrid prayed she wouldn't have some sort of tantrum.

Leshi went to Azhanda's side and wrapped a sisterly arm around her. "So, what do we do now?"

Suddenly Debley held up his hand and whispered (a bit over-dramatically, Webrid thought; perhaps he was getting bad habits from Stravin), "Whatever you decide, make it quick. I just heard some shouting and gunfire to the northeast."

It irritated Webrid that Debley pretended know where the sound was coming from. "You sure it wasn't the south-southeast? Huh? You positive? How can you even know what direction you're facing?" And immediately he regretted his outburst. The whole pack was giving him the pity-the-dumb-Yeril look. It was their new favorite thing.

"The river is to the west of the compound," said Leshi, pronouncing the words slowly, as one would to a child, "and we can hear the river."

Stravin managed a close-lipped smile. Debley made

rolled his eyes around two complete circles. Zatell was still hiding inside herself. Webrid wished to die.

Azhanda remained eerily calm. Without a word, she pulled a hand-held computer from her apron pocket and punched on some keys, as if entering several sets of codes. "The fence is deactivated," she said simply.

"Well, la-dee-da," said Zatell, emerging. "Now I'll torch a hole in it, if you don't mind."

"Might I suggest that we use the gate, ma'am?"

Debley's chuckle turned to a howl when Zatell swatted him in the shins.

"Lead us, dear," said Stravin, bowing courteously to their odd little savior. Azhanda led them along the fence.

It wasn't far to a gate, nearly hidden in the wooden fence. Debley found a handle camouflaged in a slat, and they prepared to go out.

"You there!" It was Brulo-Gee, the pimply purple guard. Webrid felt sure they'd killed him earlier, but apparently he was the one they'd just kicked in the head.

Stravin surprised Webrid with a tough-guy act. He wielded the blowtorch threateningly at Brulo-Gee and spoke in a bass voice not at all his own. "Back away."

The lavender lackey didn't move.

"I said back away." Deep and confident, that voice.

Still the purple guy stood there. And Stravin turned on the blowtorch, moving it in a slicing motion across the guard's waistband. He whooped as his pants fell down, and tripped every other step as he ran away, trying to keep hold of his trousers.

"That was really satisfying to watch," said Debley, sharing a laugh with his sister.

"Come on, you two." Stravin was already out the gate, and the others poured out after him.

"Do you mind?" Zatell grabbed for the blowtorch, which

Stravin relinquished. To the Zenivar she said, "May I torch the fence *now*, headmistress?"

"Would you like me to turn it back on first?"

"Oh, yes, please."

Numbers punched, the corner of the fence set afire, it was time to go. As the motley crew hurtled through the woods, the *zing* and *pop* of the first small explosion rang out, followed by twenty or thirty more in close succession. The leaves and tree branches behind them rattled and hissed as steaming shards of fence rained down.

"Here's the riverbank," called Debley, who was way ahead of the pack. "I can see the edge of the...Oh, gods." He froze.

Leshi galloped toward her brother. "Deb? What's wrong?"

Webrid, alarmed, wanted desperately to run in another direction, but Leshi was waving her arms wildly, beckoning them. He, Zatell, and Stravin raced to join her, navigating over the rugged ground with zig-zags and leaps.

Azhanda, of course, walked steadily and calmly. Webrid suddenly found her self-discipline so offensive that he shoved her with his elbow as he ran past her.

"Aw, sorry. Didn't see you there." Although he knew it was childish, bullying Little Miss Perfect made him feel all warm inside. He could tell by the laughter ringing at knee-height that Zatell agreed.

Eventually they straggled up to the water's edge, one by one, each of their jaws dropping in turn when they caught sight of what the fuss was about. There was something remarkable on the edge of the embankment, just south of them.

Webrid couldn't find the words. "It's. It's. It's..."

"It my Moti-Moto," gushed Stravin, "raised from the dead!" He accepted a congratulatory hug from Debley and the two of them ran along the embankment to examine the scooter.

Webrid was still stuck. "It's. It's. It's..." He felt like fainting as his eyesight misted green. Leshi took one elbow and Zatell reached up for the other. None of them spoke.

No-nonsense Azhanda cut straight to what needed saying. "You are a carter. It is best that you have your cart."

Indeed, Webrid's beloved ancestral cart was hitched to the Moti. With each step Webrid took toward it, the miracle became greater. His cart had not just been saved from its prison at the base of the cliff up-river; it had also been repaired. The sides, formerly dented and scratched, were smoothed and polished. The axles were straight. There was an extra layer of galvanized belvanium coating the corners.

"Are you sure it's your cart?" Leshi turned to Stravin. "And this is definitely your scooter?"

Webrid's affirmation knocked into Stravin's. His joy was a nectar, heady and sweet. It became desperately important to show gratitude to the saintly party who'd brought this about.

He fell to his knees in front of Zatell, who jumped back with a snarl. "Thank you," he said.

"Get up, you weirdo. It wasn't me. Try Miss Service-with-a-Smile over there." She indicated Azhanda with three of her hands.

This made sense to Webrid. He already owed the Zenivar his life, and now this. Nobody could say a Yeril wasn't grateful for favors rendered in his direction, so Webrid knee-walked until he was at Azhanda's feet. "Thank you so much."

But she just shook her furry head. "I'm sorry, sir. I was not responsible for this happy event."

For an instant, the briefest instant, Webrid saw the green mist coalesce into the words, "You're welcome." Then it was gone.

"A mirage," said Webrid, meaning the fleeting message.

"I think you mean a mystery," Stravin twittered. "I do just

love a mystery!" He was looking over every nook and cranny of his scooter. "Someone did some fine work repairing this."

Suddenly Debley had his "shush" hand in the air again, and Stravin poked him in the ribs. "Yes, love? Are the bad guys coming?"

"It's just that it's getting late. Sun's going down. Maybe we should find a place to camp."

Stravin rubbed his nose against Debley's. "Always thinking, aren't you, sweets?"

It occurred to Webrid that now would be the time to ask the giddy Stravin for a big favor or a massive loan. Or a kidney. The answer would have been yes. Then again, Webrid knew he would have done anything for anybody at that moment. His vision was clear, he had his cart, and he felt wonderful. The disconcerting mystery of it all nibbled at the corners of his happiness, but he refused to let it get him down.

Finding a place to camp was deemed a good idea. As for their quest, nobody had a clue what to do next. They couldn't read Webrid's laser, and there was nobody home in the governmental fortress. Hard to know which way to proceed.

So, to camp it was. Stravin and Debley took their usual places on the Moti. Webrid opened the cart, where he found all their old supplies plus some new food, water, and sleeping bags. Their anonymous fairy-godparent was determined to keep them healthy. A wave of misgivings sloshed over Webrid as he climbed in. Maybe it was just the big-city cynic in him, but something stank. Nobody put out for nothing. Nobody. Maybe this "helpful" person was just playing a game with them and didn't want to lose any pieces on the board.

"I'm comin' in!" Zatell vaulted into the cart next to Webrid.

"I'll just run alongside," Leshi said, helping Azhanda into the cart. "I could do with some exercise. Not too fast, guys."

"Easy does it," Debley said. He actually smiled, something Webrid had not often seen.

As they bounced along, Webrid didn't know which question to ask first of his courageous companions. But before he could decide, he saw them both drifting off. Webrid took comfort in the bumping of his cart, a warm Zenivar snuggled against his right side, and Zatell's soft hands paddling his left. Questions could wait. He fell asleep with layers of glowing green numbers prancing through his dreams.

They found a place to bed down for the night, just deep enough into the forest that they felt protected from view, but close enough to the river that the rising sun would wake them up. Nobody talked much. They ate a few supplies and sprawled out or curled up as comfortably as they could manage. The sleeping bags helped. Of course, Webrid was too large for his, and the claws of his feet poked through the bottom. This made him recall the dried shell of a Yeril claw they'd found in the fortress, but the thought made him squirm, so he banished it from his mind.

A polyphonic sound, a cross between a honk and a coo, woke Webrid at the first light of dawn. He struggled to sit up in his cart, then popped his neck vertebrae back into alignment. Zatell and Azhanda were still on either side of him, and they didn't even stir when he gingerly moved their heads to rest on suitcases and bags of dried fruit.

The noise continued, interrupted by little gasps. Someone was crying. A quick survey of his companions showed that Leshi was missing. He couldn't wait for the chance to comfort her in her hour of need, while her brother was out cold and useless.

Following the sound some twenty paces away from camp, he found Leshi folded up at the base of a bulbous tree trunk. She looked up when he approached. "Sorry I woke you." She sniffled, which sent bubbles through Webrid's bloodstream.

"What's going on? You okay?" He tried to sit down next to her, but his joints were so stiff from his long day and his cramped sleep that he fell on top of her instead. "Oof. Sorry." He almost avoided touching her anywhere ungentlemanly. His hand might have brushed against this or that. Totally by accident. By the time he settled down, she was smiling and wiping her eyes. Nice that his clumsiness served a purpose for once.

She seemed eager to talk. "It's the forest. It makes me so sad."

"Really? It just pisses me off."

"But...the trees! These wonderful, living trees."

Webrid spewed out his response, realizing even as he spoke that he should be more delicate. But he didn't do delicate. "What is *with* you and trees? What's the deal? Were you born in a tree? Did a tree save your mom's life? I just don't get it."

Leshi held her arms tightly across her chest. She spoke toward the ground, barely opening her mouth. "Trees help the environment. They help the air quality."

"No. Seriously. What's with the trees?"

Leshi looked up and stared at him so intensely that he thought she might melt his face. That would make a nice change, him melting and not the other way around. "Webrid, I honestly don't know."

"What do you mean? There must be some reason..."

"Here's the thing. I connect on so many levels with the ideas of Heesha Swaratt, but I gotta tell you: It's only the part about..." She sobbed and then steadied herself, continuing in a softer voice. "It's only the part about forestation that just tears my heart out. I really can't explain it. But it's so important to me, Webrid. I'd do anything for the Resistance to succeed in saving this forest. I was so sure we were headed in the right direction. But then this..." She put her head in her hands.

"Then what?" Webrid was dying to feel her pain. And anything else she'd let him.

"Then Eshalo didn't know what your laser said."

"He's an idiot."

"No, he's not. He's eccentric, and clearly having some financial troubles. But he's got the splinter group in his pocket."

"Yeah? So?"

"So, Debley and I thought that Eshalo and the splinter group were communicating with each other through the laser. I mean, obviously they do that, since he had a laser reader."

"What are you driving at?"

To Webrid's alarm, Leshi teared up again. "That our whole Swarattan Resistance Force is on the wrong track. Or is just wrong, period." She sniffled again.

"Wait now, wait." Webrid stroked her arm. Its flesh was silky under his rough padded fingers. "Maybe Eshalo's not involved. So what? You still have your resistance thing." This wasn't going as well as he'd planned. He couldn't come up with the words he needed. "You still have your, your list of things, your guiding..." He ground to a halt, defeated.

"Peace, Prosperity, Fairness, Justice, Community, Individuality, and..." She looked up.

Webrid finished for her. "And forestation. Yeah, that stuff. That's great. Who needs Eshalo?"

Her face darkened, and his chances of getting laid grew dimmer. "But don't you see? Can you really not understand why this is important?"

"Leshi, I just..."

"Deb and I have spent every waking moment for five years trying to root out the source of corruption in our government. All signs have pointed tc Eshalo and his influence on corrupt government factions. Now it seems like we've been totally on the wrong track. We got a message."

"What message?"

Leshi sighed, her eyes fixed on her knees. "About your laser."

"You got a message?"

"Yeah. That's how we knew to look for you, to home in on your signal when you were at the hotel in Ksacheel."

Webrid's brain spun with conflicting thoughts. He felt betrayed, but also glad to be getting a little information for a change. "Well, what was in the message?"

"That the data contains proof of the collusion between Eshalo and Rommey."

"Who?"

"Rommey Ebleneneth. Cheed Council Secretary. You said somebody mentioned him to you when you first came on board the *Draspar*. He's getting greased right up to his..." She put her hand over her mouth. "Anyway, your laser is supposed to have evidence, especially about their attempts to exploit the forest. The message said it was enough so we would be able to expose them and take Rommey out of power, maybe put them both in prison." She raised her glistening eyes. "It's what we've been working toward for years. So if Eshalo can't read the laser, then we can't connect him to Rommey. So maybe we're on the wrong track. Do you see?"

Webrid stood up. "How do you know it's totally wrong, just because Eshalo isn't involved? Maybe there were things the splinter group was doing that he didn't know about. Back on Bargival, criminals work like that all the time. They tell some people some things and other people other things.

How come it can't be like that? We'll go to this government outpost I keep hearing about, and see what's on the laser, then take it from there." He beamed what he thought was his most encouraging smile, curling both his tongues around his incisors.

Leshi no longer looked angry. "You know, you're pretty smart, actually. In your own very special way, you're a pretty smart guy." She put her hand out and Webrid pulled her to her feet. Maybe not so accidentally, he pulled a bit too hard, so she crashed into him and they kissed. Well, their lips touched, anyway. Webrid decided it counted as a kiss. His tongues rippled as she pulled away.

"I'm gonna get some breakfast," she whispered, batting her eyelids. And off she loped toward camp.

Webrid couldn't stand to be alone with his muddled, lustful thoughts, so he followed. As he approached the clearing he heard a familiar noise, much less pleasant and intriguing than the honking coo of Leshi in tears. It was someone talking, and the lisping, obsequious-yet-insulting tenor voice was unmistakable. It was an Akardian.

Of all the hemispheres on all the planets in the Raralt Circle, Webrid had not expected, here in Northern Cheed, to find a specimen of the universe's best used-car salesmen. This one was rubbing his hands in a slow, steady rhythm, his hundreds of facial lobes wobbling along.

The Akardian had Stravin trapped in his Moti seat. Debley had managed to escape and was standing behind the cart in a defensive posture. Stravin held his arms tightly across the opening of his vest, where Webrid knew he kept his indestructible pouch of Universal Dendiac notes. Webrid had to hand it to the Akardian: his type could sniff out whoever had the money.

"We can't pay you," Stravin was lying. "We don't need a guide."

A guide? Webrid was intrigued. He spoke, striding into the clearing and making everyone jump. "For an uncharted territory, there sure are a lot of folks around here."

"Uncharted. Right-o, boss." The salesman increased his hand-rubbing, lobe-wobbling velocity. "This is just what I was telling this gentleman here. You require a guide. Uncharted territory."

"But we can't afford to pay you," Stravin said with vigor.

The Akardian then formed a sentence that would have shamed his entire genetic line. "You don't need to pay me. No cost to you."

Leshi spoke up. "Maybe we *could* use a guide."

Her brother shot back. "No. Azhanda can lead us. You know where the fortress is, right?"

She nodded.

Far from being deterred, the Akardian seemed to gloat. "Ha! The fortress? You don't want to go to the fortress."

"Yes we do, you rubber-drop freakshow." Zatell rolled near him, and Webrid feared there would be fisticuffs started by her many little fists. "We need to go back to the outpost for the government splinter group."

"Then you do not want the fortress." He gulped before adding, "Lovely lady."

Debley stepped forward. "Explain."

"The fortress on the riverbank is not the government outpost. I can take you to the correct building. It's deeper, far deeper in the forest."

"Why should we trust this guy?" Zatell wanted to know.

"Who hired you?" Stravin asked.

"How did you find us?" demanded Debley.

It wasn't looking good for the Akardian in the middle of nowhere. Leshi held him against a tree while Zatell paddled at his knees. And Webrid could tell that it wasn't the soothing, gentle paddling he'd felt from her the day before.

The Akardian yelped.

"Rempener Dras!"

At the sound of that name, Webrid staggered backward, his vision clouded with flying green numbers. But he couldn't access his memory to explain the reaction.

"Rempener Dras says you must follow me! I shall take you to the government building. Please, please stop with the fast tiny slaps."

Webrid took the salesman by the neck and burped elaborately in his face. The Akardian shivered. "Who is Rempener Dras?" Webrid demanded, blinking fast to see through the cloud of numbers.

"Rempener Dras pays me."

Now Webrid remembered. "You and me both." He loosened his grip.

Stravin asked, "Is that a person or a company?"

"How should I know?"

"Will he or they be at the government outpost?"

"Don't know. Rommey will be there."

Leshi and Debley both reacted with alarm. Debley tapped the salesman hard on the chest. "You sure about Rommey? He's been trying to shut down the Resistance Force since it began."

The Akardian was nodding miserably. "I don't know about politics, people. I was just paid to take you to the government building."

"Paid by Rommey?" Debley asked.

"No, I told you. Remp..."

"Yeah, yeah. But Rommey's there, so he's behind it."

The Akardian sounded like he was reciting a memorized fact. "Mr. Rommey flew in from Southern Cheed yesterday."

"Just in time to see us," said Leshi. "How touching." She and Debley seemed to have blocked out the rest of them, including Webrid, who longed to be in on their plotting. But

Leshi never even looked his way, although he lurked at her shoulder as she spoke. "I say we should let this guy take us."

"But not the hairy Yeril!" The Akardian practically shrieked this. Now Webrid got his wish for attention. They were all looking at him.

"What?"

"Rempener Dras says the Yeril should follow his head."

"Follow my what?"

Pointing to the bnarli on Webrid's brow, the Akardian repeated, "Your head. It will lead you." Webrid suddenly remembered what the guy who'd first sold him a bnarli had told him—that his laser would guide him. Maybe he hadn't really given it a chance to do that.

The Akardian spoke to the others. "We must go now. You'll see the Yeril later on down the road. I can't wait no more." He started off into the woods.

"I think we'd better go," said Zatell, looking at Webrid with what he hoped was guilt.

Stravin patted his shoulder. "This is just as well, my dear. Sounds like we're headed into a tricky-sticky situation. Better if you're safe."

Leshi took up the refrain. "That's right. You keep that laser safe in that handsome head of yours."

It annoyed Webrid that even her cheap flattery thrilled him. "Will at least one of you come with me, wherever it is I'm going?"

"Where *are* you going?" Zatell asked.

"Straight to hell, for all I care." That was no place to travel alone, he knew. "Hey, Stravin, ol' buddy. Why don't you stick with me for this part of the adventure?"

Azhanda stepped in front of Stravin. Webrid had forgotten she was there. "Please, sir, allow me to accompany you instead."

"Oh, capital idea. That's for the best." Stravin sounded

relieved. He was probably afraid of missing something important and exciting while Webrid meandered aimlessly through the woods.

Leaning down to address the Zenivar, Leshi stirred Webrid's heart for the tenth time that morning. "I'm trusting you to keep him safe. Keep him out of trouble. That's your job, okay?"

"Yes, ma'am. My pleasure, ma'am."

First they abandon him, then they hire him a babysitter. Could he really be as much of a loser as they were making him feel? Still, he knew he could do worse than a Zenivar chaperone. Sure beat the socks off an Akardian guide any day.

He watched with a heavy chest as Leshi, Debley, Stravin, and Zatell followed the sniveling Akardian into the shadows. Then he turned to Azhanda.

"I guess it's just you and me."

She smiled a mysterious, furry smile. For just an instant, she didn't look like a flight attendant. But just as quickly, her face returned to its generic politeness. "Where does your head say we should go, sir?"

He felt stupid doing it, but Webrid closed his eyes and tried to let his head guide him. But when a magnetic pull started turning him, he instinctively fought against it. It was no use; the force was more than he could resist. He let his feet take him around and around, until the pressure stopped. Opening his eyes, he didn't bother looking. He just pointed. "That way."

So Webrid, Azhanda, and the cart went north, following the river.

"You look better, sir," said Azhanda after they'd been walking for a while. She was right. He felt calmer now.

"You can stop calling me sir, you know." Webrid admired the smooth motion of his newly repaired cart. It probably hadn't had such a thorough tune-up since it was built two generations before. And it still had those fancy military-grade wheels that Stravin's friend had put on. Picturing the sexy mechanic with the shiny black skin, Webrid paused to try to think of her name. It was no use.

Unfortunately, he *could* picture her getting paralyzed by the police. Was she dead, he wondered?

"Maybe those were Eshalo's men," he said aloud.

"Which men, sir?" Azhanda jerked her face up and rephrased: "Which men, Webrid?"

Good question. "Well, the ones who attacked me at Stim's Diner in Ksacheel, definitely. But maybe also the ones at Stravin's friend's garage."

"Garage?"

"Yeah. She was a mechanic. I think she might have gotten killed." He stopped walking and rested his upper body against the cart handle. "She got killed because she was helping me." He looked closely at his plush companion. "People die or get hurt when they're with me. You should probably join the others. They're going to the...to the..."

A realization was trying to break through into Webrid's consciousness. They say some people have a thick skull. Webrid had more of a thick brain. Signals did not move around in it easily.

"They're going to the government building," Azhanda said primly.

And the thought bubbled to the surface. "Azhanda?" Webrid spoke from deep inside his idea. His voice seemed to echo. "Azhanda, there is no government splinter group."

She started to say something, but he wouldn't be stopped. "No, Azhanda, just let me talk. Let me figure this out. The capital building. In Bargival, my city in Bexilla. That's where they took me when they kidnapped me from the *Draspar*. They couldn't get the laser out of my head while I was alive, so they were planning to kill me. This was in the capital building, Azhanda, not in some fortress in uncharted Northern Cheed. This was the established, elected government, not some criminals in hiding."

Webrid emerged from his fog and spun his cart around using the patented Ganpril family rear-wheel pivot.

Azhanda clapped with delight. "Wow! *Wow!*"

The carter had never heard her express emotion before, and he puffed with pride. "Yup, it's quite a move, isn't it? Learned it from my mom. Well, come on."

"Where are we going?"

"To save our friends."

"Pardon me, sir...I mean, Webrid. Why do they need to be saved from a government building?"

"Because," he said, patting his cart lid, "the legit government folks are the ones who want my laser. I think that's why Eshalo couldn't read it. They've worked with his gang in the past, but whatever is on my laser is so valuable that I think they're double-crossing him."

"Wow," Azhanda said again. "You must be very important if you were chosen to deliver this laser."

nd that's where Webrid's theory fell apart. He was not, in fact, important enough to be carrying such valuable information. Who was he, anyway? There must be thousands of carters in the Raralt Circle. Certainly most of them had received fewer tickets for moving and parking violations, so they would be considered more reliable.

"I'm not important," Webrid said, "but I really think my friends are in trouble. Will you help me save them?"

Azhanda grinned, showing pointy pink teeth. "By all means, Webrid."

The carter was blanketed in a new feeling of confidence as he pushed his cart back the way they'd come. And he felt reassured with Azhanda by his side. He liked Azhanda. Sweet, prim, well-mannered Azhanda.

"Webrid, shall we kick some government butt?"

The spunky phraseology caught him so off his guard that he roared with laughter until he couldn't breathe. "Oh, you crazy girl. I am *so* ready to kick some government butt, and I'm glad you're on my team." He pushed the cart with one hand, wiping tears away with the other.

And then the pain started. Webrid knew headaches. They'd plagued him all his life. And the laser in his skull had given him a whole new level of experience. But this was different. A jagged, rusty knife sliced into his blood-brain barrier and someone twisted it. With each step Webrid took, the knife was twisted again. To him, this was not a metaphor; he had the strong sense that some conscious being outside him was controlling the intensity of the pain. After about fifteen steps, he fell to his knees, weeping.

"Azhanda, what can I do to make it stop? What should I do? It's like somebody's trying to keep me from going forward."

Her fur-covered hands on the back of his neck were almost as comforting as her whisper. "Then maybe it will stop hurting if you turn the cart around again and go in the other direction."

"But they'll kill my friends," he wailed.

"Much more of this and you'll be dead, too. Then you can't help them. Somebody or something is telling you to go the other way. I think you should."

"I'm so tired of this, Azhanda." He turned to face north, still on his knees. The pain dulled slightly, and he knew she was right. Dragging himself to his feet, he struggled to turn the cart around. No fancy carter's trick-spin this time. Azhanda helped by guiding the front end.

Quieter now, with the searing lessened to an ache, Webrid asked, "Why can't I go where I want to go?"

"It seems," said Azhanda, looking at the sky, "that your laser is not just for carrying a message. Or, perhaps I should say, not just for taking a message in one direction."

"They're using me, whoever they are!" Webrid roared and reached his hands up, fingers tight and ready to claw the thing out of his skull. But before he could pierce his skin,

Azhanda stopped him with a remarkable acrobatic feat. Although only half Webrid's height, she pounced up and hung from his forearms. Those big Yeril muscles couldn't be stopped by a Zenivar featherweight, but the element of surprise did the trick. That, and the amusement factor.

"Hey, this is fun," he admitted, swinging her little furry body back and forth. She giggled. It was a sweet, girlish giggle, not the raucous sound that Zatell made. Webrid completely forgot that his innocent plaything was a trained spy and computer genius who had taken down Eshalo's entire bot fleet by pushing a few buttons.

"We should keep walking," she said.

Reluctantly, he lowered her to the ground. "Let's just stay here. My friends are that way. Why bother going in the opposite direction?"

"It seems to be your destiny."

Webrid snorted. "It's not my destiny. It's somebody trying to control me through this stupid laser."

"What's the difference?" Her question contained no trace of sarcasm. And Webrid had no answer, not being educated in the philosophical arts.

So they walked north along the river. The roar of the rushing water made Webrid feel pleasantly small and unimportant, as if he weren't worth controlling.

"I recognize this place," he said, taking a few steps closer to the water. "Yeah. The bank changes here. It goes straight down instead of sloping." Hanging onto his cart as a counterweight, he peeked over the edge. "Hey, look! It's our raft, still stuck in the cliff."

But Azhanda wasn't paying attention. Webrid was miffed to see her staring northwest and pointing.

"Yeah, yeah," he said, "I know the fortress is over there. But you gotta see how Zatell stuck our raft into the..."

He heard the mechanical whir before he saw the

chopper-bots. First they appeared as maybe a dozen specks, but they grew as they approached. These weren't the toy-sized numbers that Eshalo had used—they were big enough that Azhanda could have ridden inside one. As Webrid prepared to die once more, he strained to see whether there were any biological pilots.

"Are they yours?" Azhanda asked.

It was such a weird question that Webrid had to laugh. "Um, that would be a no."

Just then, the closest chopper, hovering halfway across the river, made an announcement. "Ganpril Webrid, First-State Universal Carter. We are yours to command."

So much for the illusion of sublime insignificance. Webrid had no idea who had sent these chopper-bots. He certainly didn't know what to do as a commander, or what to tell them to blow up.

Azhanda tugged at his tunic. "I would recommend that you ask who programmed them."

It was nice to hang out with someone who was smart, helpful, pleasant, and devoid of serious personality quirks. For an instant, Webrid considered letting his other companions fend for themselves and focusing on Azhanda. But, no. He cleared his throat and shouted, "Who programmed you?"

The hovering chopper-bot took a while to say, "Awaiting your command, Ganpril Webrid."

Webrid shot Azhanda a pleading look. She picked right up on it. "Ask the question again, but command it to answer."

Such a smart lady. Webrid took a deep breath to prepare himself. In his daily life, he never got to be in charge of anyone else, so it felt awkward. "Okay." He waggled his finger at the lead chopper-bot. "I'm gonna ask a question. You're gonna answer it. Now, tell me who programmed you."

There was no delay this time. "Data unavailable."

"Oh, for Bralganni's sake." Webrid looked at the Zenivar.

"Now what?" She spun her furry fists around each other, which Webrid took to mean that he should keep asking questions. "Okay. Try this one. Do you work for the Vox?"

"Negative."

"Do you work for the Raralt Circle government?"

"Negative."

Webrid scanned the ten or twelve other chopper-bots in formation behind their leader and pictured them turning against him if he asked the wrong thing. He decided it was time to change his approach.

Stepping to the precipice over the river and puffing out his barrel of a Yeril chest, he roared, "I command you to take Miss Azhanda and me to the government outpost in the forest and help us rescue our companions if they need rescuing." His head throbbed from the effort.

"Command received," said the lead chopper-bot. The other machines closed in fast from behind, too fast, and the front one was not moving forward.

"I believe they're going to crash," Azhanda observed with less than the appropriate urgency.

Webrid's reaction was not so understated. Screaming "Get down!" he jumped on Azhanda and rolled with her toward the forest's protective covering.

But there was no explosion or falling bot debris. Webrid's body was sheltering Azhanda's and his eyes were squeezed shut against an expected sun-bright flash when he heard the voice from the sky. "Ganpril Webrid and Zenar-Zeblanna Azhanda. It is now safe to board."

"Safe to board?" Webrid approximated the words while picking dried leaves off his right tongue. From his prostrate position under the trees, he couldn't quite make out what had become of the chopper-bots.

Somehow Azhanda had wriggled out from under him. She was standing at the cliff's edge, pointing upward.

"What's going on?" he asked.

She kept on pointing. "This is difficult to describe."

So Webrid joined her, still spitting leaves, and looked in the air. A large U-shaped black thing hovered before them. "Is it made of the chopper-bots?" he asked in genuine wonder. "They fitted themselves together?"

"So it would seem."

"That's so freaking cool."

"It certainly is." Azhanda looked up and gave him a warm smile. "Wow."

Webrid addressed the ship. "That's nice work, buddy. How do we get up there?"

The craft lowered itself so that its horizontal area was even with the cliff's edge. Pushing his cart, Webrid and his spy stepped onto the black surface.

"Okay, we're on. So how do we strap ourselves...Aaagh!" Before he could finish, they were both supine. Metal rings clicked around their middles. The cart was secured, too. The craft took off. From the position he was stuck in, Webrid could only look upward, so he had no idea where they were headed.

"Stop! Take us down! Stop! I command you!" Webrid yelled and pleaded, but these machines, *his* machines, ignored him. Hoarse from shouting, Webrid turned his head toward Azhanda. "I think we've been kidnapped. Why does this keep happening to me?"

"I don't know, Webrid." He tried to read sympathy in her eyes, but she wasn't a big one for emotional display. What she said next surprised him: "I believe they're doing what you asked."

"You don't think we've been captured?"

"No. I think we're strapped down so we don't fall off."

Webrid was deeply touched. "What a sweet little optimist you are." Maybe tears clouded his vision. Or maybe it was just pollen from all that infernal nature. Her face looked blurry, anyway.

Azhanda looked like she was about to say something, but it turned into a scream as the bot craft ripped through the tree branches in a gut-sucking descent.

Webrid's voice came out as a squeak. "I can't breathe. I can't *breathe*."

They landed with a *whump* that socked what little air remained right out of his lungs. At a pitch only a wild animal could hear, he wheezed, "Help."

In no time, his respiration returned to normal, and the clamps unlatched at his belly. But he was too scared to look around. Azhanda didn't seem ruffled at all by the landing, and she certainly wasn't afraid. As soon as the metal belts retracted, she sat right up, looking serene.

"Tell us where we are," she said.

"How the hell should I know?"

"I'm asking the bots."

"Oh."

They didn't answer. Webrid felt pretty smug about that. "Guess they only talk to me." Pulling himself up to a sitting position, he rapped on the surface of their transport craft. "Hey. Tell us where we are."

The mechanical voice responded. "As you commanded, we are in the region of Rommey Ebleneneth's summer home."

"But I asked you to take us..."

Azhanda cut in. "The Akardian and your friends mentioned Rommey. The government outpost must belong to him. That makes sense; he wouldn't want it to be public record."

Webrid had that familiar feeling of being the dumbest kid in the class. "Fine. Whatever. So, what are we waiting for? Let's go get 'em."

"Shall we make a plan for entry, mission fulfillment, and

exit?" Azhanda had pulled her tiny computer from her apron pocket.

Webrid laughed. "Knock yourself out. My plan is to kick some government butt in whatever way works best." He jumped down to the ground. It was a greater distance than he'd reckoned, and he fell on his face. Rising quickly and trying to look nonchalant, he tapped at the side of the bot craft again. "Um, I need my cart down here. And some backup."

"Zenar-Zeblanna Azhanda, please deplane," said the bot voice. Azhanda climbed down, with Webrid's help.

The cart rolled to the edge and Webrid grabbed it. Then the craft came apart at the seams. With sleek efficiency, the single unit broke into twelve black metal boxes, which now lay strewn in a circle on the forest floor.

Webrid couldn't take another mystery. "Oh, come on. What am I supposed to do with a bunch of boxes?"

"I would suggest..."Azhanda started.

"Oh, would you? You would suggest what? I bet you're controlling this whole operation. Gimme that." He swiped a handful of claws at her, trying to snag her computer. By the time his arm finished the motion, she had pulled his legs out from under him and he was flat on his back. He kept forgetting she was trained as a spy.

"So," he said, sputtering as he fought to regain his wind, "what were you going to suggest?"

"I would suggest that you place one of these boxes in your cart. If the bots operate or fly any closer to Rommey's outpost, they will be detected." She put the computer away.

Webrid knocked on the top of a nearby box. "Is that true?"

"Affirmative."

"And have you got weapons on you?"

The voice that responded from within the box sounded biological. "Oh, have I got weapons!"

The voice reminded Webrid vividly of his childhood. "Who said that?" He was picturing his mother, of all people. "Sheesh. What kind of a freakin' pansy am I turning into?"

Webrid lifted the talking box-shaped bot into his cart and peered at it. "Who was that talking?" He turned to Azhanda. "Did you hear that biological voice?"

She nodded grimly. "Whoever it is, they're monitoring us remotely through these bots."

"But I know that voice. Why do I know that voice?"

"Pardon?" Azhanda asked politely.

"Nothing." He pressed both palms down firmly on the box. "I command you to speak."

It answered in its old mechanical voice. "I am speaking."

"No, in your other voice!" Webrid dragged his claws across its top. "Talk to me in your biological voice."

"Data unavailable."

"Go to hell." Forgetting that his cart was between his foot and the box, Webrid kicked as hard as he could. He scratched the outer wall of his newly repaired cart and dislocated two toes. In pain and misery, he fell to the grass.

"I'll take care of that," said Azhanda. Without meeting his gaze, she popped his toes back into place. All business and efficiency. Webrid found it humbling.

"We'd better get going," he said, massaging his foot.

The Zenivar had the good grace to help him up without being asked. Webrid knew that discretion was in her breeding, but maybe she was just being friendly. He could use another friend.

They piled some supplies around the bot-in-a-box to make it less obvious. Once they'd secured the cart's lid, Webrid plowed a trail in and out of the remaining boxes strewn on the ground and bumped over a number of the omnipresent tree roots and weedy plants.

"Are we going the right way?" Webrid asked. He meant it rhetorically.

"Yes," the box answered, its bot-voice muted from inside the cart. "A hundred more paces in this direction."

Azhanda asked a good question: "Yeril paces or Zenivar paces?" There was a big difference.

"Yeril," the bot replied.

The answer surprised Webrid. Nobody thought of Yerils as being worth measuring the world by. Whoever had provided these bots not only knew just who he was, but could also see the world just as he did.

As they picked their way forward, Webrid even attempted to count his steps, but the trees made him zig and zag so much that it was hopeless. He longed to ask the box in his cart for directions, but when he opened his mouth to speak, Azhanda put a hand over her own lips and shook her head. She was right, he knew. Better to stay undetected as long as possible, which turned out to be only five more steps.

A reedy voice spoke from above them. "You will cease forward motion." A flying bot, about the size of Webrid's hand and held aloft by four tiny red propellers, buzzed around Webrid's head. His instinct was to swat at it, but as he moved his arm to do so, the buzzy bot froze him with its next words. "Complete ID verified. Blarin Effarbion, First State Universal Carter."

No way Webrid was getting saddled with a dorky name like that. But before he could correct the error, Azhanda spoke up. "Yes. We're here for a delivery."

"Affirmative," said the bot. "You will follow. You will follow."

So they followed. Once they had left the forest and come into a cleared area (comfortably paved in plastic, not wood), Webrid whispered to Azhanda, "What's going on?"

She just shrugged. He wasn't sure he believed that she didn't know. She had adapted to the new situation a bit too easily. Then again, she was trained for this kind of thing. She *was* really a spy, wasn't she? Webrid realized with horror that he knew nothing about her.

His suspicious train of thought was derailed as Webrid became conscious of their surroundings. That plastic pavement he'd so admired was the only thing in the large cleared area they'd entered.

"There's no building here," said Azhanda. Great, was she reading his thoughts now?

Webrid looked up at their buzzing guide. "Where's the building?"

"Blarin Effarbion, you will follow."

Webrid said, "What kind of a stupid name is Blar...what is it?"

To his alarm, Azhanda began to laugh, not her natural gentle giggle, but the forced guffaws of a lousy actor. "Ha-ha-ha. You are *so* funny," she said, "pretending you don't know your own name, Blarin Effarbion. Ha-ha-ha."

Finally, Webrid caught on. They must be on the Vox now.

Of course, that made sense, if this was government property. Webrid expanded his mouth into a mangled approximation of a smile. Fake laughter was much trickier than it looked. "Ha-ha-ha." Realizing how lame he sounded, he gave up and addressed the flying bot. "How do we get into the gov...

"Halt here," it ordered.

The huge plastic tile they had stopped on was sinking briskly beneath them. "Oh, you gotta be kidding," Webrid moaned. "Why can't I ever just take the stairs?" He patted wide-eyed Azhanda on the back as she clung to his waist. "Welcome to my life."

It was a long, fast-paced descent, and Webrid was nauseous when they bumped to a halt. Judging by Azhanda's face, she didn't feel so hot either.

The annoying little propeller-bot was as perky as ever. "You will follow. You will follow." It zipped down a hallway lined with multicolored plastic stripes, then zipped back and circled Webrid's head as if to urge them on.

"Why do all the crazy people with forest hideouts like such ugly decorations?" Webrid wasn't asking anyone in particular.

"You will be silent," the flying bot warned.

"Sheesh. Sensitive. Did you pick out this wallpaper yourself?"

Azhanda let slip a quiet giggle.

"You will enter." They were at a wide, low entranceway. Azhanda barely made it through upright, but Webrid had to double over. Fortunately, the ceilings in the large meeting hall they stepped into were somewhat higher, but still not enough for Webrid to stand upright. He bumped his head a few times before sorting out a crooked stooped position he could maintain as he walked.

It was difficult to look around with his head at such an angle, but hearing Azhanda's gasp was his first clue that he should shimmy around to face another direction. Doing so revealed a terrible sight.

Along the far wall of the room were Leshi, Debley, Stravin, and Zatell, obviously detained against their will. The three tall, two-armed people were seated, with their fingers trapped in a metal device. They looked like they were being given a forced manicure. Zatell was suspended in mid-air, her many limbs waving around slowly like a field of shebel plants in a summer's breeze. Webrid couldn't tell what was holding her there.

"Blarin Effarbion," boomed an officious biological voice.

Entranced by his friends' suffering, and having completely forgotten his fake name, Webrid didn't respond. Azhanda kicked him. "Yes, sir," he croaked. Leshi looked up with widened eyes, but said nothing.

"You have a dispatch pouch for me from the capital?"

Azhanda kicked him again. Webrid looked at her, and when she nodded her head, he repeated, "Yes, sir." He couldn't see who was speaking. Squinting at the walls, he expected to find someone else who went to Eshalo's tailor.

"They don't usually send these missives by such primitive means. Still, I received the transmission from Bargival and have been expecting you. I realize you must hand it to me directly."

"Um." That was the limit of Webrid's improvisational powers. Azhanda looked pained. Leshi seemed to suppress a smile. Webrid's other companions were noticing him one by one and their jaws were falling open.

"Well, come here, you stupid man. You're slowing the machinations of government with your dawdling. I have to sign the dispatch."

"I'm sorry, sir, I can't see..."

"Over here, you worthless civil servant. Whose nephew are you, that such an oaf should get such an important job?

It's almost beyond imagining that the Vox itself was designed by a Yeril."

"What?" The finer hairs on Webrid's chest and back stood on end. "A *Yeril* designed the Vox?"

"Poor, ignorant sod. Just bring the pouch before I molt my outer skin while I wait."

The word "molt" brought that Yeril claw they'd found back into Webrid's mind. Was the world run by invisible Yerils now? It was not a comforting thought, since it ran against everything he knew about his own people. Frankly, the thought made him feel sick, and his vision flashed green again. For the sake of his friends, he forced himself to focus on his current situation.

A jungle of microphones, speakers, cameras, and mini-monitors next to the row of captives moved forward slightly and parted. A desk and a familiar face were revealed. The face was wide and flabby, of pasty beige. As the layer of equipment parted further, Webrid realized why he recognized the figure.

"You're that politician who's always in the news for going to wild parties!" His admiration was genuine.

There were sharp intakes of breath from Azhanda, from all four prisoners, even from the soldier stationed in the corner.

"Well, now," the politician chuckled. "I like a fellow that calls 'em as he sees 'em." After a great struggle, he managed to get his feet under his bulbous bulk, although Webrid noticed that he was no taller standing than he'd been while sitting. Hence the low, wide doors.

"Yes, I'm Rommey Ebleneneth, your duly-elected Council Secretary. And, yes, I've been known to raise a glass in good company. But I ask you, who can be said to truly represent the people if he fancies himself too good to drink with them?"

Webrid really liked this guy, and promised himself to

become a voter when he returned home. He completely forgot about his companions staring at him from their various restraints. But he was quickly reminded.

"In contrast to you, um..." Rommey wheezed while bending toward a screen, "yes, in contrast to you, Blarin Effarbion, these, er, visitors are not being at all straightforward." Rommey waved a dismissive webbed hand at Stravin, who was nearest the desk. "Effi, my good man, won't you and your charming assistant step forward so I can shake your hands, if you've got 'em?" He bared his teeth in a syrupy politician's smile. "I'll shake whatever you've got."

Feeling the blood drain from his head, Webrid clutched the cart for balance. The eyes of his companions showed just how betrayed they felt. Webrid thought he knew every angle a shyster could swing, but Rommey's charisma had practically hypnotized him. Deeply shamed, he rolled past Zatell, then Leshi, then Debley, and finally Stravin. He glanced at each one for an instant; by the time he'd reached Stravin, his vision was clouded with stagnant tears. He'd wanted to be a hero, but he was too much of a worthless lug. Too weak. Too stupid.

The torchsong of self-pity rang so loudly in Webrid's mind that he didn't quite catch what Rommey was blathering on about. The phrase "laser in his head" was just seeping into Webrid's consciousness as he approached Rommey's desk and a big webbed hand reached toward his brow.

"That's a bnarli!" Rommey roared.

Webrid froze, but Azhanda sprang onto the cart lid and yanked the bnarli off. To Webrid's great disappointment, Rommey's skull didn't melt.

"Guard!" bellowed the fat politician.

"Webrid, look out!" Zatell shouted from her floating prison. Seeing the soldier raise a weapon and head toward him, Webrid ducked, grabbing Azhanda as he went down. She wriggled under the desk and disappeared. Ramming head-first into Rommey's rubbery legs, Webrid tipped the politician onto his back. Simultaneously kicking backwards, Webrid shoved his cart hard toward the soldier. Those high-grade military wheels on the smooth plastic floor made the cart roll faster than a rube loses money at Rebeten Casino. The soldier went right down.

"Got it," called Azhanda, who had crawled onto the desk chair and was busy with various knobs and buttons in the curtain of equipment. The finger-locks whirred, and Debley, Leshi, and Stravin were able to pull free. "Catch Zatell," the Zenivar ordered.

Debley reacted first, running to Zatell just as she fell from her invisible cage. She gave him a big, slurpy kiss.

The soldier, back on his feet, was trying to help Rommey up when the ceiling opened and the tile that had brought down Webrid and Azhanda now delivered a familiar motley crew.

"Put 'em up!" shouted pimply purple Brulo-Gee. There were two more gangsters on the elevator with him, each sporting a bandanna decorated with a purple triangle. Webrid was sort of insulted when they ran past him and went right for the soldier, knocking him flat again.

The elevator tile was still stationed on the lower level, but that didn't stop the chief gangster himself from making a spectacular entrance. Down floated Eshalo through the square hole in the ceiling, his rainbow-striped gown billowing like a parachute. Webrid shuddered at the view up his skirt, and he could see Stravin and Leshi turning their heads. Zatell, wisely, kept her eyes tightly shut. Nobody wanted to see a gangster's nether regions closing in on her from a great height.

"Eshalo!" shouted Rommey from his supine position. Arguably, he had the worst view of all.

"Rommey!" roared the gangster as he neared the floor. He bobbled to the side, then steadied himself.

"Eshalo!" said Webrid, just figuring out what was going on.

"You bunch of losers!" muttered Brulo-Gee, who looked a bit bruised and smelled slightly charred. He was apparently still recovering from the last time he'd seen these "losers."

"I wondered when you'd drop in," Rommey huffed from the floor.

"Cuff 'em," said Eshalo. "Leave the fat one. He ain't exactly a flight risk." Eshalo's entourage slapped electronic cuffs on Webrid and his friends. It didn't work too well on the multi-limbed Zatell, of course.

"Put her back in suspension," Rommey wheezed to a soldier. It took three of them to force the wriggling woman back into her invisible prison. Webrid felt very sorry for Zatell, but couldn't imagine how to free her.

The polychrome fabric of Eshalo's garment shimmered as he walked over to Rommey. The globular man was stuck on his back, and no amount of rocking and squirming seemed to do the trick.

"Well, well," crooned Eshalo, "you sniveling, back-stabbing bastard."

"Who, me?" Perhaps because of the weight of Rommey's chest pressing down his lungs, his voice had become very high. "What did I do to..."

"Don't give me that. I want the laser. You took it out."

"I didn't. I just got the guy in custody. I was just about to..."

"Don't waste my time. Give me the decoder."

"The what?" Rommey seemed sincerely confused.

"I got the data, but I can't decode it."

"What do you mean, you got the data?" Rommey, red with anger, found the strength to sit up. "You knew about the laser?"

"Of course I did, you double-crossing carpetbagger." The shoe with which Eshalo kicked Rommey in the ribs was of a fetching burnt ochre color. "Can't trust a politician. You really can't. I thought we were partners."

After being kicked, Rommey was again on his back. "So, what did the laser say?"

Eshalo slapped his forehead. "I've told you." He turned to Debley and Leshi. "Didn't I tell him?" And back to Rommey. "I couldn't read it because I haven't got the decoder."

Rommey was shaking his head. "There's no decoder. There was nothing in the messages about a code."

"Well, it's just random numbers then."

"Random?" Rommey snorted. "It's not random, I assure you. It's an official document. Highest clearance. How the hell did you know about it, anyway?"

"I got a message saying it was coming."

"*You* got a *message*?"

Webrid was enjoying this match more than last year's Intra-Raralt Women's Soft Hoop series, in which Bargival barely squeaked past the rookie team from Arapuns. And just like in that series, it was impossible now to tell who was winning, but everyone was giving it his all.

"I got a message, too. Straight from the top." Rommey spoke in the same haughty tone Webrid had once heard him tell a reporter, "I would never use public funds to hire a prostitute."

Eshalo blew his nose on the hem of Brulo-Gee's jacket. "Yeah? So? Mine came from the top, too. Rempener Dras."

A shiver disrupted the nap of Webrid's belly hairs. So much for Rempener Dras being some accounting cog in a corruption scheme.

Rommey also seemed startled by the name. "Rempener Dras. Well, well, well. Isn't that something?" He shoved his wide face close to Webrid's."Well, well, well." Webrid's cheeks tingled under Rommey's toxic breath.

shalo continued, "So, since it was from Rempener Dras, we figured—"

Rommey nodded sagely. "Well, sure."

Longing to ask a million questions, Webrid decided he'd get more info if he stayed quiet and just listened. In any case, his tongues felt sluggish from shock.

"But, I gotta say," said Eshalo, "I think Rempener Dras might be slipping."

Rommey harrumphed. "You think there was an error in the message? That it wasn't meant to be random numbers?"

Polishing a glazed wooden ring against Brulo-Gee's head, Eshalo sighed. "Code wasn't done properly. She's slipping, I tell you."

"Was bound to happen, I suppose." Rommey turned back to Webrid and spat as he spoke. "Don't you agree?"

He might as well have asked him the chemical formula for velancium. But Webrid had a lot of practice pretending to know what was happening. "Yeah, totally slipping," he concurred, trying to be sociable.

Eshalo ignored Webrid. "And we gave it our best shot in

the lab. I have this wonderful Zenivar working for me, and she..."

Zatell's giggles were so loud, they could probably be heard above ground. The sound of her raised spirits came as such a relief to Webrid that he couldn't help laughing, too.

Eshalo did not look relieved. "What are you slugs sniggering at? I thought I ordered you killed." He looked quickly at Rommey, who did, after all, represent the government. "I mean arrested. I thought I ordered you *arrested*. Hey! That's my Zenivar!"

Azhanda smiled sweetly and waved her furry hand as much as the cuffs would allow.

"Listen," said Rommey, finally rolling close enough to his desk to pull himself up, "I haven't looked at the data yet. I only just figured out this guy had it." He pushed a webbed thumb toward Webrid.

"What do you mean, you just figured it out? What's he doing here, then?" Eshalo put his cold, dry hand on the back of Webrid's neck. "You wouldn't be thinking of making a deal with him, would you?"

Rommey sat down so heavily that his metal chair popped a screw. "No, no. There was an ID scramble."

"Here? But you have all the latest..."

"It was professionally done. He sent me notice of an official dispatch and changed his ID in the Vox, so I let him in. This Yeril may look like a moron, but he's got some major skills."

Webrid positively beamed. The smile left his face, however, the moment he heard Zatell behind him, laughing again. He tried to turn and threaten her, but the electronic cuffs zapped him back into submission.

"You're not going anywhere, fella, so just calm down," said Brulo-Gee, using his buzz-stick to force Webrid onto the floor. Azhanda plopped down next to him without being asked, but their three tall, slender companions remained standing.

Lifting his robes, Eshalo tiptoed over to Webrid and bent to peer at his face. Webrid had had enough of those slimy yellow eyes the last time they met, so he looked away.

"No," the gang lord announced after a few seconds. "He really is a moron. I don't think he knows what's on the laser, and I am absolutely sure he can't spin the Vox." Eshalo straightened up and looked at Rommey. "I bet it's those bastards in the Swarattan Resistance. They're not so bad at the tech stuff, for a bunch of spoiled idealists."

Webrid had enough sense not to try to look at Debley or Leshi, but he heard several gasps behind him.

"Well, then," said Rommey. His webbing made a squishy sound when he rubbed his hands together. "You came to the right place. Soldiers, bring those ugly, scrawny red kids forward." He nodded to the Fekli siblings as they were dragged up to his desk. "I believe Mr. Eshalo would like a word with you two."

"These are Swarattan rebels?" Eshalo poked at Debley's shiny ribcage. "They were with the Yeril earlier at my place, and I thought they were just his guards."

"Pah!" The sound erupted from Debley. Leshi groaned.

"Your info was wrong," said Rommey. "He's a terrorist. And that," he added with a satisfied chortle, "is why it's so important to have connections in government." The two horrid men shared a laugh. Brulo-Gee took advantage of his boss's distraction to smack Webrid on the back of the head for no particular reason.

Rommey spoke from his chair. "May I present the Feklari twins, Debley and Leshi? These two underfed waifs were telling me earlier that they don't know what's on the laser. Then again, they also pretended they weren't with the resistance, or headquartered on the *Draspar*."

Lifting up the skirt of his rainbow garment, Eshalo perched on a chair near Rommey. "I think we should make them talk, you know, a bit more plainly. I like plain speaking, don't you?"

"Why, yes. I was just saying that to our Yeril friend here before you dropped in."

"A fun bunch, those Yerils, eh?" Eshalo flicked a pointy finger against the bnarli. "This one isn't as brainy as some, though, which is why they could fit the laser in." He had himself a good laugh.

Webrid imagined what it would feel like to pop one of those ghastly yellow eyeballs between his palms.

Waving a webbed hand, Rommey called, "Soldiers, hook up these poor emaciated meat sticks. Let's see if they can grow some thick skin fast enough to protect them from the Truth Pulse. Come on, hook 'em up."

Debley and Leshi were pushed into chairs, and their fingers were locked back into the forced-manicure contraptions.

"Are you familiar with these brilliant machines?" Rommey asked, pacing and pointing as if in front of a classroom. "Sure, sure, they can hold a person still. But notice the name. Truth Pulse." He turned and spoke close to Debley's face. "You tell the truth, you don't get pulsed."

"Dastardly," hissed Stravin. Webrid had never heard anyone use that word in real life before, but suddenly he understood what it meant. Brulo-Gee zapped Stravin with his buzz-stick, making the feathery man yelp. Debley gave him a pleading look.

Leaning toward Debley again, Eshalo said, "Let's start with you, shall we? Are you and your repulsive sister leaders of the Swarattan Resistance Force?"

"Hell, no," said Debley. Then he squealed with pain, and his body jerked backwards.

"Tsk-tsk. Wrong answer. You lie, you fry."

"Oh, nice. I love poetry," said Rommey.

"Are you trying to get info from the laser?"

"No. Aaaah!"

"Do you have any idea what data the laser might contain?"

"No. Aaaaaaaaaah!" Debley's body was trembling and his eyelids drooped. He seemed barely conscious.

Next to Webrid, Stravin was whimpering. Zatell had curled herself up in a ball, still suspended in the air. Only Azhanda looked calm. Calm but alert, it seemed to Webrid. He noticed that she kept her eyes fixed on his cart, although it was halfway across the room.

"This fellow is most uncooperative," said Eshalo to Rommey. "Shall we take a dip into the female side of his genetic pool?"

Rommey nodded. "By all means." Webrid's heart doubled its pace.

Grabbing his chair and pulling it up next to Leshi's finger-lock, Eshalo arranged his gown meticulously as he sat. "You've seen what happened to your brother, so I do advise you to think carefully before you answer." He cleared his throat, making his jowls bounce. "Leshi, do you have any idea what data is contained on that laser?"

She said nothing, but looked past her inquisitor, and deeply into Webrid's eyes.

"Right. I'll repeat the question. Do you think you know what's on the laser?"

Now Leshi swung her gaze to meet Eshalo's. "Yes," she answered. There was no shriek of pain, except in Webrid's heart.

"What are you doing?" Zatell called to her from her mid-air lock-up. "Don't tell them anything."

"Hush now, or you're next," Eshalo warned her, and

Rommey gurgled out a laugh. The gangster turned back to Leshi. "You will tell me what you believe is on the laser. If you do, you'll go free. I'm not a monster, you know."

This time it was Brulo-Gee who laughed, zapping Webrid with the buzz-stick again for fun. "Yeah, we're not monsters, man. Ha!"

"All right, Brulo-Gee, that will do. Leshi, your brother's not looking so well, so you'd better spill what you know."

"It's a writ," she said, taking a deep breath, "mandating complete deforestation of Cheed over the next twenty Standard Raralt Years." Her voice got stronger. "Rommey there is the author of the bill and the primary governmental liaison for the project. If the document goes public, your career is finished, and probably your freedom, too." As she lifted her chin triumphantly, Webrid tried again to figure out how she could be so brainy and so sexy at the same time.

Eshalo wasn't so impressed. "Oooh, bad for you if she's right," he said, pointing gleefully at Rommey. "But why should I be concerned about it?" He turned to Brulo-Gee. "We're wasting our time here. This ain't our problem after all."

Leshi spoke loudly. "The contract names the Triple Sunset Corporation of planet Prellga as the company contracted to process the wood." She zapped Eshalo with a poisonous glare that turned him a paler shade of gray. "That laser is supposed to contain bank routing records proving you own that company." She smiled, and Zatell tried so hard to clap her hands that she did a somersault. As Leshi's voice got louder and clearer, Webrid pictured her as Raralt Circle president, with himself as her arm candy, darling of the paparazzi. "Our work is coming to its fruition. We will save the last remaining forests of the Raralt Circle! We will save our world from your corruption! We will save the people from the Vox! Heesha Swaratt lives forever! Heesha Swaratt lives forever!"

Webrid, completely swept up in the moment, began shouting with her. "Heesha Swaratt lives forever!" Stravin and Zatell joined in, too. "Heesha Swaratt lives forever!"

"Shut up! Shut up, all of you." Eshalo glowered at Rommey. "You said this was an effective lie detector."

"It's infallible. Best of the best. Military torture grade."

"She can't be right about the laser."

"No reason to think she is, my friend. Just relax. You asked her what she *thought* was on the laser. She hasn't read it, wasn't able to decode it. She's just wishing."

Eshalo folded his arms and furrowed his brow. "The message I got said it was deep info to help us take down the Swarattans."

"Yeah," Rommey agreed. "And registration codes for their HQ. How many times have we tried to break that office-building cover? But the Vox won't let us. Now we'll be able to stop them and throw them all in prison." Rommey wobbled his fat face toward Webrid. "As I'm sure you recall, I had my people snatch you off the *Draspar* once, but they were too incompetent to hold on to you when you reached the capital. Wouldn't think someone with your build could slip away like that. Huh."

Webrid decided to let him think the escape was part of a carefully crafted stratagem. No need to mention his desperate dive through the trash chute.

"We've got to find out for sure what's on the laser," said Eshalo. "Hook him up to the reader. Let's take a look."

"Here's the thing." Rommey rubbed his webbing together contritely. "We are on a government budget, so we don't have one of those fancy new readers."

Eshalo sighed. "Well, put him in the Truth Pulse. Maybe that will work to extract the data. Maybe it's buried in his psyche."

Webrid was absolutely sure there was nothing buried in his psyche, about the laser or anything else. What you saw was what you got. But Eshalo was determined. Brulo-Gee shoved Webrid's fingers into the delicate instrument. He could feel his claws puncture some wiring when they entered. With his luck, he'd get electrocuted before they could ask the first question.

As Eshalo and Rommey moved toward him to start the interrogation, Webrid noticed Azhanda slowly reaching into her apron with her cuffed hands. He willed himself not to stare too hard and call attention to her. But he was sure he'd pass out if he didn't focus on a friendly face. He turned his head and gazed into Leshi's tear-filled eyes.

"Who are you working for?" asked Rommey.

"I thought I was working for you," said Webrid. He held his breath, but the only pulse of pain was his professional shame at not knowing his own client.

Rommey tried again. "It has to be someone really high up. How were you able to trick my bots with your ID?"

"I don't know." No pain.

"How did you send me that message to expect an official dispatch pouch so I'd let you in?"

"I don't know," Webrid said slowly, defiantly, truthfully.

"Gods curse you, man, tell me how you spun the Vox!"

"I don't know!" Webrid screamed.

Rommey heaved up his weight and waddled away. "Great gods. He's just a stupid Yeril puppet. We don't need him. Let's get the laser. We'll do it the old-fashioned way. The brain has to stay connected to the living spine while we read the data, so we'll have to remove the front of his skull. Don't see the point in sterile surgery, since he'll be out in the forest as dinner for the wild animals soon enough. Soldiers, open his skull."

Rommey's soldiers came at Webrid as his friends cried out.

"No!" said Zatell.

"You can't!" said Leshi.

"That's murder!" said Stravin.

"Let me do it," said Brulo-Gee. "I wanna do it!"

The soldiers shrugged and held Webrid down while Brulo-Gee grabbed a fire hatchet from the wall. As he was about to swing, Webrid took a close look at Brulo-Gee's pimply, purple face. A tiny dot of green jiggled across that purple nose just before the nose and its face melted. Then the skull melted. What was once Brulo-Gee's head dripped as gelatinous bone and brain matter all over the sputtering Webrid.

Azhanda stood up, pulling her little computer from her apron pocket with one cuffed hand. "Okay, I believe we're done here." As Rommey's soldiers aimed their weapons at her, she called, "Reverse polarity." Everyone's cuffs and finger-locks and mid-air prisons ceased to function. Stravin ran under Zatell just as she fell.

"Webrid, order the bot," said Azhanda.

He honestly had no idea what she meant. "What?" He was still wiping Brulo-Gee goo off his face with his sleeve.

"You know," she said, looking hard at the cart. Webrid followed her gaze and his memory kicked in.

"Bot! Come out of that cart and get us out of here!"

"Fire at the cart!" cried Rommey. But as his soldiers did so, the cart's lid clanged open and a series of black metal strips grew from it. They formed into a huge armed robot, twice as tall as Webrid, which stepped onto the floor and lurched across the room.

"Damn." Webrid ran to the cart and wrapped his hands around its comforting handle.

Then he heard a surprising sound, the distinctive whir of the Moti-Moto engine. Stravin whooped, "Oh, it's my Moti! She's come to save her daddy. Get on, loves. Let's get out of here!"

Stravin climbed onto the front seat, and Leshi, Debley, and Zatell clung onto whatever part of the scooter or its driver was closest. "I don't think we can take you two," called Zatell to Azhanda.

"Don't worry about Webrid and me. But how will you drive out of here? We're not at ground level," Azhanda warned, ducking as a soldier fired at her.

"Not to worry, dear," said Stravin. "There's a ramp up at the end of the building. That's how we got in earlier." Stravin's voice faded as the Moti disappeared down the corridor, with legs, arms, and heads flailing in every direction, like a circus act.

The bot had continued to grow, and by now it had a good ten guns clutched in all the limbs it had sprouted. Webrid braced for a bloodbath. Instead, he felt himself being lifted, cart and all. Although he was afraid to open his eyes, he felt the remaining supplies fall out of the cart and heard them hit the floor.

ramps raged through Webrid's muscles, from his hands clear up to his neck. If he'd been holding anything besides his cart, he would've just let go. But he clenched his teeth and growled against the pain as the box-bot-turned-flying-warrior soared upward.

Webrid didn't have much experience hanging from aircraft, so he kept his eyes shut until the stench of nature on the breeze made him curious. Worried that he'd puke if he looked down, he forced his head upward. There was a lot going on up there.

The bot's square head now had a huge propeller coming out of it, spinning so fast it was a blur. Oh, and there was Azhanda, clinging to the bot's shoulder, her eyes bulging and her mouth open.

"Hi," said Webrid. What else was he going to say? She didn't answer, apparently unable to move her face.

Then he looked down. He saw the cart, of course, gleaming against a background of treetops far below. The cart swung wildly, its open lid flapping on its hinges. With a great effort, Webrid tucked his feet under its rear axle to keep it from swinging so much.

Suddenly, lots of black objects came shooting upward toward him from the trees. Webrid lost his leg grip and nearly released his handhold, too. It took a few moments to figure out that these were the other eleven bots that he'd left behind on the forest floor in the shape of boxes. They were now in their chopper shapes, and closing in on each other at great speed. Webrid's ride was heading straight for them.

"Noooo!" Webrid screamed, snapping his eyes shut and hauling his cart right up to his chin in a supernatural burst of ancestral strength.

Webrid's body skidded sideways against a solid surface, and a metal belt clicked into place around his waist. His hands were still frozen around the handle of his cart, which lay on its side next to him.

"Webrid, we're on the U-craft."

Peeking around his cart, he could see Azhanda, supine and safely strapped. On either side of them rose the high black walls of the U-shaped bot vessel that had flown them to Rommey's compound earlier.

"Where are we going?" he shouted over the screaming wind and engine.

Azhanda moved her lips. "Rempener Dras."

At the sound of that name, something came unhitched in Webrid's brain. The name replayed over and over in his inner ear, knocking through his skull. The world spiraled around him, and those cursed green numbers swept across his vision at terrifying speed.

"Rempener Dras. Rempener Dras. Rempener Dras."

He blacked out.

"Hello, darling."

Webrid felt feathery fingers sliding across his cheek. He fought the weight of his eyelids.

"Oh, look, our Webrid is rejoining us."

Stravin's was the first face to enter the waking carter's vision. All his friends were there. Azhanda, with her soft, gentle smile. Zatell, her squashed face puckered with concern. Debley, sleek and handsome, peering from the back of the group, as if determined to seem aloof. Webrid's trusty cart was there, reflecting the greens and blues of the forest and river. And then there was Leshi. Lovely Leshi, her facial flesh glinting in the twilight, her deep brown eyes radiant with emotion. Was it worry? Was it love?

It didn't matter. Webrid knew that all these people loved him in one way or another. He basked in their warmth, absorbed their kind attention, gloried in an unaccustomed soul-deep calm brought about by this sweet...

"What the hell is happening to me?' Webrid sat bolt upright, desperate to stem the sappy tide drowning his brain.

"No, no," Leshi said, moving toward him. "Don't get up too fast."

He met her gaze, feeling very confused, longing to kiss her. "Something's wrong with me." His voice cracked.

"What are your symptoms?" So Debley was a doctor now?

"I feel so..." Webrid was stumped. "So...'

"Nauseous?" said Zatell.

"Dizzy?" said Azhanda.

"Achy?" said Stravin.

Rolling up onto his knees, Webrid looked at each friend in turn. "Happy. I feel totally happy and contented. This is not normal, and I don't like it, not one little bit."

Debley shrugged dismissively. "You're probably just glad you're safe. I'm sure it'll pass."

"No, it's more serious than that." Webrid let the Fekli

sibs help him to his feet. "It's a total happiness, like there's absolutely nothing wrong in the world."

"Like we're not stuck in the wilds of Northern Cheed?" Stravin asked, furrowing his brow.

"Like you're not an ugly hairball with a funky stink?" Zatell contributed.

"I think he's cute." Good old Leshi.

Azhanda looked up at the carter. "I don't quite understand, Webrid. Is contentment not desirable?"

"Not for me." Webrid forced out a lungful of air. "I mean, I don't even have a headache right now. I've had at least a minor headache pretty much constantly for the past decade. Not now. Not the slightest twinge in any joint. This is messed up."

It was then that Webrid noticed the huge metal double doors, providing a backdrop for Leshi as if she were posing for a portrait. Doors built for giants, with big black metal stripes. No visible handles or lock.

"I know this place."

"That's right, my dear, it's the entrance to the fortress. Some flying bots dropped us here. Picked up the Moti with us hanging on, flew us north following the river, and then just left us. Practically disappeared before our eyes. Not long after, you and Azhanda showed up in a big black aircraft. So here we are, back at the fortress." Stravin gestured extravagantly. "Isn't it just like old times?"

"Just like yesterday, you mean," grumbled Debley.

This made Webrid's overwhelming sense of well-being an even greater mystery. "Last time I was here, you guys used a scary machine to suck out my brains."

Leshi huffed. "We extracted data. Your brains were left intact."

"Which isn't saying much," quipped Zatell. Debley snickered.

"Okay, okay, fine. But it was really unpleasant. And then those gangsters came, and I accidentally melted two of their heads..."

"Which was just exquisite," said Stravin earnestly.

"Thanks, but then I got kidnapped."

"Hey!" Zatell swatted him on the shin. "We all got kidnapped."

"You didn't." Debley was towering over Zatell, his arms crossed.

"He's right, darling," said Stravin. "You got away, remember?"

They weren't getting the point. Webrid *had* to make them understand. "What I'm trying to say, people, is that I have all kinds of bad memories about this place. So why am I happy to be here? I should not be happy right now. I should be the total opposite of happy. But I feel like... I feel like..." Expressing feelings wasn't really a Yeril thing, so it took a while to spit it out. "Like I'm home and never want to leave."

Something very soft enveloped Webrid's clenched fist. Looking down, he saw Azhanda, her eyes wide and shiny. "Maybe you've found what you were seeking."

The suggestion was so stunning that Webrid couldn't immediately respond. But Stravin reached out and scratched the Zenivar between the ears. "You're an enigmatic one, aren't you, love?"

"No, I know what she means," Webrid heard himself say.

Leshi came up to his side and spoke quietly. "Tell us."

"She means I'm here."

"Where?"

"The place where I'm supposed to make my delivery."

Zatell let loose one of her ill-timed laughs. "But you were just saying we were here before."

"Yeah, but it's different now."

Leshi whispered, "How?"

Webrid felt as close to wisdom as he ever expected to be. "It's not the place, it's who's *in* the place."

"But we were all here before," said Debley.

Zatell pointed three limbs at Azhanda. "She wasn't."

"But, my dear," said Stravin, "Webrid's been with her all day."

Pulling his hand out of Azhanda's and pressing it against his forehead, Webrid knew. He just knew. "It's the client. The one who hired me to carry the laser is here now, but wasn't here before."

At that moment, the great double doors began to open inward. A voice said, "Would you care to come in, or are you going to stand there talking on the porch all night? I could bring out some drinks and snacks."

Webrid was hurtled back in time to his childhood again, the squalid back alleyway, his mother and aunts watching him play. No question in Webrid's mind, this was the same biological voice that had come from the box-bot in the woods. Now Webrid also remembered where he'd heard the voice before that. "The bot that put the laser into my head, on the street in Bargival. You talked to me through that bot." It felt like he'd solved one of the greatest puzzles of the cosmos.

And then more enlightenment dawned. "You're Rempener Dras! The Vox said your name when I asked who gave me all that money. You're the one who changed my license status to..."

The voice finished for him, "First State Universal Carter. You got it, Ganpril Webrid."

Debley cleared his throat. "Not that this isn't fascinating, but the night air's kind of chilly."

"I'm with Deb on this one," said Stravin, taking Debley's arm. "Let's go inside." They all muttered agreement and walked through the doors.

Webrid sighed and pushed his cart in behind his friends.

"That's more like it," said the voice of Rempener Dras. The doors closed slowly and steadily behind them. "Webrid, I'm sure you can lead the way from here."

It was true. As his companions moved to the side, Webrid pushed his cart past them and down the hallway without hesitation. He could see a soft green glow in front of him, not a focused laser beam or a million floating numbers, but a healing green shimmer floating on the air. That diffuse light tugged him firmly onward, around corners, into an elevator, into another hallway, around some more corners, and up to a sliding door. Although the door was locked with a code pad, Webrid punched in the numbers as if his fingers had done it daily for years.

He regained his self-awareness in a room decorated with metal panels of a black darker than the forest night. Webrid felt a little let down to see that his friends were still there with him. He figured he'd passed through some special carter-only portal. But somehow all these folks had come along, too. Still, he felt honored to be experiencing this magnetism, this transcendental...

"Holy hoongofls." Zatell's outburst shook Webrid from his mystic state.

"By all the gods," was Stravin's way of putting it.

Leshi and Debley backed up silently, their faces tense with alarm. Azhanda smiled and waved.

Turning slowly to his right, Webrid tried to prepare himself for whatever horror had shown itself. He failed.

"Hello, Ganpril Webrid. I'm Rempener Dras."

Webrid was looking at—well, at himself. Or at least a version of himself.

Webrid could form only one word. "Mom?"

The Yeril in front of him laughed heartily, curling both her tongues. "Everyone used to say I looked like your mother. Don't you recognize me, Webrid? Come on, now. I used to play with you all the time."

Dumbstruck, Webrid pressed his elbows and most of his weight against the cart lid. He couldn't even blink. But Azhanda walked right up to the mystery Yeril and said, "Good evening, ma'am. Nice to see you again."

"A delight, Azhanda. You did your job to perfection. Thanks so much."

"You're...you're..." Webrid squeaked. "You're my Auntie Naggrid."

"That's right, dear."

"What's going on?" asked Zatell. She had squeezed all her limbs tight around her face, presumably in self-defense.

Leshi shrugged. "It seems that the great Rempener Dras is Webrid's aunt."

It took a while for the peals of laughter from Stravin and Zatell to stop ringing against the walls and ceiling.

A seriously awful thought occurred to Webrid. "Was this my mom's idea?"

"Oh, please!"

Webrid shivered at how much Rempener Dras sounded like his mother. She had the same baritone voice that scooped upward with each breath. That, and the edge of sarcasm.

"I haven't seen your mother since I ran away to Cheed over twenty years ago. Came here because of the forests. My beautiful, beautiful forests." She sighed, pausing to gaze at a monitor on the wall that showed the woods outside. "I'd learned all about trees when I was secretly paying attention in school."

"Why'd you change your name, though?" he asked. "Nobody would have known you here."

"I was starting fresh. 'Rempener Dras' means 'savior of trees' in the extinct tribal language of Northern Cheed."

A high-pitched "Ha!" popped out of Debley's mouth.

"You're kidding!"

She drew herself up proudly. "I am certainly not kidding. I enrolled in the Excheeli Monarchic Academy and studied mathematics and science. Got recruited on my graduation day by the Cheed government as a programmer."

"That was before the Raralt Circle unified government?" Leshi's voice was filled with wonder.

"Aren't you a smart girlie?" Rempener Dras looked at Leshi and suddenly began to laugh. No, she positively cackled. It was alarming, and everyone took a step away from her.

Struggling to keep the conversation going, the way one does with disturbing old relatives, Webrid said, "So, um, don't you miss Bargival?"

The cackle heightened, then died away. Wiping tears from her eyes, Webrid's aunt snorted in a very Yeril-like way. "There was nothing for me there. I sure wasn't going to waste my life as a simple old carter."

Webrid looked down at his cart, depressed and ashamed. He thought about his grandfather, and hoped the old geezer's ghost was busy somewhere else at the moment.

Leshi, bless her heart, stood up for Webrid. "But you needed a carter. You hired a carter. Looking around here, I'm gathering that you're some kind of a genius, but you still couldn't get along without a carter. Can you really say they're not important?

"And who do you think you are, anyway, dragging Webrid all over creation, putting that thing in his head, nearly getting him killed a bunch of times?"

Moved beyond words, Webrid straightened up and embraced the fleshy Fekli. Then he gave her a good, long, two-tongued kiss, right there in front of Auntie and everyone.

ebrid and Leshi backed away from each other. There was much clearing of throats. As Debley came toward him, Webrid prepared to do battle for his gleaming fuchsia princess.

"Wait, my sweet." Stravin hurried into Debley's path. "You can deal with family honor later. There are more pressing issues."

"Yeah, like I've got a question," said Zatell, pointing to Rempener Dras and then to Azhanda. "How does this female hairball in a red pantsuit know that flight attendant?"

"Her name is Azhanda," Webrid snapped. He was still struggling to get his blood pressure down to normal.

Their hostess seemed unperturbed. "I hired Azhanda to get some info about Eshalo's crew."

Debley stepped up close to her, anger clearly still pumping through his veins. "Aha! So, you're the government?"

Rempener Dras did not back away. "I once was."

Leshi took up her brother's hostile stance. "What do you mean, once? You live in the Vox zone here. You must be an official now, or they'd come and get you."

"Well, I was director of Vox programming. I..." She looked at the floor. "I *invented* the Vox."

"You're the Yeril..." Webrid couldn't even continue. This was, indeed, the stuff of legend.

Stravin breathed in through pursed lips. "Impressive!"

And then Rempener Dras started to cry. It reminded Webrid of the last time he'd gone to visit his mother in the nursing home, and she couldn't chew well enough to eat the meal they were serving. It was that kind of pathetic, demented weeping that left visitors feeling helpless.

"They poisoned it. Poisoned it! The Vox was mine. It was good. It spoke. It helped. But they took it. They stole it. They corrupted it. They made it listen. They made it *watch*. They made it evil! Evil!" She staggered over to Webrid and pinned him against his cart, her hands open near his face in supplication. He noticed that she was missing some claws, and hoped that it was hormonal imbalance from molting that was making her so wacked out.

For once, he was relieved to hear Debley's voice. "I thought I'd noticed the Vox had changed over the years."

Rather than focus her into a rational conversation, his comment made things worse. She dug her fingers into Webrid's shoulders and began screaming. "Rommey! Rommey did it! He made me change it. Made me reprogram it. He wanted to rule everything. Hooked up with that Eshalo. Greedy, evil bastards, trying to sell off the forest. Rape the forest. And I...I...I...I...I..."

Rempener Dras fell silent, closing her eyes and relaxing her grip on the paralyzed Webrid. No one seemed to have the nerve to speak. When she opened her eyes again, she was once more the calm, calculating person who had drawn them into this bizarre nexus.

"I'm not proud of being the creator of the Vox. But it makes it easy for me to get around surveillance."

Zatell and Stravin exchanged glances, as did Leshi and Debley. Webrid, looking at his aunt's pensive face, wondered if he had imagined her outburst. He thought he'd better take advantage of this window of cognizant thought. "Forget the stupid Vox. Tell me about the damned laser."

"Well, as you've surmised, I had the laser implanted in you."

"Yeah, but why?"

"I needed you to carry it for me. You didn't mind doing that little favor for your auntie, right, Poochikins?"

Webrid brought his head down onto his cart lid in frustration. "Don't *call* me that." The pain that ripped through his skull was colored bright green.

"What's the matter? Did I not pay you enough?"

She had, of course, paid Webrid more for this one job than he had expected ever to make in his lifetime—in ten lifetimes. But he looked up, defiant. "Who cares how much you paid me, if I'm running from the law forever?" And as an afterthought, he added, "Or dead?"

She snickered.

He knew that family brand of condescending laughter. "Never mind, just tell me how you found me on Bargival."

"A better question is," she said, smoothing her silky red pantsuit, "how did *you* find *me*?"

"Oooh!" Behind Webrid, Debley's arm shot straight up.

"This ain't school. Just spit out what's on your mind," said Webrid to Debley, the goody-two-shoes.

After flashing Webrid the evil eye, Debley touched his fingers to his forehead. "The laser led you here."

"Very good, Feklari Debley."

To Webrid's stressed mind, his aunt sounded like his Historical Colonization teacher back in school. The association released a torrent of repressed angst. Words tumbled out as fast as he could speak them. "Okay, okay, maybe the laser led me here. But what do all the green math equations mean? And the flashing tree? And why did you need me to carry this stuff in my skull instead of in a pouch? And why, oh why, oh *why* did it have to be *me*?"

Leshi stepped forward and spoke soothingly to Webrid. "Embedded communication lasers are often used for classified..."

"Don't." He backed away from her. "Just *don't*. I don't want to hear from anybody except her." He pointed at Rempener Dras. "You've got a lot of explaining to do, lady."

The others shifted their weight and glanced at each other, but Webrid refused to be embarrassed or to apologize. He *would* get some satisfactory answers.

"May I have permission to speak?" said Azhanda. She looked at Webrid uncertainly, but he'd blown the brunt of his anger on his previous outburst. Anyway, she was so businesslike that he had no grounds to object. He nodded.

The little Zenivar clasped her hands primly in front of her apron. "Madam Rempener, Webrid and his friends have many questions. Perhaps we would be more comfortable having this discussion in the parlor?"

"What a treasure you are, Azhanda." Putting a clawed hand to her chest, their hostess spoke to all assembled. "Yes, indeed. Yesterday when I was out, I picked up a dozen clods of Bretchriven jamboro cakes. We'll have those, and some tea."

Tea? Had she seriously just invited them to tea? As Webrid stood there dumbfounded, his companions stepped around him, murmuring about the varying quality of jamboro cakes and how long it had been since they'd eaten. They all followed Rempener Dras out of the room, leaving Webrid alone with his cart.

"Come along, Ganpril Webrid," said the voice of his Auntie Naggrid, broadcast from the ceiling. "We're all waiting. And leave the cart. We don't need that dirty old thing in my nice, clean parlor."

Suddenly Webrid was a kid again, getting a talking-to. He shook his fist at the ceiling. "The cart goes where I go. That's final. You wanted a carter? Well, the cart's part of the package."

"Fine, fine. Now, no more fuss. Come and eat your cake."

"Yes, Auntie."

Through that fog of bloodline guilt from which no species is ever completely free, Webrid pushed his cart through the door where the others had exited. The green mist from his laser led him around a few turns to a cozy room where everyone else was already settled into soft furniture, passing around pieces of cake.

"Darling, you really must try this." Stravin popped up and handed Webrid a plated clod. "It's even better than the stuff I get from...from my client."

The moment the jamboro cake was under his nose, Webrid felt faint with hunger. He opened his jaws to their full amplitude and shoved the whole clod between his tongues. After a few cursory chews, he swallowed it down.

"And that," said Rempener Dras, indicating Webrid as she nibbled her cake daintily, "is why I ran away from my Yeril community."

To Webrid's dismay, Leshi, Debley, and Stravin nodded in sympathy. Bunch of traitors. Azhanda and Zatell were busy serving tea.

"So," said Webrid's newfound, long-lost relative, "what is it you wanted to ask?"

It was just as well that Webrid's throat was coated with jamboro cake, since he had no idea which of his million questions to start with.

Zatell was apparently hampered by neither stickiness nor confusion. She rolled right to the shins of Rempener

Dras and pointed several index fingers up at her. "How come the last time we came here, Webrid didn't get all weird and happy like this time?"

"Because I wasn't here."

That answer sent a jolt of confidence through Webrid. "So you don't know everything. You weren't expecting me last time."

"Oh, I knew exactly where you were. It's just that I knew you'd catch my vibe if I was here."

He snorted. "Seriously? 'Catch your vibe'?"

"Yes. So I left. You had more to do, and I didn't want you to get that feeling of completion just yet. I know how you carting Yerils are when you're on assignment. So, I left you some lunch and went out shopping."

Zatell treated them all to a cascade of giggles. "There's shopping in the forests of Northern Cheed?"

"Oh dear gods, no. I popped over to that big mall just outside Effalania on Prellga."

Stravin sat up straighter. "You left the planet? Fantastic!"

"Sure. I have a little rocket, so I can go to whatever planet I want whenever I feel like it." Rempener Dras leaned down to speak directly to Zatell. "You've got a nice business of that sort, haven't you? I've been watching you for years."

With several hands covering her blushing face, Zatell muttered, "Gee, thanks..."

"And I can show you my plans for the thrusters so landing is..."

"Oh, no you don't," said Webrid. "Don't you dare co-opt my friends by flattering them. You!" He whistled and pointed at Zatell. "You're on my side, and don't forget it."

"Just relax, hairball." Zatell plated another jamboro clod. "Here. Have some more cake."

"I don't want more cake." He shoved more cake into his mouth. "What I want," he struggled to say without spitting crumbs, "is to get this thing out of my head." He tapped his forehead. "Delivery made. Please collect your merchandise."

"Oh, you poor thing." Their hostess trotted up to him and put her hands against his cheeks. He remembered how Auntie Naggrid always used to do that when he skinned his knee. "Let's take care of that right away."

It was the first sensible idea Webrid had heard in quite some time.

But nothing could be simple. The Fekli sibs perked right up and whispered to each other in a suspicious way. Then Leshi addressed the hostess, seeming to choose every word with care. "Would you be willing to share the data you extract? It would be invaluable to our..." She stopped and shared a meaningful glance with her brother. "...to the project we're working on."

Without looking at Leshi, their hostess spoke as she led the way out of the room. "Data? What data?"

The consternation of his companions made Webrid laugh in spite of his foul mood. He followed the group, pushing his cart into a lab he recognized from his previous visit. The equipment he had broken seemed in pristine condition now. "Do I have to go in that awful machine again? The one that traps my head and wrists?"

"Just to start with, dear." Stravin put his hand on Webrid's arm. "After she takes some readings, you'll go to the surgery."

Rempener Dras said nothing, but held up a small black sphere and touched it briefly to Webrid's forehead. He felt the tiniest pinprick.

Webrid began to sway, but Stravin steadied him. "Now, now. I'm sure she's got the best surgical machinery. You'll recover in no time. She'd never have put anything in your head that she couldn't take out." He turned to Webrid's client. "Right?"

Rempener Dras said nothing. Her face was blank. Webrid

did not find that reassuring.

"Hey, Leshi, look at this." Debley was over by the equipment they'd used earlier, the laser-reading machine and monitors. "This is weird. Stravin, what do you think?"

Stravin, Zatell, and Leshi all gathered around him as he pointed to a monitor.

"Look at those numbers," said Zatell. "It's that same sequence we extracted from the laser before."

"You're right, my dear." Stravin leaned in toward the monitor. "And it's time-stamped from our previous visit." He turned toward their hostess. "What's up with that?"

Rempener Dras said nothing.

Suddenly Leshi spun toward her and lunged. Grasping the lapels of the Yeril's pantsuit, she drew her face near her own. Webrid found the aggressive stance a serious turn-on; he couldn't wait to see what would happen next. Some wrestling would be nice. Too bad one of the women was his aunt, but still.

Sadly, no wrestling ensued.

"You already had the data," Leshi hissed. "It's been right here on your machine, ever since we put it there."

Still Rempener Dras said nothing. She just smiled.

Stravin went to stand at Leshi's side. "And if you already had the data, why did you make us wander around for an extra two days and nearly get killed?"

Rempener Dras said nothing. Her smile broadened.

Debley was scrolling through pages of numbers. "You haven't even run an analysis on this. It's untouched."

Zatell spoke up. "You already know what it says, don't you? You didn't need to analyze it."

"You have to tell us," said Leshi, releasing her grip and opening her hands in a pleading gesture. "The message that we intercepted made it very clear that this data was essential for the revolution. For a return to the Swarattan tenets."

Rempener Dras said nothing. Webrid decided he'd had enough of her smile, and of all his so-called friends.

Banging on his cart lid to call this mad meeting to order, he spoke. It was, after all, *his* laser in *his* skull. "You know what? You're all crazy. And you're all a bunch of selfish jerks. None of you really cares what happens to me." He put his hand up for silence as they all began to protest.

"No. There's only one of you here with any sense. And that's Azhanda." He indicated the Zenivar, who stood demurely in the corner. "She does her job well, she speaks straight when she speaks at all. That's what I like in a person. So, Azhanda, tell it to me straight. Say something that makes sense, or I'm gonna lose my mind."

With small, quick steps, Azhanda padded into the middle of the floor until she reached Webrid. When she indicated that he should bend forward, he did so, and she spoke.

"There is no longer a green light in your forehead."

Everyone gasped. Rempener Dras held up the tiny black sphere. The smile had never left her lips.

"That's it?" asked Webrid. "It's in there?"

"You took it out already?" said Leshi.

"He doesn't need major surgery?" asked Zatell. Webrid thought she sounded slightly disappointed.

Come to think of it, Webrid was himself slightly disappointed. "But it was stuck in there so deep. And it had a weapon and stuff. And all that data. Wait, I bet she didn't really take it out. It'll be lodged in there forever. She just shut off the light."

"No, Ganpril Webrid, I assure you, your brain is as perfect as the day my bot found you on Bargival."

Zatell laughed so hard, she rolled over a couple of times.

"But what about the data?" said Leshi. "What about the revolution? We got a message..."

"I sent that message myself, Feklari Leshi. As you know,

I also sent one to the Underlord Eshalo and to Council Secretary Rommey. You were all seeking the data about my precious forests."

Debley put his hands on his head. He seemed at wits' end. "So, give us the data. Now."

"You've *seen* the data," she said.

"Yes, but what does it mean?"

"Nothing."

"Nothing?"

Leshi's voice cracked. "But it was supposed to help the revolution."

"Believe me," said Rempener Dras, "it *has* helped the revolution."

Lanky Leshi lashed out, pushing the pantsuited Yeril hard against a wall. "What do you know about the Swarattan Revolution?"

Still as unflappable as a flag in the Windless Deserts of Engrappillon, Rempener Dras brushed Leshi aside and took her fine time getting comfortable in a chair. She had such presence, such a powerful aura, that no one uttered a word. Once seated, she looked directly at Leshi.

"You should not presume to tell me about the Swarattan Revolution. I knew Heesha Swaratt's daughter, Arusha. She and I, not her famous mother, codified and published her founding principles."

Rempener Dras pointed one of her new finger claws at Leshi. "You are part of the Revolution because I made you so."

eshi's chin trembled as she spoke. "How dare you! I became a resistance fighter because I had a dream about Heesha Swaratt..."

"You certainly did," said Rempener Dras. "I was your dream." She laughed, a resounding cackle that made Zatell's raucous laugh seem like a delicate spring breeze. "I saw how intelligent you were, yet how sensitive and easily swayed. So I spoke to you through the Vox one night, inventing this whole resistance movement. I've been helping out your cause ever since."

Debley came forward, "You bitch. You manipulative, lying bitch. How dare you say we haven't done all this ourselves? We even managed to commandeer a ship to use as our headquarters."

"The *S.R.S. Draspar*. Yes, yes. I'm glad it's working out for you. I named the *Draspar* after myself," said Rempener Dras. "Wasn't it brilliant to make a floating office available for your HQ? It made you very hard to trace."

Leshi was sobbing inconsolably now. Zatell and Webrid exchanged looks. Maybe he couldn't tell a political ideal from a hole in his head, but he sure knew what it was like to feel you weren't in control. He realized he was still missing some important info, too. Gently pushing Leshi out of the way, he stood up to his creepy relative and her dastardly cackle.

"Why could I kill people with that laser? Some people, but not everybody?"

"Oh, my dear little nephew." She reached forward and pinched his cheek, scratching him with her claw. "So innocent. *You* didn't kill anyone. *I* killed a few people."

"You did?"

"Certainly, certainly. Only when necessary. I don't believe in gratuitous violence."

Webrid considered arguing with that last statement, but there were more pressing issues. "So that's why I couldn't control it? You were doing it?"

Rempener Dras nodded, a dreamy expression on her face.

Stravin stepped forward. "How did you know what was going on? Just because Webrid had a data laser..."

"Oh, you damn fools." The sweet auntie had been swallowed up by an impatient crone. "Can't you figure this out?" She paced in a big circle around her guests as she spoke, as if corralling them in the middle of the lab. "There's no data laser. There was never any data. It was a camera, a Vox ID port, and a gun, with a little program of nonsense numbers to stymie folks who tried to read it."

Webrid and his companions looked at each other, their jaws slack, their eyes wide.

Zatell rushed forward, waving at least twelve arms. "What gives you the right? You think you're so high and mighty that..."

Leshi shushed her. "Wait, I want more info." She stepped out of the circle and cut off Rempener Dras's next orbit. "What were you trying to find out with your camera?"

"I needed Webrid to collect evidence."

"About what?" Webrid thought he had a right to know.

"About the plot to sell off my forest and use the money to fund an underworld power that would control the government. Rommey and Eshalo were in league over this."

"But that's crazy," said Debley. "How could you know that Webrid would gain access to Rommey or Eshalo, let alone both?"

Webrid's aunt got a coy look on her face. "Well, I *did* send them a message telling them that Webrid was carrying a data laser containing essential info about the Swarattan Resistance..."

"And you sent us the messages saying we'd get data to help imprison Rommey!" Leshi exclaimed.

"Yes, I needed you involved. I wanted the resistance to witness what was going on. See, I'm trying to strengthen your cause. So don't be so crabby."

"What cause, exactly?" Stravin asked. "I don't get a strong vibe of Swarattan ideals from you. Except the tree obsession."

"Forestation is the only ideal that matters!" Rempener Dras screeched.

Zatell said, "Why do you care so much about the..."

"My trees! They're my friends! They're my only friends!" She was dragging her new claws through her facial hair. "They're the only ones who won't betray me. And I'm the only one who won't betray them."

The was a moment of silence as the companions put more distance between themselves and Webrid's loony aunt.

"You're just trying to control everyone," Webrid said. "That's all you're trying to do. Just for the stupid trees?" He felt a desperate urge to run out into the forest and rake his claws through every trunk he passed.

"That's right," Zatell said. "You got no respect for people." Webrid was touched by her support. "You had no right to use everybody."

"Yeah." Webrid was getting into the swing now. "You may have paid me a ton of money, but that was for carting. You never paid to control me or take over my life. Nobody gets to buy that."

"Yeah," said Zatell. "It ain't right to make someone bait, even an ugly hairball like him."

"Yeah," said Webrid.

"Oh, would you two stop that?" Debley glared at them. He turned to their hostess. "Now explain this to me—what was the point, really? What was the ultimate purpose of getting all this info? Are you starting a lawsuit? A smear campaign? A..."

Rempener Dras was emitting a new kind of laugh, one that Webrid had never heard come out of a Yeril before. It sounded like an emergency siren, and was so loud that it drowned out Debley's voice. Then, suddenly, she stopped laughing and spoke in a whisper, making fleeting eye contact with each in turn. "They've been killing me for years. They killed my soul. And now they're going to kill all my trees. Once I was sure of their plans, I told them Ganpril Webrid was coming here. That he has the data laser. They should be here any minute."

"Madam Rempener!" It was Azhanda's voice projected through a comm speaker. Webrid realized he hadn't seen her in a while. "There are choppers. And soldiers. You need to raise the defenses, ma'am."

"No, no. We want them here. Shut down security on the east side of the fortress, sides and roof."

"But, ma'am, they're heavily armed."

"Oh, yes. I know." Rempener Dras sounded perfectly calm. "Do as I say."

"What the hell are you doing?" Stravin demanded of this bipolar megalomaniac. She ignored him, even when he started to throttle her. "Tell us. Tell us! What are you planning?"

She broke away from him and spoke into a comm unit. "Azhanda, are Rommey and Eshalo present?"

"Yes, ma'am," said Azhanda's voice. Webrid wondered where she was speaking from.

"Have they entered the building?" asked Rempener Dras. If Webrid hadn't seen how her eyes swam loosely in their sockets, he might have thought she was asking about dinner guests.

There was a short radio silence before Azhanda answered. "Eshalo is inside, ma'am. Rommey's troops are landing on the roof. Aaaaand...now he's in the building, too."

Rempener Dras looked pleased in a light, trivial way, like she'd found a sale on a dress she'd been wanting. "That's excellent. Please detonate all explosives in the east sector."

"Ma'am?"

Her face grew darker and her voice stronger, lower. She repeated the order. "Detonate all explosives in the east sector."

"That will..."

"Yes. It will obliterate the east sector. Do it. Kill those bastards."

"No, ma'am." Azhanda's voice shook.

"Fine, I'll do it myself." Rempener Dras shouted at the bank of monitors in front of her. "Override." She was talking to the air, now, or to somebody no one else could see. "They made me into a monster. They made me betray the whole world. None of us deserve to live. None of us! Only the trees should live. Only the trees!"

Webrid noticed his companions inching toward the exit. He agreed—it was time to make a run for it. But he had his cart to worry about. And he was fascinated by the insane Yeril whose mind seemed to be self-destructing right in front of him.

"Detonate all explosives in the east sector," she roared.

Zatell, Stravin, Leshi, and Debley bolted from the lab. At the same time, a series of explosions blasted in the distance. Although it was in another part of the building, the lab shook hard, and several machines capsized.

Webrid's aunt looked suddenly serene. "Nobody could have survived that. I could have blown up one of the smaller Fregnis planets with that, wouldn't you agree?" Given her tone of voice, she might have been discussing vacation plans.

"Um, Auntie?"

"Yes, dear?"

"We should maybe leave."

"Why?" She really didn't seem to sense any danger, although just then a bolt of electricity shot out of a vent, causing the laser reader to catch fire.

"Um, I think this whole place is gonna blow."

"Yes, you're quite right."

"So..."

"So, we'll die. So the trees can live." She was talking louder and faster. "So the Vox can be destroyed. So the Raralt Circle can be purified." She spun around, clapping her hands in rhythm, like a child dancing at a picnic. Flames burst out of the monitor near her. "Die!" she screamed over and over. "We all deserve to die."

Hearing the barmy chanting of his Auntie Naggrid, who was now completely removed from her sanity, Webrid was visited by a deep and abiding truth. "We have to go *now*, Auntie!"

Rempener Dras had started foaming at the mouth and tearing at the air with her claws, so Webrid assumed she wasn't listening. It surprised him, then, when she answered in an eerie shriek.

"It's all because of the Vox," she wailed. "It's all my fault. Letting them destroy my wonderful trees! I had to stop them.

And I have to stop myself. It's my punishment. It's my fate!"

Her eyes, reflecting the surrounding flames, gave Webrid the illusion that she was burning from the inside. She turned those fiery orbs toward her trembling nephew.

"Ganpril Webrid. Be proud that you're a Yeril. It is your heritage. Be proud that you're a carter. It's the reason you were born. If you try to deny your destiny, it will destroy you."

Webrid looked around, stepping out of the way as a burning ceiling tile fell toward him. He could feel the flames singeing his fur. "Looks like this old carter's come to the end of the road."

"No!" she screamed. "Follow your cart. Let it lead you to safety. Let it deliver you."

"Um, it was the laser that could lead me, Auntie Naggrid. The cart can't..."

"Follow your cart, Ganpril Webrid. Follow your cart!"

There wasn't time to argue. The flames grew higher. Explosions were nearer. Pieces of the ceiling and walls were breaking and melting loose.

"Come with me, Auntie." Webrid stretched out his hand. She did not reach back, but sat wide-eyed and still as a prison of flames shot up around her and she was blocked from Webrid's view.

If he wanted to live, he needed to move. There was only one exit still accessible. But between Webrid and that doorway was all manner of detritus. He couldn't roll his cart in that direction. He stood there as the heat closed in on his mind, praying for guidance. It came.

"Webrid!" He couldn't see who was calling him. "Webrid! Over here!" It was Leshi's voice, coming from the hallway.

And with an inner strength wired back from Webrid's heart through every Yeril who ever lived and loved, the carter lifted up his cart, carrying it over the smoldering obstacle course and out of the lab. As he stepped through the doorway, there was a massive explosion and flash behind him. Flames billowed through the lab, and Webrid forced the door closed to block them.

Someone yelled, "We gotta go." Webrid hadn't taken stock of who was present. He was too busy wrapping his arms around Leshi, who buried her silky, skinless face against his leather-tough neck.

"I said move it, hairball." Zatell was paddling his calves. She didn't wait, but rolled recklessly limb to limb down the smoking hallway.

Stravin and Debley were there, too. Something was wrong with Stravin. He looked lopsided, and his face was taut with pain.

"You okay?" Webrid asked.

Stravin shook his head slowly. "Broken arm. Never mind. Just move." He turned to Debley. "Go. Take your sister."

Debley kicked Webrid's cart. "Just leave this damned thing behind," he barked as he passed sideways between the cart and the wall. "It'll slow you down and get you killed."

Leshi gave Webrid a sympathetic peck on the cheek, but took her brother's hand. "Stay safe," she said.

With a feeling of abandonment that roared louder than the fires around the fortress, Webrid watched Debley and Leshi sprint into the smoke, in the same direction Zatell had gone. Stravin straggled along next, steadying himself with a hand against the wall every few paces. Webrid pushed his cart as fast as he could over the shaking floor, but soon he fell behind.

Explosions were more frequent now. Some boomed far across the fortress; some were so close that they shattered the edges of the ceiling along the corridor. What with the smoke and the dust, the fear and the exertion, Webrid felt like his lungs had been pierced by a thousand metal shards. But his fear was greater than his pain, so he kept going.

huge crash around the corner in front of Webrid made him wonder if he should find another way out. But the flames trying to lick his rear end cleared that quandary right up.

"Whatever happened up there," he assured his cart, "we can always crawl over it."

So forward they went. As they rounded the bend, Webrid rammed his cart right into Stravin, who was sobbing so hard he couldn't get any words out.

Webrid heard Zatell squealing near the ground, so he reversed in case he'd caught one of her limbs with a wheel.

"You've gotta help!" Zatell shouted. She was shifting her weight from one limb to another in a dance of terror. "It's Debley. Come on!" The three of them got the cart through some debris as Zatell explained.

"I got caught when the ceiling came down over there." She pointed to a pile of rubble. "Deb grabbed me and pulled me. He got me loose, but then he got buried. We can't move the metal plate that fell on him."

They had reached the smoking junkheap that had

trapped Debley, and Stravin ran around the pile and knelt down. Before Webrid would turn his attention to Debley, though, there was something he needed to know. "Where's Leshi?"

Zatell pointed toward a tall shaft of light down the hallway. "The main entrance is down there. She went out to try to get the Vox to send help."

Relief coursed through Webrid's chest. But horror pushed it out as he looked down at Debley. He was trapped at mid-thigh, his leg continuing at a strange angle below his hip. There was a pool of blood forming around his head. Stravin knelt next to him, stroking his cheek and speaking too softly for Webrid to hear.

Webrid did the obvious thing. He grabbed the metal plate that was weighting down the pile atop Debley's leg, and he pulled upward. He pulled with every ounce of Yeril strength he had. It gave only a little, but then Webrid had to make the awful decision to lower it again in order to save his own back. Debley let out a demonic wail, and Stravin echoed it.

"Lever!" screamed Zatell.

"What?"

"Use your cart as a lever." She was pushing it toward Webrid and trying to tip it over.

"What the hell are you doing?"

"Just help me lower the front. The corners are galvanized, right?"

Stravin seemed to wrench himself out of mourning. "Oh, darling, that's brilliant." He stood shakily. "There's not much I can do with this bum arm, but I'll give what I've got." He blew a kiss to Debley, who seemed to be slipping from consciousness.

At last Webrid got the picture. "The cart can't take the whole weight of that metal."

"No," said Zatell, "but if we jam it under and I pull down

on the other side, and you use all that hairball brawn to get the plate up..."

"That should be just enough to pull him out!" Webrid liked the plan.

"Which is my job," Stravin said. He put his good hand on Debley's belt and straddled his feet for balance.

They caught the front corner of the cart under the plate. Zatell heaved down on the handle for all she was worth, screaming with the effort, and Webrid yanked up on the plate with a resounding roar. It moved a little more than last time.

"Pull him! Pull him! *Now!*" Webrid cried. Then he let go. His muscles had nothing more to offer. He was afraid to open his eyes, for fear he would find he'd killed Debley instead of saving him.

His eyes popped open when Stravin said, "Quick, Webrid, get him in the cart." Debley was alive. With Stravin and Zatell to help, Webrid carted him over the debris, down the hallway, and across the foyer that opened out into the main entrance of the fortress.

The mammoth double doors were standing open. Passing through the doorway, they found themselves on the familiar front porch near the river. Leshi was a few paces away at the water's edge, calling to the sky, "Help! Help! Send help!"

"We got him, Lesh," Stravin shouted before collapsing to the ground. He rocked back and forth, weeping and holding his broken arm.

Leshi turned and froze. As if suddenly realizing what she was looking at, she ran forward. In tears, she covered her unconscious brother with kisses, sparing a few for Webrid, who barely noticed. This was all too much for him, so he stood still, comforted by the feeling of the cart handle under his fingers.

"He can heal himself, right?" said Zatell.

"Not something this serious." Sighing, Leshi bent down and kissed Zatell's forehead, but she wiped it off her face.

"We gotta get help," said Zatell. "Any sign from the Vox?"

"Nothing."

"Figures. They watch you when you don't want them to and ignore you when you need them."

Then Webrid noticed something disturbing. "Guys, there's flames. In the hallway." Sizzling tongues of orange could be seen in the section of corridor where Debley had been trapped. The foyer they'd just run through would soon be ablaze.

A bot voice, crackling through melting wires, announced, "Forest fire prevention mode. Building sealed in thirty, twenty-nine, twenty-eight..." The two doors, big enough for a giants' castle, were swinging slowly toward each other.

"Well, that's for the best," said Stravin, starting to recover himself but still sitting on the ground. "Those thick doors should keep us safe from the flames."

"Twenty, nineteen, eighteen..."

"Webrid! Webrid!" It was Azhanda, inside the building, running from the hallway into the foyer toward the door. The fire was licking at her heels. A piece of ceiling fell in front of her, and she jumped back.

"Sixteen, fifteen..."

The doors were more than halfway closed. Leshi and Zatell pushed outward on one and Webrid on the other, but they just kept closing.

"I'll run and help her," said Leshi. But she didn't move. They all knew there wasn't time.

"Twelve, eleven, ten..."

"Webrid!" Azhanda was back on her feet, running around the chunks of melting plastic and metal, holding out her furry hands toward the carter.

It wasn't a conscious decision. Webrid didn't think it through. The world around him disappeared and he moved with absolute surety. In the time it took him to breathe once, Webrid pulled Debley from the cart. In a second breath, he kicked his cart forward as hard as he could into the gap between the closing doors.

The massive doors hit the cart and caught it. Even its galvanized velancium sides weren't strong enough to stop the inexorable motion inward, but it slowed the mechanism slightly. Leshi reached her long, thin body halfway in and grabbed Azhanda's hands, pulling her out, just before the doors sheared the cart in two. Webrid's lifelong metal friend screeched and creaked with the agony of a slow, twisting death.

Standing numb in front of his severed cart, Webrid grabbed its handle one last time as he heard the doors' bolts shooting into place.

"Fortress sealed," said the bot voice.

Webrid lay in a soft, clean bed staring at the ceiling of his suite at the Royal Ksacheeli Hotel. There really was a lot to be said for living the high life. Next to him, Leshi stirred. She draped a long red arm across his belly.

"What time is it?" she asked, blinking sleep from her eyes.

"Hell, I don't even know what day it is." He burrowed back down into the covers and pulled her close.

"Really? Again?" She backed away with a playful laugh.

It had been a fun few days of love and luxury. Before the explosions, Azhanda had programmed the bots to configure into their U-craft and transport all of them to the *Draspar* in Southern Cheed. After the fortress was destroyed, the Vox system had begun behaving erratically. Its policing services stopped functioning altogether. Stravin had taken advantage of the weakened state of security to clean up everyone's ID status. Webrid, in particular, fared well. All the millions of dendiacs Rempener Dras had paid him were now accessible. Hence the fancy digs.

Debley was in the hospital, seriously injured but healing quickly, thanks to his remarkable Fekli genes.

Now Webrid looked at his lover. "You want to order some food? Or drinks? Or a massage? Maybe a spinal cord transplant? They've got everything here."

Leshi was laughing, her head pushed back into her pillow, her body completely relaxed. Webrid couldn't stop his tongues from asking the forbidden question. He sat up.

"So, now what? You know, after." He'd never asked a woman that before.

Still lying down, Leshi turned her head to look at him. "Well, I guess you could stay here."

He made a big show of misunderstanding. "In this hotel? I'd go nuts from all the pampering."

"No, silly. Here on Cheed." She looked away. "With me."

Webrid sighed a long, deep, lung-flattening sigh. Then he did it again. He might not know much about women, but he knew about needing to be free.

"You don't really want me to stay, do you?"

Now she sat up, sounding flustered. "No, no. I mean, yes. Of course. You can stay if you want, I mean I want you to..."

Webrid leaned across the bed and gave her a long, hard kiss. "It's okay. You've got your life here. I've got my life back in Bargival."

She looked sad, so he gently took her face in both his hands and lifted her chin. "It's been fun, though."

"Yeah," she said with a wistful smile. "It's been great."

A burst of knocking at the door broke the mood. Long,

slow pounding mixed with a quick *rat-a-tat*.

"Open the door, you ugly hoongofl," came Zatell's voice.

Once Webrid and Leshi were decent in robes and their over-used bedroom demurely closed off from the rest of the suite, Webrid opened the door. Zatell rolled in first, followed by Stravin, wearing an arm cast.

Last to enter was Azhanda, in a black and white striped dress. It was more businesslike than her old blue apron, but it still couldn't prevent her from looking cute. With her face somber—a contrast to the chummy smiles and embraces from the others—she handed Webrid an egg-shaped metal object.

"For me?" He resisted the impulse to pat her furry head.

"Yes. Please watch it."

"Okay." Webrid held the thing in his clawed hand and stared at it. "What's it gonna do?"

Zatell let rip a cascade of giggles. The others were chuckling, and even Azhanda seemed to be biting her cheeks to prevent a smile.

"Here, darling." Stravin took the egg. "It's much more interesting to watch if you turn it on." When he held it up and pressed on its side, the egg lit up and projected an image onto a bare wall of the hotel room.

Suddenly there was Rempener Dras, life-sized and in living color, looking several degrees saner than she had when Webrid had witnessed her self-immolation a few days before. Webrid sat on the arm of a chair and watched his long-lost Auntie Naggrid recite her last will and testament.

"...and upon my death, the bulk of my funds will be transferred to the operating account of the Swarattan Resistance Force. My auto-attorney has already filed the documents and licensing fees to make the SRF a legal organization."

Leshi gasped. "Wait 'til I tell my brother!"

"But I vow I'll not have my cause forgotten. Trees are not simply a rarified symbol for life. They *are* life. Where they are gone, the atmosphere will change and the..."

On and on went her harangue about the trees. Webrid lost his focus and soon drifted off into sleep. He was awakened by Zatell slapping him and saying, "You gotta hear this."

He sat up and listened again.

"So I've programmed the policing function of the Vox to die with me," Rempener Dras was saying. "You're on your own. To replace it, you'll need to redesign it. It will be chaotic for a while, but you'll be better off in the long run.

"When the holders of this video pod play its contents, said contents will be broadcast simultaneously on every screen in the Raralt Circle. Peace, prosperity, and personal freedom to you all, and a world filled with trees." The image disappeared.

Zatell shook her limbs. "She really was a good person before she went all, all..." She stopped, looking at Webrid guiltily. But he knew what she meant. She was a nut job. Still, he was glad his Auntie Naggrid had made a good impression. She'd impressed him, too. Not many days before, if someone had told him that a Yeril invented the Vox, he would have spit up his lunch through his nose.

Webrid and his companions were congratulating each other and ordering up drinks when he heard Auntie's voice again very softly, although her image was gone.

"Ganpril Webrid." The sound was coming from the little video egg. Its white light pulsed. Webrid went into the bedroom, holding the egg to his ear. It spoke again. "Ganpril Webrid. First State Universal Carter."

"Yeah?" he answered, feeling stupid talking to a dead person in an egg.

"If you want it, there's a new cart waiting in your

apartment in Bargival."

Webrid was too choked up to speak.

"Thank you, Ganpril Webrid. You have done your family proud." The egg went dark.

"So," said Zatell as Webrid came out of the bedroom, "are you guys coming back to Bexilla with me, or what?"

Stravin looked at the floor after a quick glance at Leshi. "I thought I'd stay on Cheed. You know, until Deb's better."

"Ugh. You're such a hoongofl, abandoning me like that. What about you, hairball?"

Webrid looked at Leshi, who smiled supportively. "Yeah, I'm going back to Bargival." He smirked at the rocket scientist at his feet. "Think I'll take a commercial flight this time, though. No offense."

Zatell snorted as the rest of them laughed.

"Will you still be a carter?" asked Azhanda.

"Well, sure," he answered without hesitation, picturing the shiny new cart that awaited him at home.

"But you've got money now," said Zatell. "What's the big deal about carting?"

"It's an important job, carrying stuff from one place to another." Webrid touched the scar in the middle of his forehead. He could have sworn he saw a green glow.

ACKNOWLEDGMENTS

This book would not have been possible without
the enthusiastic support of Kate Sullivan at
Candlemark & Gleam. Lucky for me, she was
Webrid's biggest fan from the moment she met him.

I'm also forever grateful to the brilliant friends
and family who always agree to read my new
manuscripts when they could be spending
that time reading an edited, published novel
by somebody famous.

And a bow of respect to the memory of
Raymond Chandler and Douglas Adams.
I'm glad Earth happened to be the planet
where they both lived for a while.

Photo by Ken Munch

Anne E. Johnson has taught the history and theory
of music and written a fair amount of non-fiction,
but in truth, all she really wants to do is make things
up. She lives in Brooklyn with her husband,
playwright Ken Munch.

You can learn all about her long and short fiction at
AnneEJohnson.com.